The Trail
of the
Butterfly

Blood Ties

by

Calvin Bowden

Llumina
Press

Requests for permission to make copies of any part of this work should be mailed to Permissions Department, Llumina Press, 7915 W. McNab Rd., Tamarac, FL 33321

ISBN: 978-1-62550-444-9 (PB)

Chapter I

Straining to see by the light of a half-moon filtered through tall trees along each side of the blacktop, Blin Burge reined his big brown horse to a stop on the grassy shoulder. He tightened his grip on his pack mule's lead rope, knowing he couldn't survive long in the wilderness without supplies.

The deep shadows were an ominous sight to a man who had lived his early life on barren West Texas plains and recent years in brightly lit concrete jungles.

Unable to see the ground along the drainage ditch, he dared not risk one of the animals breaking a leg. He would have to wait for daylight to cross, unless he could find that break in the timber he'd spotted three days before while scouting the area. Oh, to find that break and enter the safety of the big timber before daylight. It wouldn't be so dark there. He turned his horse, Catcher, back toward the asphalt.

Openings between the trees' branches extending over the blacktop let in enough light for him to ride to his present location from where he had camped for two days some five miles back. If he could find that break in the timber, the killers looking for him wouldn't be able to find him. Luck had been with him: he couldn't afford to risk it running out on him.

The silence was eerie, threatening. To break its hold, he nudged Catcher's sides with his heels and the steady *clip, clop, clip, clop* of the horse's hooves against the asphalt broke the spell. *Hope my seat and thighs can hold on long enough to find a safe campsite deep inside the forest.*

His misgivings about his desolate refuge were offset somewhat by thoughts of Dora, his only sister; Bella, the singer at his club in Houston; and others sacrificed to drug addiction. He remembered friends complaining about the rotten state of the world around them. "Somebody's got to do something," they'd said. "The politicians won't. They've all been bought off. That means folks like us must take a stand."

Well, he had done something. He had taken a stand. Now he was on the run from gangsters wanting to kill him. Where were all those good citizens now who whined about rampant crime, illegal drugs, and violence? Blissfully sitting in plush recliners behind locked doors, swigging cold beer and watching cable television.

He considered using his flashlight to see his way across the drainage ditch, but decided against it for fear someone in the distance might spot the light. The nearest house was at least two miles away, but light could be seen much further than clopping hooves could be heard.

He looked up at the ribbon of stars shining through a narrow opening in the trees and thought: *Even the sky has eyes. I hope they're friendly.* Dropping the reins on the saddle horn, he bowed, stretching his arms wide. Looking at the stars again, he said, "Good evening, bright eyes. How are you? I'm not so hot myself. A city man on the run in the dead of night. Yep, there are plenty places I could be tonight where you'd be just as impressive, but I'd be too scared to take the time to look up and say howdy."

He lowered his arms and clucked the animals forward while mentally backtracking five miles to the two-day campsite in thick underbrush. He had abandoned the hidden trailer and car, stripped of plates and all identifying papers, and covered his trail on the ride out to the blacktop.

Finding no break in the tree line, he looked again at the stars. "Lord, Big Man in the Sky, or whatever you prefer to be called, guess you know all about those government big shots in Houston pleading with me to help them take a stand against organized crime, promising me they'd back me all the way, guaranteeing me I wouldn't end up holding the end of the stick with the stink on it if something sent our plans belly up."

He glanced ahead and backwards for approaching headlights and went on, "For all my trouble, I got ballyhooed and tattooed. Not only did I get the dirty end of the stick, they shoved it into a very sensitive, unnatural point of entry." He paused, adding, "I would've used the vernacular term, but didn't want to show disrespect for such a high authority in surroundings that man hasn't messed up yet."

The sound of his voice did not shake the dismal mood threatening him, or hold back the quiet of the night that came rushing back, as if to taunt him for daring to hope his problems would be important to a Higher Power. He sensed that his primal surroundings cared even less. *Nobody cares, not even nature—or, I'm beginning to suspect, not even God.*

Blin peered toward the ditch again and at the wall of darkness beyond, which threatened to pull him into its sinister embrace. The sight was in sharp contrast to the peace he had observed while driving through,

2

looking for a suitable point of entry to the wooded refuge. In spite of the remoteness, however, he had found it a beautiful setting in daylight, a much-needed comfort following his narrow escape in Houston the previous week.

He reined Catcher to a stop and again strained to hear approaching traffic. He'd been told that rural east Texans got out and about long before sunup. Nothing but silence now. Total silence.

He jumped when Catcher snorted suddenly. Sighing, he patted his mount's neck. "You're a good boy. But next time, give me a little warning before blowing your nose, okay?"

Like the promise of safety the primitive surroundings offered, his gentle horse and the sound of his own voice provided a certain degree of reassurance. Finding comfort in such simple things struck him as odd. He tapped the horse's sides to begin moving again.

His new map showed the big woods beyond the ditch stretching many miles in three directions over an uninhabited land. A safe haven until the furor created by his recent actions in the big city died down. By remaining undetected, maybe the breath of death at the hands of assassins would fade and eventually disappear.

During the ride from his abandoned campsite in the thicket, he told himself that danger, like pain, faded quickly once endured, in direct proportion to the distance between it and its victim. He also told himself that his struggle to survive in the remote area would take first priority over pursuing killers and government bungling. Living alone in the big woods would also give him the time needed to sort the limited options open to him and reconcile his anger over having lost everything for doing what he thought would help his fellow man and save his businesses and his home.

His lover had turned against him. Hard-earned savings were lost. Gone also was the belief that any average, well-meaning man can challenge the rich, powerful leaders of the criminal underworld if he had the force of his federal government backing him. The latter myth exploded like a cheap balloon in that federal courtroom in Houston following an aborted trial, triggering a rude awakening about the games lawyers play and the worthless promises of government officials.

So now, it appeared the only valuable things left were memories, especially of his early life with his Native American grandmother, Laura Bartee, who reared him. Their common heritage and alliance against racial intolerance had fostered a unique, unbreakable bond between them.

It was his long-ago promise to her that brought him to the big woods adjoining her childhood home for sanctuary, a place to hide or die.

A native of the Alabama-Coushatta tribe, his late grandmother had told him, "In order to know and survive the world as a man, you must first understand yourself. Know that person inside you, Bright Light in Night."

She gave that name to him after serving as midwife on the night of his birth. Afterwards, upon walking outside under a clear sky, she saw an extra-bright star, probably Venus. His father objected, but his ailing mother insisted, so it became his official name. His grandmother told him how it was said in her native language, but since it could not be properly translated into English, it was never used. Elementary school officials later refused to use the entire English version, using instead the first letter of each word: Blin.

Her advice held little meaning to him at the time, but he hoped life alone in the big woods would allow him to discover its significance. There would be no distractions except his thoughts and fears, the forces of nature, and solitude. Most of his grandmother's teachings about how best to live his life stuck in his memory, and as he grew older, he occasionally had thoughts of them, but never as much as he had since his comfortable world collapsed. Until then, he had always thought of himself as what he always wanted to be: a regular American, like all the full-blooded Caucasians he had known and worked with. In spite of recent setbacks, he still believed that, but something about that jolting experience in the courtroom caused him to feel the pain his Native American grandmother must have endured living in hostile West Texas, far from her own kind. He checked his surroundings. No lights. No sound except creaking leather beneath him.

He remembered clearly something else the stoic Laura Bartee said about the big woods. In a soft, reverent voice she'd told him, "One who spends much time in the big woods where I once played will find comfort of mind and spirit." She said the forest would do that for him provided he lived a sufficient time there with a hungry mind.

So now he was about to enter that special place his grandmother loved, but not without a heavy sense of guilt for not having heeded her advice for good living before becoming callused about matters of mind and spirit. He doubted the forest would offer more than a place to hide, but to a skeptic, that was a victory of sorts. As long as there's life, there's hope. However, he doubted the pristine area would give him insight on how to regain material possessions that had brought him comfort and pleasure in recent years. Or any mystical powers that restored faith in himself, government, women, or people.

His newfound bitterness, however, did not override his grandmother's words, which had guided him through high school and into successful business endeavors. The ugly realities of a dog-eat-dog existence and his betrayal by federal authorities had changed his attitude, increased his skepticism, and finally caused him to push his grandmother's teachings aside. He considered them buried for sure as he fled Houston in a hail of bullets.

In view of bad experiences in a tough world his grandmother never knew, he was pleasantly surprised and comforted remembering her wise observations. In view of recent events, he doubted being able to live by such basic rules again, and that troubling possibility rekindled his yearning to return to the simple ways, most noticeable following another failed love affair or business downturn. Now that the most troubling time of his life was at hand, his grandmother's values had returned, stronger than ever.

While looking for the crossing as his horse walked slowly through the darkness, he recalled more of Grandmother Bartee's stories centering on the big timber country. He began calling her Mama when she moved into their ramshackle home to replace his mother. His grandfather was already dead. Early on, Mama made him promise to some day travel to the Alabama-Coushatta Reservation, her childhood home, even if she was dead or too old to make the trip herself. It would still be for her sake, she said, because one's spirit never dies.

Shame on you, he chided himself, *failing to keep the promise before Mama became too ill to travel.* His guilt intensified when it occurred to him that he might never have come at all had the bottom not fallen out. Previously, his promise had been superseded by an unrelenting drive to become wealthy and put poverty and deprivation behind him forever. He was convinced such an achievement would insure him against future adversities. That was another myth shattered by recent developments.

Eager to leave the road, Blin glanced to the east for signs of daybreak. Seeing no sign of dawn or the ditch crossing, he pulled Catcher to a halt and reached into his saddlebag for his flashlight. *Chances of the light being spotted are less than being caught on the road by the next motorist.*

The flashlight produced only a dim glow. Apparently, the switch had slipped on during the ride from the campsite. He returned it to the saddlebag, unable to reach his fresh batteries without unpacking the mule.

"How about let's cross and rest a while, big boy," he said, nodding Catcher toward the ditch. "There are lots of miles ahead of us."

The horse responded gingerly, but suddenly swerved upon nearing the dark void, almost throwing Blin out of the saddle.

"Come on, boy," he said. "It's okay. I'm sure it's a shallow ditch."

Catcher moved slowly down the gentle slope, and when his front feet found the opposite embankment, he lunged forward, jerking the lead rope through Blin's fingers, burning them. The mule, munching on some grass, had not sensed the urgency of the move.

Blin yanked the rope. "Come on, Ears, I'd starve without those supplies on your back. There'll be plenty of grass where we're going."

Geez, he thought. *I haven't said anything to a mule since plowing the family garden as a kid.* He could almost feel the soft, clean dirt against his bare feet, and his heart swelled when he remembered looking behind him at a straight furrow.

After Catcher and Ears scrambled up the incline to a black wall of brush, Blin remembered another thing from his childhood. Beginning with his mother's death, he had associated darkness with death and evil. Okay, you're no longer a child. You are thirty-three years old. Get over it.

Moving only a few yards, they encountered a solid wall of underbrush, so Blin decided to give the animals a rest while waiting for more light. It shouldn't be a long delay, and he was far enough off the road not to be seen.

The pre-dawn stillness pressed upon him. He strained his ears and eyes for some indication of a human presence, but heard nothing but buzzing mosquitoes, the animals' breathing, and the squeak of the saddle when he stood to relieve his aching muscles. He told himself, *Relax. Stop looking for assassins behind every bush and turn.* That didn't appease the tightness in his gut. The last year had made him too aware of the tremendous power and reach of organized crime.

His soreness dampened his sense of victory at having arrived safely at his destination and increased his resentment for having to resort to such a drastic change of lifestyle. *Did I make the right choice coming to this place?*

He had run out of reassuring thoughts and relief that his undercover work for the government was finished. Fighting illegal drug trafficking had been an eye-opener to someone of his limited experience. Besides introducing him to the ugly reality that tends to kill idealism, it also robbed him of a sense of satisfaction for a job well done. It made enemies, turned friends into strangers. The law abiding were too afraid. Everybody was afraid.

Ironic that he had believed Mama, who told him all honorable men took a stand against evil. She said, "Do right and you won't fear being the victim of another man's anger. Work hard at honest labor, and you will receive sweet rewards that no person can take away. Do these things, and stay in tune with the earth and what comes from it, and your mind will forever be at peace." He had believed it all, never considered questioning anything she told him. She was his anchor.

He looked east and wished it didn't take the sun so long to come up. In daylight, he believed, his surroundings would be less threatening. He could move far into the big woods and enjoy the safety it offered.

He stood in the stirrups to relieve his backside, but decided dismounting would best serve that purpose. Climbing down, with nothing to do but wait and think, he recalled the previous week and learning just how alone he was in a cold, unfriendly world.

He'd believed he had at last found a woman who cared enough to stand by him in a crisis, until he stopped to pick up Veronica upon fleeing the Houston federal building. Refusing to let him inside her apartment, she'd screamed, "What are you trying to do? Get me killed, too? Get away from me, loser! Stay away!"

Before Veronica Stedham, there had been many women in his life, all self-possessed, good-time girls. He was tired of short-term affairs; it was time to settle down and have a family. He wanted a permanent relationship with a woman who loved him, one who would support him during good and bad times. He hungered for a home full of love and kindness, living proof that he had overcome the cruelties and rejection of his early years with his father.

Veronica's rejection freshened bad memories of his boyhood in his dilapidated, West Texas home, and confirmed how calloused and untrustworthy some women could be. It was then that he realized that the only woman who had ever truly loved him was Mama. His sister Dora had, too, before her boyfriend got her hooked on hard drugs and coerced her into running away from home. By that time, Mama was dead, leaving him without family as he tried to earn more than enough to get by.

He suspected his longing for virtuous women to trust and love was a result of being robbed of his birth mother's affection and the fear of losing his aging Mama. Whatever the reason, he must have tried too hard to find a partner who fulfilled his expectations; the most promising ones seemed to be frightened off after a short courtship. He had clear mental pictures of the puzzled, fearful looks they gave him during and immediately following their intimate moments, as if they saw something sinister in him. He wondered sometimes if something they associated with his Indian heritage trigged their reactions. Proud of his heritage, he had never attempted to conceal his genealogy. Those close to him would not have known he was one-eighth Native American if he hadn't told them. Although he did have a slightly olive complexion, dark eyes, and the black hair of his Indian ancestors, he was believed by all to be white unless he told them otherwise.

What advice would his dear mama give him now? Maybe she would explain how she had endured her own hardships and defeated her inner demons when her world changed drastically after she abandoned her ancestral home. He had always marveled at how she retained her stoic, patient manner and positive outlook under such adverse circumstances while caring for him, his sister, and his alcoholic dad in the West Texas shack they called home.

Blin was three when his mother died and Mama came to live with them. He had no memory of his mother, only a picture of her on his apple box dresser. She looked ill in the picture. Perhaps her poor health had contributed to his being a sickly child, a problem that plagued him throughout elementary school.

He doubted his grandmother could answer the many questions now burning in his mind. Her simple ways, based on a mysterious inner faith he never understood, belonged to another world, another time. Gone now, like the comforting remembrances of bare feet against freshly plowed ground.

He welcomed the cool May breeze moving gently through the tall pines. It was a soft, soothing sound, unlike any he had ever heard, almost a whisper, saying, "You'll be safe in the big woods where Mama once played."

Riding horseback to that point under cover of darkness had allowed him to complete the last leg of his journey without being overtaken by those looking for him or spotted by someone along the highway who might alert them. His undercover experiences taught him that dealers had many allies and supporters imbedded in the roots of American society. Drug usage was the open, golden door to young people craving excitement, new experiences, and escape; the suppliers' greed in a freewheeling society guaranteed availability. The dealers and pushers possessed unlimited money, and therefore influence on some public office holders.

Many of those caught up in the illegal drug market had neither wealth nor power, but an even more compelling reason to participate in the sordid business. They were the addicts. Enslaved by their habit, they maintained fanatic allegiances to dealers and pushers.

Blin first learned about the all-consuming power of illegal drugs over ordinary peoples' lives when his sister Dora, and more recently Bella, a singer in one of his clubs, became addicted. Witnessing their horrible experiences turned his desire to eradicate hard drugs into a mission.

He sighed, remembering the events leading up to his decision to work as a federal undercover agent. After Mama told him she did not feel up to making the long trip to visit her people on the reservation, he used the money saved doing odd jobs after graduating from high school to look for his sister. He'd heard the year before that she had become a drug addict and been turned out as a prostitute by her boyfriend. By the time Blin found her in Los Angeles, Dora had died from an overdose of heroin, according to the coroner's report. Angry and bent on revenge, he tried to find her boyfriend dealer, but the good-for-nothing had left town.

Using the remainder of his savings, Blin traveled around the country looking for work he could excel at and eventually buy into and prosper. He found many menial jobs that offered no future. He came back to Texas, stopping in Dallas. He bounced from pillar to post for several months then moved to Houston in search of something more promising. Realizing he would never become independently wealthy working for someone else, he weighed his options. Gigs in the food service industry had helped him overcome his shyness and develop a winning way with people, so he enrolled in bartenders' school with the long-term goal of some day owning his own bar or club.

After three years of serving drinks and saving every penny he could, he bought a lounge. Five years later, at age twenty-five, he went broke and was back behind somebody else's bar. He saved enough money in four more years to shop for another property, and by then had attracted a good clientele. When a run-down country and western nightclub became available, he bought it.

Utilizing his carpentry skills at night after closing the bar where he was employed, he refurbished the new place and opened for business two months later. Shortly thereafter, he leased another building down the block. He offered live music and a singer popular with older customers at the second place, believing they would be more orderly and have more money to spend. Then, he opened a back room where, for a hundred-dollar cover, special customers could gamble with no limit on bets. There was a private bar, and pretty, scantily clad waitresses to serve players.

The game room hadn't been in operation a year when Blin began to suspect a numbers racket had moved in, but he didn't interfere because patrons behaved themselves and the money was good. He had drawn the line on two things only: organized prostitution and illegal drugs. Attractive, drug-free hookers worked the place early on, but because they caused no disturbances and were well received by customers, he didn't have them thrown out.

After three years, he smelled success. He had a sizable bank account, nice clothes, a luxurious home in River Oaks, and a stereo system almost as wide as that West Texas shack he lived in as a boy. To crown his list of achievements, he ordered what was, to him, the ultimate symbol of affluence: a new Cadillac. Finally, he had done what he had set out to do, and poverty and all the other handicaps that had plagued "Teepee Peewee" Burge soon faded into dim memory. He felt invincible in his success and the entourage of pretty women surrounding him.

Occasionally, however, he lapsed into a guilt trip, berating himself for violating Mama's moral teachings to achieve his goals, but he quickly recovered by telling himself the rewards were ample justification for a little shadiness. Besides, by then, Mama was dead, as was the kind of life she thought best. These different times and different circumstances demanded a realignment of values.

His first indication of serious trouble in paradise came when Pack Pascal, his black bandleader at the ballroom, told him about an affair between his lead singer, Bella Devereaux, and an associate of Frank Deno, their best customer. Blin had made many friends in the nightclub business, but none came close to handsome Frank Deno.

Frank and his associates were all good customers of the back room. Some of Frank's friends were in "the business," as he put it, and they, in turn, brought friends in to drink, gamble, and be catered to by the waitresses and call girls.

Pack told him that one of Frank's friends in "the business" had introduced Bella to drugs, marijuana at first, cocaine and heroin soon after. He said she was hooked badly, and Frank was threatening to have her supply cut off if she didn't start turning tricks for them. That was Blin's first piece of evidence about Frank's "business."

In view of what had happened to Dora, the news about Bella infuriated him. He promised Pack to escort Frank and his friends out and ban them from the club the next time they came in. He said he'd put Bella in a treatment program, although Pack told him he had already tried. Pack said his efforts resulted in a visit by a couple of Frank Deno's muscle men, stating clearly, "Come near Bella again; find yourself dead in an alley."

When Blin urged Pack to go to the police, the bandleader replied, "I already did, and when I said I wanted to file a complaint against Frank Deno, the cops got really interested. They said to tell you not to kick Frank out or do anything else to run him off. They want him bad. That brings me to the other thing I came to tell you. Two of the cops I talked to are out there now, waiting to talk to you."

Pack's unexpected news caught Blin off guard, and because he did not want to work with the police, who had done nothing to save Dora, he was in the embarrassing position of having to turn down the request of a friend and valued employee. After some pleading on Pack's part, he agreed to meet the officers.

Pack returned to Blin's office with the two policemen, both young and casually dressed in sport shirts and jeans. One had long black hair and a full beard. His partner didn't look any better with an untrimmed goatee. Both were cocky to the point of arrogance. They introduced themselves as narcotics agents who had been working undercover for the state and federal governments, trying desperately to make a case on Frank Deno's drug and prostitution operation for over two years.

The agent working for the federal Drug Enforcement Agency told Blin they didn't want Frank nearly as much as they wanted the ones heading his organization. Identifying the drug leaders would show how Frank's operation fit into the big picture. They told him Frank Deno was just the tip of the iceberg of what could be the biggest case they'd ever worked on, with suspected headquarters outside the state—the country, even.

Blin listened as they explained that Frank Deno was merely a small cog in a well-established, national organization that flourished in many cities, controlling local and state politicians with payoffs. They said Blin could help convict Frank and the kingpins by taking advantage of his friendship with Frank to work his way into the organization as an undercover agent.

Blin turned them down. "My business is running nightclubs, not working as a policeman."

Then they played the Dora card. "We thought you'd want to help because of what happened to your sister."

Using her as a recruitment tool angered him. Next, they played the vengeance card. "If you work undercover, agents will find Dora's murderer."

Remembering his own failed search, he decided their plan might be his only chance to punish the man responsible for her degradation and death. "I need time to think about your proposition," he said. "And figure out a way to run my businesses if I do."

At that point, they softened the sell, asking him to allow Frank Deno to continue coming to his club in the meantime. That would at least give them a chance of making a local case against him.

A second bomb rocked his safe new world the following night. A bouncer rushed into his office reporting that strangers had entered both clubs and tried selling pot and crack cocaine. A fight broke out when customers tried to throw them out. When local police rushed in to break up the melee at his big band dance club, his bandleader and a bouncer were placed under arrest for assault and battery. By the time Blin arrived, the gambling room had been discovered and the dealer handcuffed. The lieutenant in charge ordered all customers out of both businesses and padlocked all exterior doors.

The two narcotics officers appeared at Blin's home the next morning, saying that unless he helped them, both clubs would remain locked. Two detectives, working under orders of the mayor's office, along with representatives of the local congressman and the governor, came to his home shortly thereafter to explain how he could strike a blow for all clean-living young people of the country by working with law enforcement. They praised his entrepreneurial skills, work ethic, and business achievements, and expressed concern that he might lose everything if his businesses remained closed indefinitely. They were very convincing.

Seeing no other option, he reluctantly agreed to work undercover for the DEA. The attorney for the Southern District of Texas promised to protect him at all times from the drug dealers and their political friends. He also said, "Once you gather enough evidence for a case, we'll keep all defendants in jail without bond until sent to prison."

His early efforts as an undercover agent produced an unexpected sense of satisfaction and accomplishment. The bubble exploded when he found out at the aborted trial how empty the government's promises were.

He patted Catcher's neck. "Good boy. I'll take the saddle off as soon as we get to a safe campsite. Then you and Ears can fill up with green grass and roll in the dirt."

He looked and listened again, relieved that no cars had come by since crossing the ditch. Only three vehicles had met or passed him since leaving the trailer and car. When their headlights appeared in the distance, he'd ridden into the trees along the right-of-way until they passed. He wondered if he would ever feel safe again, or trust anybody.

As the sun began fading the darkness about a half-mile later, they came upon a pipeline easement. "Well, look at this, guys. A cleared path. Thank you, Sun Oil Company."

Forty-five minutes later by his watch, he reined Catcher toward the big timber and tightened his hand on the mule's lead rope to make sure he followed. His body ached fiercely, but he pressed on, rather than dismount to get relief. By the time the sun came into full view above the tallest trees, he guessed they had moved more than a mile into the heavier growth of pines and hardwoods.

Coming to the crest of a high hill, he stopped, stood up in the stirrups, and looked back over the trees at distant openings along the farm-to-market right of way. *The last evidence of modern life you'll see for a long time.* A daunting thought.

He studied the dense growth of timber and bushes, wondering if he could survive the challenges ahead. *There's no turning back now.* He would find out if a man could escape evil by running from it and if the forest would be a safe haven. Would it hold the rejuvenating powers Mama said it offered? Lowering his sensitive backside into the saddle, he decided to walk a while to relieve both buttocks and bladder.

According to his calculations, they should veer north to avoid the Big Thicket. Research indicated impassable spots of heavy bushes, vines, and briars there, even pools of quicksand. *Definitely not for a city slicker.*

Turning his attention to the flesh wound on the outside of his left thigh, he thought, *you're lucky to be alive.* He was marked for death. He had teamed up with the feds expecting to take risks, but had been surprised by how badly the government failed to carry out its part of the agreement. That failure caused his world to crash and burn and made him keenly aware of being betrayed and alone in a room filled with alleged friends and allies. He was overcome with disgust for the legal system and those who ran it and feared for his safety. This adult fear surpassed the worst he had known as a puny, dark-skinned boy in elementary school, bullied and beaten and called "Teepee Peewee" and "Squaw Boy."

How ironic it was, he thought, that the Houston tragedy happened in a courtroom emblazoned with flags and other symbols of authority and permanence. Looking back, he realized he should not have been surprised, not after learning while undercover that outside the government's "Halls of Justice," there existed a much stronger order, made up of a vast array of tough, money-hungry, criminally oriented people and their lackeys. He knew because it had been his job to develop their friendship and learn their methods of operation to provide evidence to the U.S. attorney.

He remounted and rode down the back slope of the hill, snapping open his compass to make sure he was still moving northeast. The last thing he wanted was to get lost in such the vast stretch of trees, hills, and brush. If he should break or lose his compass, that's what would happen if heavy clouds moved over the sun. He glanced at the bright sun over his right shoulder at about the ten o'clock position and returned the compass to his pocket, making a mental note to store it in his supply pack for safekeeping before pitching camp. He didn't want to chance it falling out of his pocket as he went about his chores or hunted game to supplement the canned provisions.

He surveyed an endless sea of pine trees with a liberal spattering of gum, oak, and hickory. The virgin pines were straight and sleek, many seventy feet tall on a thirty-inch base. Many varieties of weeds and grasses grew around them.

In small clearings, he smiled at honeybees and butterflies gathering nectar from wildflower blossoms. *If such fragile creatures thrive in the forest, surely I can endure for a few months.* He hoped the grandeur of it all would turn his mind from ugly developments to sort things out and plan his future.

He recalled riding his paternal grandparents' paint horse on the country roads west of Midland, one of the few pleasant memories of those early years, other than the kind guidance of Mama. No pleasure in having nothing to eat beside what they picked from their garden. No gratification in failing to keep the cutting winter winds off your bones in a dilapidated, old clapboard house with cracks in the walls and no panes in some of its windows. No joy in seeing Mama crying each time Dad came home drunk after being laid off from another roughneck job in the oil fields. No security in Dad's failure to hold a steady job. An uneducated man with no special skills, his father was the first laid off in a business slump and the last called back. Even half-hearted attempts at growing cotton or food to eat on rented land always failed for one reason or another. More failures brought on more drinking, and more drinking blurred him to the needs and feelings of his family.

Blin hated that part of his life, and early on vowed to not become a man with such limitations. He swore to graduate from high school, even if he had no lunch, no shoes to wear, and no clothes without patches. He vowed to make lots of money, because only the wealthy had control of their lives.

Mama told him her only child, his mother, was forty-one when he was born, and his sister Dora told him how their father abused her. Dora said their infuriated dad would knock their mother down and yell, "You dumb squaw!" Only the calm assurance and patience of their widowed Indian grandmother gave him and his sister the strength to survive their troubled childhood.

A faint smile touched his lips, as if some mysterious inner force might have swept over him. Mama was sixty-five when he was born, ancient by some standards. But in spite of increased problems associated with aging, she stood straight and proud, seemingly unaware of her many winters of hard living and the deep wrinkles on her face. Her dark brown eyes, shining with an inner strength, reflected an acceptance of hardship in hostile surroundings and the conviction to survive in spite of it. He sensed at times her misgivings about the choices she had made as a young woman, but she always exuded pride in her Native American roots. Her brown, round face, kind and ever pleasant, would forever remain his anchor in rough waters.

Mama lived with her tribe on the reservation until age eighteen, when she, ignoring her people's strong objections, married a white logger and moved to West Texas. Her husband, who worked as a farm laborer, was killed in a bar room brawl shortly after Blin was born.

Long talks with his grandmother remained fresh in Blin's mind. About his burning ambition to be rich, she advised, "Bright Light in Night, my grandson, richness is peace of mind and a strong spirit, not money and power. Wealth and greed will lead you to much trouble and give you no one to turn to. Those who become your friends because of your money will turn their faces from you."

He remembered the detached, far-away look in Mama's eyes near the end of her life when she spoke of her homeland and the old ways. She told him, "When everything is against you, do as I would do now, if I could. Go to the big woods. There a person can find power that will lift him from the grave of his troubled spirit."

He had given her a puzzled look and asked, "What power, Mama?"

He would never forget the longing for things lost he saw in her eyes when she responded. Staring across the fields in front of their little house, she said softly, "Long ago, I left my people. Their bones lie far away from this place. I hear that the new ways of the white man have scattered our young even more since that day. If that is true, our line is weak, and it is too late for those who are left to ride the old trails again and change the young back to the good ways. It is too late for tears. You will know when you have found the Power. The Great Spirit that all call God will come to you in the form of something seen or heard that you will understand. It will give you strength to ride out any storm."

Skeptical of the old ways, he said, "A man with money has power, Mama. He never needs any other kind of help."

She gave him a reprimanding look. "You will need a special power when you come to the blackest time of your life. Your money will be like feathers in a great wind."

Blin stopped the horse and glanced at his watch to find he was two hours away from the pipeline. Convinced that more walking would relieve his soreness, he climbed down.

His legs felt as if he were still astride the horse. After briskly rubbing aching muscles, he tied the reins around a sapling and walked around the mule, examining cinches and tie-ropes. "Feels like I've already been in the woods a week and it's only nine-thirty on my first day. Seems like the sun's been gone two days."

Surprised that he had again spoken as if another human were present, he glanced at the animals. Both ignored him.

After leading Catcher for another half hour, fighting underbrush and briar vines, he climbed stiffly back into the saddle. Oh, for a tub of warm, soapy water to soak in for at least an hour. A good massage by loving, feminine hands would be even better. Veronica had magic fingers.

He looked back at the gentle beast of burden plodding along, as if time and distance was of no consequence. Catcher was more spirited and responsive, but he also appeared content with his plight.

Blin wondered how much more aggressive the horse would be if he had not been gelded. The castration of a horse apparently caused fewer traumatic changes than it did with a man, but it seemed a pity to

16

have robbed such a beautiful animal of his most prized possession. Blin shuddered at the thought of such a thing happening to him, but guessed it would make being alone in the forest less stressful. What a tragedy it was that Veronica had turned against him.

Wonder if I'm crossing paths Mama and her friends used long ago. The thought of her having been there gave him comfort, but also another guilt attack for never having brought her back to her girlhood home while she was still able to travel. He, at least, had brought her letters inside his metal first aid kit. Some were addressed to him, others to the present chief on the reservation and her living relatives. He would need them, she said, to prove his ties to her tribe.

To ease his guilty feelings, he reminded himself that while in school, he had been financially unable to bring Mama back, and after graduating, he'd gone to work. His goal at the time was to save enough to pay down on a car with some left over for the trip. But by the time he was ready, she was tied up caring for his ill father. Ten years later, when his dad died, her poor health made travel impossible.

She told him, "I'll be content to live out my life with only memories of my innocent years if you give your sacred promise to one day go in my stead. Find and talk to my surviving relatives and bring back word of who is left and what has changed." Mama added sadly, "Maybe it's best I didn't go back, after all. I have outlived all my close relatives. My memories might stop being my strength if I saw it now, but there is comfort in knowing some things never change. The pines. The oaks. The hills. The birds. The beautiful butterflies of many colors and sizes. Seeing all those things will make you stronger."

He jumped suddenly and jerked Catcher to a stop as a loud crash nearby jolted him back to the present. He scrambled down, convinced it was the crack of a rifle fired by Houston gunmen that had overtaken him.

Chapter II

When Blin's feet hit the ground, he jerked his pistol from its belt holster. A second sound told him a heavy object had struck the ground, perhaps a large man jumping from a hiding place. He searched the brush for the assassin and spotted swaying branches near a tall, dead tree. Raising his eyes, he saw the stub of a large, rotten limb.

Grinning sheepishly, he stood up, shaking his head in disbelief at how jumpy he was. Several attempts were required before he got his .357 Ruger revolver back in his holster. His heart was beating like a big drum. "My first day in the woods, and I'm already as nervous as a rookie policeman working the graveyard shift in Houston's Fifth Ward."

Neither animal seemed disturbed by the sudden sounds or his remark. The mule was munching grass, and the horse was standing quietly by, its ears flipped forward as he looked at something in the trees. Blin looked, but saw nothing. Catcher lowered his head and began grazing.

Blin climbed back into the saddle and urged Catcher forward, still shaking his head in disbelief that he was talking to himself. It was enough to make him wonder how long it would be before he began having steady one-way conversations with Catcher and Ears.

"I'm falling apart, Catcher," he said. There! He was doing it already. At least his voice sounded normal, so perhaps he should consider himself sane as long as he didn't hear the animals talking back.

Remembering his gunshot wound, he examined the bulge in the leg of his trousers. The bandage was still tight, and there was no new bleeding from the shallow graze. He turned his attention back to the brush and trees on each side and ahead of him. He must remain alert for both the normal sounds and those that signaled danger. No exciting task, so as he did that and studied the slowly passing scenery, he found his mind going back to the time he became an undercover agent.

Following a swearing-in ceremony and an interview with the agent in charge of the Houston DEA office and Assistant U.S. Attorney George Madsen at the federal courthouse the next day, he was advised of his responsibilities as an officer and the laws governing admissible evidence. At his request, he was not supplied with identification papers or a badge. Through his contacts with Frank Deno and his associates, Blin was instructed to learn locations, methods of operation, and names of prime movers in their illegal enterprises, and to make regular reports of his findings to the supervising agent assigned to the case or George Madsen.

Madsen assured him that as soon as he had ample evidence on Frank and his associates, or on any member of an organized crime unit in any part of the country, he would have all indicted and would request such high bonds none of the defendants would be released. Blin was further advised that he would be required to testify for the prosecution at any federal trial or trials that followed.

Overwhelmed by the gravity of the mission he had undertaken, Blin had remained silent for several moments after receiving his instructions. He was overwhelmed, having never expected to work as an undercover officer, but when he thought of refusing the assignment, he remembered his businesses and his home. He remembered Dora and Bella, and thought about the other young people that might suffer their fate.

He was allowed to re-open his businesses the next day, and charges against his employees were dropped. Summoning Pack to his office, Blin asked him to be his manager when he was out of the city, and when those times occurred between the first and the fifth days of the month, to make payments on the bank loans still outstanding on both places and his home. Pack reluctantly accepted and agreed to accompany Blin to the bank to sign the necessary papers allowing him to do that, but said he hoped the arrangement was temporary, as he did not feel qualified for such heavy responsibility. Blin also had reservations about allowing his affairs to be run by someone else, but he didn't believe at the time that his new responsibilities would take him out of Houston for more than a couple of days at a time. That was just one of the many misconceptions he had of what was about to happen.

It didn't take long to develop deeper ties with Frank and his associates, because he allowed Frank to continue bringing his party girls and drug pushers into his clubs. To further convince his gangster friend that he was fully committed to becoming a loyal partner in his criminal operations, Blin told him he wanted part of the action in his local enterprises.

While Pack operated his businesses, Blin gathered vital information for the feds and transported secret messages and huge sums of dirty money to different parts of the country for Frank and his bosses. In that capacity, he developed a working relationship with several key members of the different branches of criminal organizations in several states. At the urging of George Madsen and the drug enforcement agent in charge, he allowed his ballroom to be used as a meeting place for the various criminal operations, the details of which were duly recorded by him or videotaped by other undercover agents hidden in adjoining rooms.

Shortly after getting involved with his new duties, Blin's beloved Mama died at age ninety-eight. Grief-stricken, he informed the federal authorities and his criminal associates that he would have to leave town for a few days. His mob friends were very suspicious, but reluctantly agreed to let him go, telling him they would not accompany him, as one of their men had gone to Midland to confirm his reason for leaving.

It was a very sad time for him, made especially painful by the fact that he had not taken time from his selfish pursuits to visit his grandmother's homeland and give her an account of his findings before she died. He suspected his guilt would burden him the rest of his years. He was, after all, bone of her bones and blood of her blood.

After attending Mama's funeral, he remained in the Midland vicinity for two weeks to sell the old house and two acres to help pay her medical bills. He spent much of that time sitting in Mama's old rocker reading letters previously received, which he kept in a metal box in his car, plus two she did not mail. One he found on the cot he slept on as a boy; a nurse who cared for her prior to her death delivered the other to him. That letter contained unexpected revelations about a side of Mama he never knew, and with her list of relatives whose descendants she wanted him to visit when he went to the reservation was an outline of his tribal responsibilities as her closest still living male family member.

The letter on his cot contained her usual statements of love with a request regarding his earlier promise to visit her childhood home. It read, in part, "When you go before the old ones in my home place, beg those who remember me to forgive my failures. Do that so I can be at peace on my long journey."

Concluding that his grandmother would not have approved of his grieving over things he could not change, he returned to Houston with her letters safely stored in the trunk of his car for future reference.

He found his businesses not going as well as he had hoped. Some of the employees at the country and western club were unhappy with Pack's style of management and had walked off the job, and there was barely enough income that month to pay his overhead, not to mention his mortgage payments. He encouraged the disgruntled Pack to replace the departed employees with people of his own choosing, but realized, too late, that unless he fulfilled his undercover obligations soon and returned to run things full time, he would lose his businesses.

Frank and his associates were relieved that he was back. Frank told him that as a result of his work, he had placed huge sums of money in a secret account in his name at a local bank. Blin reported that to Frank Madsen per instructions received when sworn in.

After working undercover for fourteen months, Blin found himself able to name most of the principal participants in criminal organizations in several states. He possessed first-hand knowledge of their various illegal activities and the names of public officials and business men to whom they were paying bribes. The extent of their criminal operations was so complex and far-reaching that all states involved turned their cases over to the federal government in Houston for prosecution. Blin was told that simultaneous indictments against all offenders could be best handled that way.

Blin had been very thorough, convinced that his sister's death had been avenged and he had performed a valuable service for his fellow man. After believing for so long that wealth was the only worthwhile pursuit for someone of his humble beginnings, the pride that came with having struck a blow for the good of all was a new experience for him. And with that righteous thought was spawned a few other noble opinions that proved to be idealistic nonsense.

It had been a very dangerous undertaking, but one that was exciting, challenging, and emotionally rewarding. And at the time, he smugly told himself, as soon as the trials were over, the bad guys would pay, and Blin Burge would walk safely away from it all, rebuild his struggling businesses, and get on with the good life.

Catcher stumbled suddenly, almost tossing him out of the saddle. Grabbing the saddle horn to keep from falling, he pulled the horse to a stop. Climbing down, he ran his hand along his mount's front legs. Patting them, he said, "You're okay, thank God." He looked back and saw a fresh mound of dirt with a hole pushed into it. "Watch out for gofer holes."

He climbed stiffly into the saddle, muttering, "What else can happen? I don't need another falling limb to cripple me or my horse to break his leg."

He looked at his surroundings, which looked the same as they did an hour before and the hour before that. He looked forward to getting far enough into the forest to start searching for a suitable campsite. In the meantime, there was nothing to do but observe the passing scenery and think about recent developments.

George Madsen told him the head of the Houston branch of the crime syndicate and his lieutenants and enforcers would be tried first. Blin was assured, that when they were found guilty, all their underlings would make pleas or turn state's evidence in return for light sentences. Madsen also told him that those developments would relieve him of having to give further testimony. He said the same thing would happen in big cities all over the country where they had ample evidence to file charges.

Blin was also advised that when local indictments were made, he would have ample time to get his affairs in order before being taken into protective custody somewhere outside the city.

Blin first sensed not everything was going according to plan while waiting in a locked witness room to be called as the government's lead witness. Madsen entered the room with a strained look on his face.

Blin asked, "How's the trial going? Ready for me now?"

"The trial hasn't started," Madsen replied. "We're still hearing motions outside the presence of the jury. Motions to suppress and for acquittal."

"So?" he replied, still full of confidence. "When *will* the trial start?"

"Unless we can convince the judge to let us use the evidence we've got, there won't be a trial." Madsen finally met his gaze. "Right now, it looks like he's leaning toward granting all defense motions."

Blin thought he had misunderstood Madsen, but when he realized he hadn't, he was shocked and angry. "What the hell kind of prosecutor are you, Madsen?" he demanded, jumping angrily to his feet. "With the evidence I gave you, the cases should be a snap. It'll make you the next U.S. Attorney for the southern district, for Christ's sake. I'm surprised the defendants didn't plead guilty when they found out about the evidence you have."

"That won't happen if I'm not allowed to use it," the somber-faced Madsen replied. "That's what I need you for now—to testify on the motions."

"You're saying you want me to show up in there as a witness, not knowing the judge won't throw out the case and turn all those criminals loose? You're crazy. Committing suicide wasn't part of our agreement."

"Calm down, Burge. Don't cry on my shoulder if everything doesn't turn out all roses. You knew the chance you'd be taking. Without you, we'll never get to try any of the men in there, not if the present charges are dismissed. We'd have to have you back to testify before a new grand jury to get new indictments. Without you to testify on defense motions now, your gangster friends are going to be turned loose for sure, and they'll know who furnished most of the evidence that got them brought before the bench today."

Blin paced the floor, at a loss for words as he struggled to regain his composure. He finally told Madsen, "If you get lucky and win on the motions with my testimony, will the judge refuse new bonds so they'll have to remain in jail until tried and sentenced?"

"Won't know what he'll do until we get through this phase, but he probably won't, the way things are going. I don't believe they have this judge on their payroll, but he has rules of procedure and legal precedents to follow. If I do manage to pull it out, all you have to do is stay in hiding somewhere until their trials are over, or until I need you for new indictments."

"Me, hide? I'm not the criminal here. And what if you *don't* pull it out? Those guys will be free to do what they've always done, and their first priority will be to kill me. My head's on the block here, Madsen!"

"Like I said, if the judge grants the defense's motions, you and I will get together with other agents and come up with new charges we can prove. Every crook in there would be re-indicted."

"If you can't prosecute with the evidence I gave you, I don't believe you ever will, but even if you did try, new indictments and trials would take weeks—months, even. You don't think their trigger men could find me in that time? There's no safe place in the country I could hide."

"You used to be a country boy," Madsen said smugly. "I'm sure you can find a place where the gangs don't have connections. Just go there and let me know where you are so I can send for you when I need you again."

"If this thing blows up and I have to run, you'll never see me again."

"That kind of thinking can get you into lots of trouble, Burge," he said angrily. "You've sworn to uphold the law, and you're under subpoena. The only chance you have now to stay alive is to cooperate with us. Now, let's get in there and get this over with."

Up to that point, none of the other witnesses involved knew Blin's role in the investigations; but their finding out was not what he was worried about when he entered the courtroom that day. His sole concern was what the gangsters would do after *they* found out.

An anxious murmur was heard at the defendants' table when he walked past them. Some spoke or nodded, apparently believing he was appearing on their behalf. All were silent when he walked before the clerk to be sworn in. He glanced at them; he recognized them all.

When Madsen stepped forward instead of the defense counsel and introduced Blin to the judge as a government agent, all abruptly sat erect, and their puzzled silence turned into a murmur of boiling hostility. When Blin looked at the local boss, Daussa "Doss" Saavedra, and his lieutenants, Moro "the Greek" Tischi and "Walrus" Walsaka, he found their cold eyes fixed on him, their expressions frozen in disbelief and hate. Their head enforcers, Victor "the Cat" Catori and "Graveyard" Boze, a black man, sat next to them, and the message in their expressions was just as deadly.

When Blin turned his eyes back to Catori, the gangster touched his fingertips to his lips and opened his hand in Blin's direction. Blin had never seen the gesture except in old movies, but he recognized it as the "kiss of death."

In spite of the unexpected turn of events, Blin still dared to believe his testimony would save the case, but within seconds of the time he stepped out of the witness box, things happened quickly. Defense counsels jumped to their feet with a flurry of protests, the main ones being "entrapment" and "probable cause." The lead counsels demanded that their motions for acquittal be granted, and after a hasty conference before the bench, the bomb was dropped: all charges were dismissed and all defendants were ordered released.

As if in a dream, Blin heard the judge's announcement, followed by cheering and shouting from the defendants' table. Catori and Boze charged toward Blin and would have reached him if three deputy marshals had not stopped them.

Blin ran to his car without being caught or shot, but two men in a black Lincoln chased him when he drove out of the parking lot. Concern for his personal safety quickly replaced his anger and disillusionment.

He knew enough about organized crime to know the order for his death had gone out immediately, and for that reason, he did not dare drop by his home to pick up clothes. He had some cash in his billfold, but not enough for an extended trip. If he had not left his checkbook in the glove compartment of his car, he would have had to rely on credit cards.

As he maneuvered desperately through the north side of Houston, he lost his pursuers and headed for the westbound freeway. Moving quickly out of town, he continued into the next county without spotting the black Lincoln. He began searching his brain for a place to hide. The gangs had too many connections in the major cities, so he could not take refuge in any of them. That was when he remembered his promise to Mama and concluded that the big woods near the reservation would be a safe place to hide if he could get there undetected.

So now, he was where he hoped he would be safe. So far, however, the big woods had not given him the sense of well being he hoped they would. The proportions were too mind-boggling, the remoteness too threatening. The eerie silence produced a sense of aloneness like none he had felt before. Veronica would have let him avoid the latter problem. Too bad all he got when he went by to get her before fleeing the city was a shallow gunshot wound in his left thigh when one of the gunmen pursuing him opened fire. The words Veronica screamed at him as he raced back to his car still rang in his ears: "Sure, we had some good times, but you were on top of things then. Now, you're nothing but a dirty snitch looking for a place to die!"

He reined Catcher to a stop and dismounted to relieve an aching backside and legs that were becoming more of a problem with each passing hour. Catcher breathed deeply, as if glad to be relieved of his burden.

The sun bathed the forest with increasing warmth, giving him hope that heat would relieve some of the discomfort. Tying Catcher to a bush in a bed of grass, he cleared a small area of leaves and built a small fire with dead twigs. He had to have coffee.

The coffee made in the tiny aluminum percolator with water from his canteen was strong, so a cup of it with a can of pork and beans was refreshing. Still feeling the need to relieve his soreness, he stretched out on the leaves in the shade of a large oak to rest, and became keenly aware of the absence of human sounds and the rush of traffic. The silence was broken only by the singing of an occasional bird—the cawing of a crow, a blue jay's shrill call—and the animals munching on grass. It made him aware of how much noise had become a part of his life.

In spite of her rejection, he could not stop thinking about Veronica. It would have been so much better if she had come with him. Thinking of her prompted him to remember how generous many of his female customers had been with their tips and smiles when he worked as a barkeeper. Some told him he was handsome with his slightly olive skin, black hair, and brown eyes. Such flattery was a real boost to his ego, which to that point, had never completely recovered from the many negative experiences early in life. Being called "Teepee Peewee," later shortened to "T.P.," was humiliating. Students continued calling him T.P. even after he'd had a growth spurt and begun excelling in track and baseball. By graduation, he had reached his present height and weight: five-feet-nine, one hundred forty-five pounds. He had gained no more than fifteen pounds since.

Welcoming the relief to his loneliness that pleasant memories brought him, he thought more of his female bar customers during the years preceding his going into business. They told him they loved his quiet, caring manner, apparently not distracted by his slightly crooked nose, inherited from one of the many fights he'd had in elementary school or the scars over his left eye, chin, and upper lip from fights in high school. Some bullies hated Indians or anyone too small to best them in a fair fight.

The lady customers also did not seem to notice the gap in the top of his left ear. It had been bitten off while fighting a big white boy who called his grandmother a "filthy squaw." He reasoned that his and Mama's abuse at the hands of racists had deepened the bond between them.

The attention showered on him by his lady customers helped him to overcome much of the shyness inherited from his childhood and early school years. They came in all ages and classes, and some were wealthy. He could tell which ones were married; they came to the bar alone and were the most eager to go to bed. They were also the ones least likely to hang on afterwards, or talk about their brief encounter.

He pushed back his white Panama, rolled his head to look toward a rustling sound in the leaves nearby, and saw a tiny brown bird hopping about in search of something to eat, apparently undisturbed by his presence. He thought, "If something that small can survive in this wilderness, why can't I?"

Aside from an occasional rustling in the leaves, bird sounds, and the buzzing of a bee's wings, he had heard nothing since lying down. But as he listened more closely, there came the gentle whisper of a soft wind in the tops of the pines. It was a soothing sound, but ominous in its newness.

Gazing up at the gathering clouds high above the trees, he said, "Hello, clouds. Can you tell me if anybody under your cover gives a gnat's poot whether I live or die in this wilderness?"

Getting up, he examined the ropes holding the supply pack to the mule's back. The docile animal seemed unaware of his presence, as if completely content to eat grass and carry whatever was placed on his back. Blin envied the animal's ability to accept his fate without protest. A noble asset.

The horse was blessed with the same attribute, to a lesser degree. Blin saw great strength in their tolerance, a quality he lost in his hurry to become a financial success. How ironic it was, he thought, that he should find such enviable qualities in two dumb animals.

He patted the mule's neck. "You and Catcher have another thing in common, too. You're both the end of your line."

His statement caused an alarming thought to flash through his mind. Maybe he was the end of his family line, too.

He raked dirt over the dying fire, returned the percolator to his saddlebag, and climbed back into the saddle. Turning Catcher's head eastward, he swayed with the movements of his horse in an effort to lessen his discomfort. The leather beneath him had become harder.

To relieve the boredom, he began studying the different kinds of birds to see how many he could identify, but he soon realized that living in West Texas had not qualified him for the task. His turned his mind to the trees.

The part of the forest he rode through now was made up mostly of tall, tight-barked pines, but there was a liberal sprinkling of oak, gum, and hickory. There were other varieties he could not identify, grape vines loaded with green fruit and small trees with purple and white blooms.

When he made cautious inquiries about the area where he purchased the animals and trailer, he was told that Louisiana Pacific owned the many thousands of acres of land and timber at his intended destination. Upon studying his map later, he determined that no roads ran through it. That was a factor he considered in choosing his point of entry. No roads meant no homes, and no homes meant no prying eyes to discover his presence.

He told himself that somewhere up ahead, near the base of a high hill, he would find a campsite where he could live until the turmoil created by his court appearance died down. Organized crime leaders would never completely stop looking for him, but after several weeks, he hoped, they would begin looking for him outside the state. Then he could move on to the reservation and complete his mission. By then, it would be safe to visit Mama's people without fear of bringing them harm.

He was startled suddenly by the unexpected sound of an approaching airplane. Kicking Catcher hard with his heels, he reined him toward thicker cover. The mule didn't feel the same sense of urgency, jerking Blin from the saddle when he refused to let go of the lead rope.

Jumping to his feet, Blin pulled both the mule and Catcher under the wide, protecting branches of a big gum tree as a small red monoplane flashed by at what appeared to be no more than two hundred feet above the trees. It had come from the direction of the pipeline easement.

Shaken by the airplane's appearance, Blin moved cautiously from under the tree to peer after it as he searched his mind for a reason for it being in his vicinity. Had the pilot been inspecting the pipeline? If so, why was he flying so far from it? Maybe the pilot spotted the animals' hoof prints and followed them. Maybe someone had seen him leaving the blacktop with the animals and had reported him to Louisiana Pacific or the local authorities. In that case, the pilot would probably swing back his way and continue his search.

After waiting ten minutes, Blin was convinced the little airplane wouldn't return, so he mounted up. He had just ridden from cover when he saw something that gave him another shock. He jerked hard on the reins.

In the clearing where the animals had been grazing, in clear view of anyone flying low, were two piles of fresh animal manure. *Did the pilot spot that? If he did, I'm in big trouble.*

He rode back under the tree as a precaution, but after several more minutes of waiting was convinced the mounds weren't spotted, so he rode away in search of a proper campsite. The airplane's unexpected appearance prompted more misgivings about the benefits of his chosen sanctuary. Although the pilot didn't circle back again, he could very well have seen the animal droppings, which he could report to his headquarters. If he did, it would prompt a more thorough search of the area. It was a disturbing thought.

After riding less than an hour, his fears about the airplane were rekindled when he heard the fast-approaching sound of it returning. Convinced the pilot had spotted the animal droppings after all, he guided the animals towards the cover of the nearest tree. Ears was more cooperative this time, but he had barely walked under the branches than Blin saw a flash of red sweep by. He was sure it was the same monoplane. He remained still for several moments to see if the plane would circle back. When it didn't, he left cover again, more disturbed than before.

The possibility that the airplane might reappear at any time required him to take extra precautions. He could not light a fire and would have to avoid the widest openings. He regretted having made one fire already. Perhaps the smoke had attracted the pilot. The owners of the timber most likely employed someone to watch for forest fires. Perhaps the pilot worked for them. Regardless of whom he was working for, Blin knew he had to move a considerable distance before pitching camp.

The underbrush had become denser, but riding around large groves of it didn't make him lose his direction, thanks to the compass. After another hour, he stopped again to rest the animals, and upon dismounting, found that he was very tired from not having slept the night before and his exertions of the day. He began walking, leading the animals, telling himself he could not sleep before pitching camp.

He saw no signs of a recent human presence in the area, and that pleased him. From the beginning, he had watched for hunters, but the farther he moved from the highway, the more confident he became of not encountering any.

At the point of exhaustion a short time later, he climbed back on the horse, but stopped every half-hour the rest of the day to give Catcher and Ears a breather. It was pleasing to know that he had come so far without serious mishap, but as he pushed deeper into the forest, he became keenly aware of the growing intimidation of his surroundings.

The cooler late afternoon breeze revived him somewhat as he continued to move through the forest, but his misgivings about his ability to cope doubled. Surviving in such an environment was, without question, the strongest challenge he had faced since those early school years in West Texas. *Have I undertaken a task I can't handle?*

As the sun sank behind the trees over his left shoulder, he approached the crest of the highest hill he had yet encountered. Riding to the top of it, he found that he could see for miles in all directions, in spite of thickening clouds that had gathered south of him. He dismounted to flex his muscles and survey the magnificent scene.

He concluded the spot would be unsafe place to pitch camp because his campfires could be too easily seen from afar, so he remounted and scouted the area at the foot of the hill. Finding a stream cutting through the area between high banks, he dismounted and led the animals in search of an opening that would allow them access to water. After Catcher and Ears quenched their thirst, he led them out of the streambed, a short distance up the slope, where he tethered them and set about untying ropes holding the pack containing his food supplies and tent. Concluding he was too tired to unpack and set up the tent before resting, he looked around for a place to lie down.

He lay back on a thick bed of leaves beneath a large white oak with a long sigh, too exhausted to care that it was not as comfortable as his king-size foam mattress in Houston. What he needed now was rest on any kind of surface. He did not remember ever having been so exhausted.

Awakening some time later in complete darkness, he jumped to his feet, disgusted with himself for not unpacking while there was light. He would need new batteries in his flashlight before he could set up his tent and unpack his supplies.

Unable to see the animals, he was still recovering from the disappointment of being caught in the dark when a lightning flash lit up the area. It reflected off treetops swaying in a strong wind, and a frightened Catcher pulling back wildly on his halter rope. Blin stumbled toward the horse as another lightning bolt grounded nearby, making a sound so loud it caused him to jump and stumble.

As he checked the halter ropes on the animals by the light of constant flashes, another bolt struck nearby, lighting the area with the brilliance of a noon sun. It was followed by an even more threatening sound that reminded him of something from his childhood in West Texas. Stopping to watch and listen to nature's awesome display, he determined that the steady roar came from the southwest. Such a sound meant a tornado was approaching.

He shook his head in disbelief. Like the airplane, the storm had caught him completely unprepared, making him realize just how badly he had failed to measure up to his first real challenges in primeval surroundings.

Chapter III

*R*ain began falling in sheets, drenching him immediately in spite of the heavy foliage, and as the storm's intensity grew, nature's awesome display of lightning flashes and rolls of thunder were continuous. Trees swayed violently as branches snapped off on the crest of the hill. Somewhere close by, a tearing, cracking sound followed by a *thump* told him a tree had been sheared off by the raging wind. Lightning struck a tree near him with an ear-splitting sound, telling him he should not be taking cover under them.

He ran from the tree by the light of the continuing flashes and jumped into a shallow ditch, but abandoned it when water began rushing through it. As he frantically looked about for another ditch, he heard Catcher neighing and stamping wildly, causing him to push concern for his safety aside and rush to him. He caught hold of the rearing Catcher's halter rope and pulled him down, then moved close enough to talk to him. Catcher calmed, and when Blin turned to the mule, he found him standing calmly in the downpour, watching him.

Fearing Catcher would become frightened again and break his tether, Blin remained with him and the mule until the peak of the storm passed. Soaked and shaken, he moved to a big tree, sat down, and leaned against it to wait for daylight, thankful the tornado had not come closer.

The rain slowed to a soft, steady drizzle, and he found himself dozing off before the light of a new day brightened his surroundings enough to see. He looked up at dark, low-hanging clouds though openings in the trees and climbed stiffly to his feet to begin looking for dead sticks for a fire.

The larger twigs were too wet to burn, but after breaking several of the smaller ones and holding matches to broken ends, a tiny flicker appeared. He stacked more small sticks on it, following those with larger ones as the flame grew.

Removing the saddle from Catcher's back, he placed it on a dead stump and pulled his hatchet out of the saddlebag to chop down two small bushes with forks in their tops. Cutting them to the desired length, he

31

pushed them into the ground on opposite sides of the fire, resting the cut-off lower half of one in the forks. Leading the mule closer, he removed the supply pack and re-tethered him. He untied the ropes binding the tarp and took out a full bag of coffee and a plastic bag containing clothes purchased at a country store on the way. Sliding his hands through his other supplies, he found his extra batteries and closed the tarp to move to the fire. He put on dry clothes and hung his wet ones over a nearby branch.

Following a breakfast of black coffee and canned peaches, he set about making camp in the cool morning air under heavy cloud cover. Looking around for a suitable location for his tent, he settled for a level spot under two towering oaks whose limbs would prevent him from being spotted by the pilot of the red airplane if he should fly that far from the pipeline easement when the weather cleared. The belt of heavy underbrush on three sides of the site gave him protection from prying eyes at ground level in the unlikely event a hunter should pass.

The stream would provide him and the animals with an ample supply of water, plus enough for bathing and washing clothes. He could supplement his canned food with rabbits and squirrels, and with luck, a small buck that he could take with his .22 Remington rifle.

The thought of settling down in a place safe from organized crime's assassins eased some of his concerns about the weather and other immediate matters. It also increased his confidence in being able to withstand the hazards of living in the forest as long as required.

Replacing the spent batteries in the flashlight, he returned to the tarp and pulled out his tent, still folded inside a small cardboard box. It didn't take long to join and erect the sections of aluminum tubing from which the fabric would hang and drive metal spikes into the ground for the anchor cords. Unfolding the fresh vinyl, he spread it over the aluminum supports, pulled it down tight, and secured it to the stakes and anchoring spikes. He unzipped the door and crawled inside to straighten out wrinkles in the floor and lower the window flaps, then went back outside to admire his finished project.

Pleased with something he'd done well in the forest for a change, he removed his sleeping bag, rifle, and first aid kit from the tarp and placed them inside the tent, rolling out his sleeping bag. He reached into his side pocket for his compass, intending to place it next to his rifle, but it wasn't there.

Afraid he'd lost the vital instrument, he searched through the items remaining in the tarp and the area where he opened his supply pack and found it where it had apparently fallen out of his pocket when he removed his pocketknife. Since he had no need for it in the tent, he pushed it inside the tarp with the rest of his supplies and returned to the vinyl structure with his hunting knife and three boxes of ammunition for the rifle.

He filled the rifle's tubular magazine with long-rifle cartridges, placed the gun next to the sleeping bag, and hung the hunting knife on his belt just behind his revolver. The pistol gave him a sense of security he sorely needed, and after examining its moving parts, he was glad to see it was not damaged after being drenched.

Outside, he tucked in the tarp around his extra clothes, canned vegetables, coffee, meat, and fish and picked up his half-gallon canteen. He led the animals down the slope in search of a place in the stream's banks that wasn't as steep as their previous entry point.

He found an easy access and had no problem in getting Catcher and Ears to follow him to the branch's sandy bed, where they immediately lowered their heads to drink. Blin watched as tiny white granules of sand swirled briefly around their hooves before drifting downstream with the current, allowing the water to become crystal clear again.

The mule raised its head, but the horse continued to drink. Suddenly remembering that horses would founder if allowed to drink too much, Blin pulled Catcher back. "That's enough, big boy," he said.

After leading the animals up the bank and tying their halter ropes to saplings, he walked further upstream in search of a place to get water for drinking and cooking and a hole deep enough for bathing. He wished the sun would come out, because the darkness not only made it difficult to explore the area, it made his surroundings more ominous.

About fifty feet from where he watered the animals, he found a smaller stream intersecting the larger one. Following it, he walked no more than forty feet before arriving at its source at the base of a weed-covered embankment some ten feet high. In a bed of white sand about three feet wide, inside a circle of green ferns, a spring bubbled.

Stepping through the ferns, he got down on hands and knees to scoop out sand from the spring's center until he'd dug a hole six inches deep and twice as wide. He watched, transfixed, as white granules swirled about like tiny tornados before settling back to the bottom of the cavity to leave the water clear again. Lowering the canteen into the hole, he filled it and headed back to his campsite, looking up on the way to find the clouds as dark and thick as before. He suspected another storm was in the making.

Stopping in a small clearing near his tent, he sat down on a wet, dead log and studied the clouds more, this time spotting small clusters of white clouds beneath the darker ones that were moving south to north, as if pushed by a disturbance on the Texas coast or in the Gulf. He listened for sounds of birds or animals, but heard nothing but the creak of the trees' rain-laden branches and drops of water cascading from them with each gust of wind. It was the first time he had not heard a bird or sounds of animal life at that time of day. That reminded him of something Mama told him—that wild creatures in the big woods had a way of knowing when dangerous weather was imminent.

As he studied his surroundings and waited for the comforting sounds of animal life, the wind calmed and the lower clouds ceased moving. It became quieter, making him feel more threatened and keenly aware of his aloneness. It triggered memories of his shyness as a boy and teenager. In spite of that handicap, however, he'd never felt alone, because of Mama's presence. She was always there.

Once he'd overcome his shyness in his struggle to become a success, the former sensations became alien to him. The constant companionship of others was something he had taken for granted and never fully appreciated prior to coming here.

When he moved to Dallas and Houston after graduation, he had carried with him a trait other than shyness: a love for quiet, unrushed surroundings. He at first hated the rush and harsh noises of the city, but as time passed, he become so accustomed to them he seldom noticed either. Engrossed with finding ways to earn quick money, he learned to shut out the most invasive sounds. It struck him as unusual that a person accustomed to the quiet of country life could become so indifferent to such things. Perhaps a man's acquired immunity to discord was just nature's way of protecting one's sanity.

His new life in the competitive business world required him to accept many things that contradicted Mama's theory of how following the natural order of things best promoted internal harmony. He sighed. Somewhere along the way, insensitivity became a necessity, and in its shadow, he had accepted its ugly cousin, cynicism.

He was glad Mama had not witnessed such drastic changes in his priorities. If she had, he wondered if they would still share the bond that always existed between them. True, she was gone now, but he remained bone of her bones and blood of her blood. Although raised in a white world, attending their schools and one of their churches, his Indian grandmother's influence was stronger than ever, following him like a shadow, guiding and admonishing. If her spiritual presence gave him the strength to survive, he vowed to return to the kind of living Mama thought best.

After a few days alone in rural settings, his ears had already become more attuned to the sounds of remote places. The physical toils of outdoor living would harden his entire body, thereby increasing his chances of survival. He had not, however, experienced anything that had helped him overcome his recently acquired cynicism. Resentment and skepticism were not pleasant companions.

He glanced at his watch, as if the hour was of the essence, and found it was only eight o'clock. He had to stay busy so time wouldn't drag so, but what could he do in a place where options were so limited? He reasoned it offered nothing that would appease his hunger for self-gratification. Self-denial was the rule now, replacing self-indulgence. But even while he had been living amid luxury, he recalled how, from time to time, he had sensed that something was missing from his life. The certainty came during those nights when he was exhausted and alone by choice, or during other times of solitude while besieged by a wave of self-examination. Each time it happened, Mama's rules for living came to mind, causing him to suspect that his conscience was disturbed by the difference between his new lifestyle and her rules. He easily recalled her teachings pertaining to the accumulation of wealth and other matters, but could not recall her ever making any announcements regarding a man's private relationship with women. His father never discussed such matters with him, and the only thing he remembered Mama saying that might pertain to a man's personal life was said following his high school graduation. She said, "There is but one wind. It is strong and it blows the same for man and woman. At times, they both must put up walls to block it so it will not run wild and destroy what must be kept holy."

He remembered the knowing expression in Mama's eyes following his high school graduation ceremony when he told her he wished he had a steady girlfriend to share his sense of accomplishment. He knew then that she sensed his mental turmoil over not having developed a meaningful relationship with a girl who would make his life complete.

In spite of his many romantic encounters while attending bar, he continued to sense that something was missing. He chided himself for having such thoughts, telling himself it was ridiculous for a man of his age to be bothered by sentimentality. But the matter continued coming to mind from time to time, making him feel a touch of guilt about enjoying the company of so many women outside marriage.

He retrieved his radio from the tent and returned to the log. Finding a clear station, he listened to bluegrass music while waiting for a news program at the end of the hour, anxious to find out if the recent happenings in Houston were still critical in the minds of listeners and local officials.

He didn't bother listening to news broadcasts after two days because he resented the reporters' derogatory comments. Among other things, they said, "The crime bosses' Judas and the justice department's wild card turned out to be a joker." The commentators attacked him again the next day, saying, "The justice department's witness, Wild Card Burge, who apparently attempted to entrap alleged criminals with illegally obtained testimony, has taken off for parts unknown. Assistant Federal District Attorney George Madsen is searching frantically for him, as are the criminals, but for different reasons, we're told. Mr. Madsen tells us that it is imperative that he find Wild Card Burge to testify before a new grand jury about other felony charges that might be filed. He also told us Burge is needed by the state D.A., who is considering filling charges against local alleged criminals. Mr. Madsen has requested we issue an urgent appeal to his star witness to immediately report his whereabouts to him if he hears this broadcast." The news announcement went to say Veronica Stedham had filed on him in state court for "assault with intent to kidnap." She'd lost no time in joining the winners.

At ten o'clock, the newscast began, but it was barely audible. Near the end, he did make out, "George Madsen's wild card, Blin Burge, the joker that ran away, has still not been found, a fact that leads some to speculate that he has either fled the state or been killed." Blin snapped off the radio.

Rubbing his beard, he considered shaving, but decided to wait until the next day, when he pulled more of his supplies from the tarp. He did make more coffee, and after drinking two cups, set off with the rifle to explore the woods along the stream.

After walking downstream for what he guessed to be at least two miles, he crossed the stream and returned to his campsite with no game, exhausted and hungry. In spite of his failure to find fresh meat, he remained convinced he had chosen the right place for his temporary home because he had seen no signs of human presence or any indication that anyone had passed through the area of late.

He had looked for places in the stream wide and deep enough to support eating-size bass or catfish, but had found only three holes containing small sun perch. He attributed the disappearance of deer and squirrel to the threatening weather. The clouds were still dark and thick, and there was no breeze.

He rekindled the fire and warmed a can of beef and a can of peas for lunch. After eating, he stretched out in his tent for a brief nap, but found he was too keyed up to sleep. He went back outside and sat down on the dead log until boredom drove him to taking a small plastic box from the tarp, in which he had stored a couple of fishing lines fitted with hooks and corks. Cutting down a small, slick-barked bush for a fishing pole, he set out for the nearest large hole in the stream. He saw a fallen dead pine tree on the way and stripped its bark until he found several wood sawyers he needed for bait.

He returned to camp tired and muddy just before dark with only six sun perch, all smaller than his hand. After scaling and cleaning them, he fried them in a small, Teflon-coated skillet. When done, he carefully pulled tiny pieces of meat from the bones and ate them with a can of shoestring potatoes. Both were tasty, but not filling.

He looked up at the dark clouds again in hopes of spotting light from the setting sun and was disappointed. Walking to a large pine tree, he sat down and leaned against it to listen for sounds that would tell him the small animals had sensed that good weather would be returning the next morning and were stirring about in the fading light, but heard nothing. Disappointed, he settled back to wait for total darkness, which came earlier than usual.

He found himself wishing again for somebody to talk to. He would be happy to have a deaf mute with him—anybody—just as long as he could look over and see another human face. He thought about Veronica again, and how disappointed he was that she had joined the ranks of his enemies. He wondered which of the gangsters she would sleep with tonight.

He wished he had a book to read, but that would require him to burn precious Coleman fluid. He would use it conservatively, as he didn't know how much fresh game he would be cooking, or for how long he would be heating canned food.

Darkness came, and when the fire went out, he could see nothing around him, not even his tent, which was no more than twenty feet away.

The animals had stopped munching grass and settled down for another night of doing what horses and mules do in the dark. An owl hooted in the tree over him, causing him to jump with an excited grunt. He immediately felt foolish for reacting that way to something harmless.

He remembered hearing frogs and katydids at the thicket where he camped with the animals before moving up the blacktop to enter the big woods. He heard no such sounds now, and could think of no reason for it except the threatening weather. He hoped another storm didn't blow through during the night.

He felt his way to the tent and crawled inside, and in spite of his nervous state, the exertions of the day's ride and his hikes along the stream caused him to drift off into a deep sleep.

He didn't know how long he had been asleep when he was awakened by a furtive sound he could not identify. Sitting up, he listened closely, pulse pounding, but the sound stopped. Several moments passed, during which he did not again hear anything, not even the stirring of leaves by the wind. It was as if the world about him had stopped. Suddenly possessed by a strong sense of foreboding, he stood and looked through the screen door at the black wall outside, but still heard nothing. It was eerie.

Feeling about on the floor of the tent until he found his flashlight, he pressed it against the nylon screen and turned its beam slowly around the perimeter of the small clearing, but didn't see anything but trees and bushes. Thinking the sound was made by something his animals did, he decided to go down and check on them.

Finding everything to be satisfactory with Catcher and Ears, he returned to the tent and stripped down to his shorts to go back to sleep, but his sense of foreboding grew.

"It's so quiet!" he muttered. "Never knew quiet was louder than thunder." He finally relaxed and began drifting off.

Sometime later, he was aroused to a state of partial awareness, and for a while drifted back and forth from that to a light sleep until he was suddenly made fully alert by another furtive sound alongside the tent. He sat up, nervous and anxious.

At first, his sleepy brain could not comprehend the meaning of the sounds, but as he became more alert, he heard similar noises on the opposite side of his flimsy shelter. He remained still, his mind whirling with anticipation. They were soft, rustling sounds in the leaves, like none he had ever heard. Of one thing he was certain, however—some*one* or some*thing* was moving about in the leaves outside the walls of his tent.

Heart racing, he rose to his knees as the strange sounds grew louder. He heard sniffing, followed by scratching and growling, then vicious, snapping sounds. From the woods nearby came a high-pitched howl, followed by wailing and barking that triggered a deep sense of dread. He had never heard of dogs running in large packs in the wild and had always been told that coyotes never attacked humans.

The sounds could mean only one thing: he was surrounded by killer wolves!

Chapter IV

Overwhelmed by fear and disbelief, Blin tried desperately to think of a way to save himself from yet another unexpected threat. He berated himself for not thinking about the possibility of wolves in such a vast uninhabited wilderness.

Heart pounding, he sat still and listened as the sounds stopped. Had he been dreaming? Perhaps the wind had awakened him, and the things he thought he heard were the result of an over-active imagination. Then the sounds came again, sweeping away all doubt as to their source. The predators were present in large numbers, and they were about to tear through the flimsy walls of his shelter.

He slid his hands along the vinyl floor in a frantic search for his revolver, angry with himself for not having placed it under the edge of the sleeping bag. He could see nothing in the darkness, but he finally found the pistol and began feeling about wildly for the flashlight. There were rustling sounds on all four sides of the tent now, and there was more scratching and pulling at the vinyl walls.

His hand struck the flashlight, but in his haste, he caused it to skid out of his reach. Cursing his clumsiness, he reached for his trousers and the matches, but before he could locate them, the wolves began tearing through the nylon screen door, whining and growling in their frenzied efforts to break in.

Blin pointed the pistol toward the tearing sounds and fired. The flash lit up the tent for an instant, and a pained yelp told him he'd hit at least one of the predators. The flash revealed many pairs of shining eyes pressed against the flimsy barrier.

Rustling sounds in the leaves told him the killers were falling back as he knelt on one knee and strained his eyes against the darkness hoping he had driven the wolves away. Remembering his flashlight, he felt along the floor to find it, in case they attacked again.

As he searched, he listened for rustling sounds in the leaves, but heard nothing except his hand rubbing against the vinyl and his own heavy breathing. He stopped searching for the light, and he had just finished pulling on his trousers when the scratching and snapping sounds began again. It would be only seconds before the animals tore through the walls, and stopping them would be impossible.

He fired three quick shots through three walls, and the sound of feet running through leaves told him the animals had fallen back again, once more leaving him in a silent, black world, but moments later, they moved in again and resumed tearing at the walls. When he raised his pistol to shoot, he heard another sound that was as puzzling as it was unexpected: a soft, low whistle from the direction of the stream.

The wolves fell silent, and when another whistle came, they immediately scampered away from the tent down the hill. After several minutes without hearing anything to indicate their return, he stretched out on his sleeping bag with a sigh of relief, shaken and spent, relieved that the killers had departed.

Had he been mistaken about the animals being wolves? The whistle down by the stream suggested they might have been somebody's hunting dogs, called back by their master. He had heard of people hunting raccoons and foxes at night. The animals could have been wild dogs, even. But who would call wild dogs? If they were wild, they wouldn't respond to human commands.

He got up, found the flashlight, and snapped it on, but all he could see beyond the screened door was bushes and trees. Still shaking from his ordeal, he shined the light on the walls to survey the damage and found the tent to be in good condition except for the bullet holes and narrow rips in the door's screen and two side walls.

He had just told himself how lucky he was when he heard a sudden burst of snarling and growling down the hill, followed by the thumping of hooves and the frantic whinnying of his horse. The wolves hadn't left after all. They were attacking the animals.

He grabbed his boots, but after pulling them on, he found that the door's zipper was stuck. Moaning in desperation, he grappled with it as the attack on his animals grew more intense. They would be maimed or killed if he didn't get to them immediately.

Ripping open the screen with his knife, he crawled outside, but stopped when he remembered there were only two live rounds remaining in his revolver. He crawled back inside, picked up the rifle and a box of cartridges, and raced toward his animals by the light of his flashlight's beam.

Ignoring the branches whipping at his face and bare arms, he fired the last two rounds in his pistol into the air and shouted wildly, but the attack continued. He ran faster, tripping and falling when he hung his foot on something. He dropped the flashlight. Jumping to his feet, he found it and continued racing down the incline.

The mule was the first to show up in Blin's light. Ears was already down, kicking at its attackers but obviously losing the battle. Blin fired the rifle into the furry mass and one wolf fell. He continued shooting, slowly and methodically, hitting several others before the survivors turned and charged Catcher.

Focusing the beam on his horse, Blin found him still on his feet, rearing and kicking at his attackers. Blin fired at the wolves closest to Catcher, then at one on his back. As that one fell, he turned the light toward Catcher's head, where another predator was struggling to get his teeth into the horse's throat. It fell when he fired, and at that point, the others disappeared into the cover of the surrounding brush.

Blin ran over to take hold of Catcher's halter rope pulling him down and speaking softly to him. The big horse calmed, but his shoulder muscles continued to tremble.

Examining his horse, Blin found scratches and shallow cuts on his legs, neck, and back. The deepest lacerations were on his back, and they were bleeding.

"Whoa, boy," he said. "Everything's gonna be okay now. I'll get you fixed up in no time."

Swinging the flashlight's beam to the mule, Blin found that animal's legs badly torn and blood running from an ugly wound in his throat. It was a sickening sight.

"I'm sorry, Ears." He walked over to him. "I'm sorry I let this happen to you." Blin examined the wounds more closely and shook his head in disgust.

The only humane thing to do was to put Ears out of his misery, but the thought of doing that to such a faithful friend sent a wave of revulsion through him. Steeling himself for the dreaded task, he placed the rifle's barrel between the mule's eyes and pulled the trigger. The mule's muscles jerked convulsively, then he shuddered and became still.

Placing the light under his left arm, Blin refilled the rifle's magazine as he walked back to his campsite for the stove, the salve in his first aid kit, and a container of water. He also grabbed his shirt while there, and on the way back to the horse, shined the light around him in search of the wolves.

He had cleaned Catcher's wounds and reached for the salve when a twig snapped behind him. Whirling, he saw the reflections of many sets of shining eyes.

"Damn!" He reached for the rifle.

He fired twice as the pack charged. One fell as others rushed, snarling, into the clearing with teeth bared. He thought he heard something move at his campsite, but didn't dare turn his attention from the wolves.

He began firing at the animals nearest him and Catcher. Two more fell, and their yelps caused the others to race back into the bushes.

Blin took advantage of their retreat to light the burner of the camp stove. He was still concerned about the noise at his campsite, but the rush of gas from the butane canister kept him from hearing that far away. It must have been a falling limb, or the rush of an owl's wings through the trees.

The round burner's blue flame made a circle of light some thirty feet wide, wide enough for him to spot the animals and fire before they reached him. He would use the flashlight to spot the ones in the brush.

He moved into the shadow of a tree and shined his flashlight's beam up the incline toward his campsite, but bushes blocked his view. He moved back to stand by the stove and listen for sounds in the leaves, but he heard nothing above the steady rush of gas.

Turning his attention to the outer circle of light nearest the horse, he looked for more shining eyes, and when he saw none, he emptied the box of .22 cartridges into his left front pocket and refilled the magazine.

He had no idea what time it was, and when he looked up to see if he could spot the moon, he saw nothing. The cloud cover was still solid.

Nervously fingering the trigger of the rifle, he told himself every shot from then on must count, because there was no more than half a box of cartridges remaining. He wished he had a shotgun.

He spotted a shaking bush at the edge of the circle of light, but none of the predators moved into view. The wolves were holding back because of the light. If the stove ran out of fuel or he fired all his cartridges before daylight, he would be as dead as his mule when the sun came up.

Chapter V

*A*n outburst of growling and snapping in the underbrush told Blin the wolves were still present, and when they became quiet again, he assumed they were creeping closer for another attack. When a pair of eyes reflected the light, he fired, and the eyes disappeared. Hearing a rushing sound behind him, he whirled in time to shoot the first of two wolves charging him. He fired again, and the second one whirled and disappeared.

Because the tree's shadow partially blocked his view of what was behind him, Blin moved nearer Catcher to put more space between him and that area. He kept the rifle at the ready and waited. When several wolves charged from the shadows nearest his horse, he fired, and Catcher jerked back hard on the halter rope, whinnying wildly. Blin continued firing until the wolves ran out of sight. Lowering his rifle, he stroked Catcher's neck and talked to him, and the horse calmed.

He heard snarling and snapping in the darkness as the killers moved about him on three sides. Catcher again pulled back to whinny and prance. Fearing a charge from three directions, Blin fired into the brush on all sides, and the wolves became quiet again. Moments later, one growled and snapped at another, and he fired at the sound.

He refilled the rifle's magazine with shaking fingers as shining eyes reappeared at the outer rim of light. Catcher moved about more briskly, and Blin worried about him jumping into his line of fire when the next attack came. He spoke to the horse to calm him, at the same time searching the circle of darkness for the next wave of attackers. He fired at one set of eyes but missed.

Moments later, Blin thought he heard a whistle down by the stream, but couldn't be sure because of the stove. The shining eyes disappeared, and a rush through the brush toward the stream told him the killers were leaving. He dropped to the ground, exhausted, but glad to be alive.

Time dragged by, and the black world began to grow lighter. He turned off the stove, and moments later heard the waking sounds of the forest—faint at first, then louder as their surroundings became brighter.

First came the chirping of one bird, then two. In a nearby tree, he heard the scraping sounds of a running squirrel's claws against bark, then the call of a crow and a blue jay. They were welcome sounds. Perhaps it meant the cloud cover was moving out.

His hopes for a clear day were shattered when it became light enough for him to see the same heavy clouds. The absence of the sun made his surroundings seem as dismal and threatening as before.

He knew by the low flames of his little stove that it was about out of fuel, and upon checking his rifle, he found he had only six rounds remaining, but like the blackness of the night, the wolves had slipped away.

He lay down on the damp earth near Catcher and fell into a deep sleep, waking some time later to find no change in the weather. Remembering the wolves, he grabbed the rifle and jumped to his feet, seeing six dead ones.

The lifeless animals resembled German shepherd dogs, only they were thinner and had smaller heads, sharper noses, and more slanted eyes. Their coloring was a mix of brown, gray, white, and black, with a predominance of the darker colors, suggesting a cross between wolves and dogs. None of their furs possessed the luster of domestic dogs.

Blin recalled boyhood tales about the interbreeding of dogs and wolves in the wild, but had never known hybrids to be taken from their natural habitat and trained to obey commands. It explained the whistling down by the stream. Had the animals attacked him prior to their master's arrival on the scene, or were they following their owner's commands? Outside the assassins, what reason could anyone have to kill him? And his animals posed no threat to anyone. That thought made him wonder if the man who had whistled had wanted them dead, or had used them to get him outside his tent. He looked around, half-expecting to find their master watching him, poised to shoot. He saw no one.

He flexed his sore muscles and patted Catcher's neck, checking his wounds. When he touched the ugliest one on his back and a smaller tear on his shoulder, the horse jumped. The other wounds were minor, but the one on his back would prevent Blin from riding him for a couple of days.

Blin looked at the dead mule and wondered how he would survive without him when he moved on. He could exist without his tent, but not his food. His guilt about the animal's fate was made more bearable by his being alive and unhurt, but that another negative followed uplifting thought: this particular area of the forest was no longer the safe haven he'd hoped it would be. He had to move on and hope the owner of the hybrids didn't follow.

Where were the whistler and his hybrids now? He picked up his canteen and walked stiffly down the hill to the cut in the bank, where he saw the predators' tracks running from it, crossing the stream's shores up the opposite embankment. He guessed there were at least a dozen survivors.

He also saw something more disturbing. Dropping the canteen, he moved to the water's edge for a closer look at a large shoeprint in the sand. Pushed deep into the soft earth, it told him its wearer was a big man and that he had departed in the direction of the hybrids' retreat. His shoes were at least a size twelve, and each toe was turned inward. The pigeon-toed man crossed the stream near the animals' tracks.

He climbed the opposite embankment but found no more shoeprints in the heavy leaf cover. Further out, where leaves had been washed away by the heavy rain, he found the same large footprints leading away from the stream. Where had the man come from? Did he live nearby? Had the pilot of the red airplane sent someone to drive out the trespasser in the timber? But why would a timber company resort to such drastic means over a minor infraction?

Whatever the motive for the hybrids' attack, they were gone, and so was their master. In view of the man's loss of six animals, he might not want to risk losing more. Blin couldn't risk that.

He re-crossed the stream and walked past Catcher, looking for signs that indicted more than one human stalker, and saw drag marks in the leaves that sent a chill up his spine. There were two of them, about three feet apart, deep enough to tell him they were supporting a heavy object, and between them were more large shoeprints, leading away from his campsite.

"Oh, no!" he moaned. Running to his campsite, he found the tarp containing his supplies gone.

The thought of having no food in the remote area sent a wave of fear over him, much like the one that struck him as he fled the federal courthouse. It also triggered memories of that morning long ago when Mama kissed and hugged him upon leaving him that first time at the door of the elementary school, which was filled with angry eyes. He was in much the same predicament now: alone in a hostile world, a reality made worse by the thought of dying from starvation.

Even if he still possessed the strength to walk miles back to the blacktop, he couldn't find it without the compass in the tarp, and if he got lucky, the prospect of encountering Doss Saavedra's killers there or somewhere on the highway was daunting. He had to find his supplies and retrieve his compass and enough canned food to get him to the reservation.

Chapter VI

*H*e was relieved to find his first-aid kit containing Mama's letters still under his bedroll in the tent. The small box of matches in it meant he could cook meat or fish he caught, if he didn't find his supplies. There were only six cartridges remaining in his rifle and none for his pistol, so each shot had to get game. Back outside, he studied the heavy cloud cover to find the approximate location of the sun, to no use. In an attempt to get his directions straight, he retraced his movements.

He recalled setting out from his last rest stop in a northeast direction, but also remembered making many turns after that, so many he could not now be sure he had held that course all the way to his present location. Without knowing for sure, he did not know which direction to take to reach the southern boundary of the reservation.

He searched the ground where the tarp had been, hoping the compass had fallen out when the thieves dragged it away, but he didn't find it. Sitting down on the dead log with a disgusted sigh, he told himself he had to remain calm if he wanted to stay alive long enough to keep his sacred promise to Mama. He believed his initial decision not to return to the highway was the best choice. He believed the reservation was closer, and heading toward it after finding his supplies would take him further from the wolf man and his hybrid killers.

He wished he could remain in the forest longer, as visiting Mama's relatives too soon might attract members of the news media. That would be dangerous for both him and his relatives. The gangsters wouldn't care who they killed as long as they got him.

He knew there were at least two thieves to contend with because his supplies were dragged away while the hybrids' master was still down by the stream. Confronting the hybrids' owner would be risky enough, but getting his supplies back from *two* outlaws would be even riskier, but the dangers involved were no more harsh than starving.

He would follow the drag marks to where the thieves had stored his tarp and bundle up as many canned items as he could in his shirt and pockets. He could get more supplies if Catcher's back was well enough to carry a pack; but lumbering through the woods with the large animal would make it impossible to approach the thieves' camp undetected, and Catcher would likely let go with one of his unexpected snorts.

He folded the tent around his empty pistol and dropped them into a shallow ditch, covering the bundle with leaves. He pushed the first-aid kit and flashlight under the leaves beside it; he would retrieve them and his canteen when he returned for Catcher.

Rifle in hand, he followed the skid marks at a fast walk, soon arriving at a clearing not far from the spring where they crossed the stream to converge with the tracks of the pigeon-toed man. Blin moved on. Stopping often to listen and study the area ahead to make sure he wasn't walking into a trap, he pressed on in the warm humid air. Within an hour, he'd arrived at a place in the dead leaves where the thieves had stopped to rest and smoke a couple of cigarettes. He sniffed a butt and found it to be marijuana. That surprised him, as he had not expected people in such a rural area to be potheads, having always associated the practice with large cities, large public schools, and other places where young people hung out.

An hour later by his watch, he stopped and lay down to rest, tired and hungry. The trail had made so many turns around and over hills and ravines that he had lost all sense of direction. If it should rain, he would be unable to follow the drag marks back to his campsite, and he wasn't sure he was still moving parallel to the stream. The sky was so dark he already had difficulty following the parallel scrapes in the heavy ground cover.

He set out again, more keenly aware of his thirst and growing hunger. He was exhausted, too, a problem that apparently had not hampered the thieves, as there were no signs showing they had stopped again to rest. He wondered how two men could drag such a heavy load so far without becoming completely exhausted.

Later, he saw a ravine to his left that wound along the foot of the slopes and hills, and sensed it was something he had seen before. Spotting a gnarled, dead oak in an open area, he realized the gorge was the stream he had followed the day before in search of places to fish. That must have been when the thieves became aware of his presence. About an hour later, at quarter to ten, he heard what sounded like a barking dog in the distance. Stopping, he determined the barking was ahead of him.

He knew the hybrids had traveled all the way with the two thieves, because he had spotted their tracks and seen their droppings from time to time. They were likely barking after having arrived at their home base. He would have to proceed more slowly now.

Moments later, he saw a narrow clearing in the timber ahead. He stopped to study the scene and listen, but he saw and heard nothing. His mouth and throat were parched, and the gnawing in his stomach was fierce, but he was convinced he had made the right choice.

Making sure he didn't step on a dead twig or shake a bush, he moved forward until he came upon a narrow, sandy road cutting through the timber. There were tire marks, but too close together to have been made by a car. The tread marks were wider than an automobile's and left deeper indentions in the sand—definitely made by ATVs.

Following a course parallel to the ATV passageway, he arrived to where the drag marks moved out into it, following it toward a larger opening in the woods ahead. Near a turn some fifty feet from him, the ATV tracks disappeared.

At the turn, he had a better view of still another clearing. In it, he saw a crudely built frame cabin under tall trees. It had no windows or door on the two sides he could see. Just past the corner of the cabin, he saw the rear end of a red, mud-splattered four-wheeler. He listened for sounds in the house, but heard none.

The small clearing in front of the cabin was filled with tall, green plants with narrow, pointed leaves, the sight of which presented another surprise. His experiences as an undercover agent told him they were the leaves of the *cannabis sativa* plant, more commonly referred to as marijuana.

The thieves were growing the weed in a clearing that appeared to be no more than thirty feet wide and one hundred feet long. There was enough of the contraband to support a sizable commercial operation.

Beneath the big trees, along the backside of the plants, he saw ropes hanging from limbs the entire length of the clearing, and upon following the only rope he could see at that distance, found it running through a pulley attached to the top of a tall four-by-four, then over to the opposite side of the clearing to another. From the second one, it extended to the ground to what appeared to be a bundle of camouflaged netting. He saw the tips of other fourbyfours along each side of the plants, all the way to the end of the rows.

He was impressed by the ingenuity of the pot farmers. Rather than risk having their cash crop spotted from the air, they pulled the mesh over it when away or when an airplane or a helicopter was in the area. The illegal operation offered another reason for the red airplane's presence and the attempt on his life.

An unusual odor told him the thieves were also producing methamphetamine inside the cabin. Meth was a moneymaker. Blin theorized he had not come close enough to the house the day before to smell the drug or the plants, but close enough for the hybrids to catch his scent.

He couldn't see a kennel, but suspected there was one and that it was concealed in the brush on the other side of the cabin. The exhausted and wounded animals were probably resting in it while their masters did the same inside. He had arrived at a good time, but the possibility of the hybrids catching his scent and alarming the thieves made him realize there was no time to waste. He had to find his supplies quickly and leave.

He eased the cartridge ejector back a bit on his rifle to make sure a cartridge was in the firing chamber in case he was discovered. He didn't have enough ammunition for a drawn-out firefight; his best chance of survival lay in his ability to locate his pack and slip away unnoticed. Besides, he was too hungry and exhausted to wait for nightfall, and he had to be able to see the skid marks on his return trip.

He eased forward a few yards and saw the hybrid dogs lying down inside a pen near the far end of the cabin, apparently asleep. Since he didn't see the thieves, he was convinced they, too, were taking a nap. Glancing at his watch and the clouds, he told himself he had to hurry for another reason: it could start raining at any moment. But where were his supplies? If they were inside the cabin, he would have to wait until the thieves left the premises, a possibility he preferred not to think about.

He moved up to less than one hundred feet of the shack, where he could see around the last sharp turn in the narrow road, and spotted his tarp leaning against a tall pine at the end of what appeared to be a freshly cut path leading off the main passageway, still tied to the drag poles.

Encouraged, he studied the path leading to his supply pack more closely, as well as the heavily used one from which it ran. On the main trail just beyond the point where the two passageways separated was a brush barrier that prevented him from approaching his supplies from that point. He attached no significance to that fact or to what appeared to be fresh dirt in the new path leading to his supplies because parallel drag marks ran though the spot.

Confident of success, he headed for his pack at a brisk walk and had just entered the new branch of the trail when the earth suddenly gave way, sending him crashing downward in a shower of sticks and dirt. He was almost knocked unconscious when he landed on his back on the earthen bottom of a deep, dark pit.

Stunned and breathless for a moment, he flailed about in an attempt to get up, grunting and cursing his recklessness. Back on his feet, he brushed off sticks and dirt and looked up at the rectangular patch of light above. He jumped as high as he could, but the top of the pit was beyond his reach. He was trapped.

"What a fool I am," he said aloud. "The thieves laid down a trail a blind man could follow, then left my supplies in clear view to make sure I found them when I got here. They don't want my supplies. They want *me*."

He heard footsteps and the high-pitched voice of a man say, "Didn't I tell you all cops are stupid, Hulie? I told Uncle Emmett he'd follow us and let us do what his pets couldn't last night."

"Him and his precious pets," a man replied. "He called 'em off because too many were getting killed. I guess he wouldn't let you shoot the cop because he was afraid you'd hit another one."

"Naah, that wasn't the reason. He wouldn't kill him over there because the cop's buddies would find his corpse full o' bullet holes and snoop around in the woods 'til they found our operation and hung a murder rap on us. He said he ain't never going back to the slammer. Well, he won't have to worry about havin' to do that now, because handlin' the cop my way won't leave any evidence for anybody to find. It'll be just like it was when I took care of that little—"

"Shut up, High!" the second man said. "There are a couple of ears down in that pit."

"So what, little brother? Makes no difference what ears on a dead man hear."

"He's not dead yet, and I don't think we oughta do anything to him 'til we talk to Papa, or before Uncle Emmett gets back."

"We're not waitin' for nobody or talkin' to nobody. I'm in charge now, and I say let's get rid of him. Uncle Emmett ain't the only one who has to worry about goin' to the pen. Our uncle will be proud of me for doin' it in a way that won't get him involved, and it'll prove to both of you that cleanin' out that old pit was a good idea after all. Now, help me throw some brush in that hole."

Blin got down on hands and knees to search for his rifle, but couldn't find it. He must have dropped it on the embankment. He was really in a fix now.

"Hey, cop!" the high voice called down. "Did the fall kill you, or are we still gonna have to build a fire?"

Blin looked up. "I'm not a cop, and I have no interest in you. I just want some of my supplies back. Throw me a rope." He didn't see a face. "Let me out, and you'll never see me again."

"If I was you, I'd say the same thing, cop," the high-pitched voice replied. "We know why you're sneakin' around in these woods. We've had plenty experience with cops doin' that."

"I'm not sneaking, just camping out for a while before moving on." He jumped, but still couldn't reach the rim. The hole was at least nine feet deep.

"We're not stupid, stupid," the high voice replied. "But not to worry, cop. We're just gonna practice a little gospel, as my papa would put it. Have you ever heard preachers use the expression 'ashes to ashes'?" He laughed. "I've heard my ol' daddy say it lots of times. We're gonna fulfill a little scripture, is all."

Blin slid his boots along the black bottom of the pit, still hoping to find the rifle. The dirt was soft and mushy, and gave off a sickening odor, much like garbage or rotting flesh.

There was a muffled exchange between his captors, with Blin making out only one word that sounded like "line" or "lime." The high voice became more excited when he told his partner, "I should shoot him first, Hulie. I've got a right to do that since I'm the one that caught him."

"You're always wantin' to shoot somebody. Control yourself. You don't want to leave a bullet in him the law could trace if they ever dig up his body. Uncle Emmett would really crawl up your frame if you did that. Uncle Emmett wouldn't let you shoot him last night, and I'm not gonna let you now. The cop comin' here makes me as much a part of this as you and him."

"But that lime is gonna eat up what the fire don't burn."

"You're forgetting what Uncle Emmett told us about doin' anything to anybody that can be traced to us. And you know what Papa would do to us all if he found out you killed somebody else."

"We could find out who sent him first. That would tell us if any more are comin' and what he was lookin' for."

"Makes no difference if he is a narc or a Holsomback man. We're lettin' Uncle Emmett or Papa decide what to do with him."

Alarmed by what he was hearing, Blin again tried to catch hold of the rim. Failing, he felt along the earthen walls for a crevice or root big enough for a step while he kept his ears tuned to what was being said above him.

High said, "But Papa and Uncle Emmett ain't here. Besides, I've got more to lose than anybody. That's why I ain't lettin' anybody stop me from doin' what I gotta do. I've still got my Beretta. If you try to stop me, I'll shoot you. But as much as I want to kill him, I'm not gettin' shot tryin'."

"Shot with what?" Hulie answered. "There's his gun right there. Try talkin' to him. Maybe that'll make you feel better."

Without his rifle, Blin's only chance to stay alive depended on his being able to get out of the pit and escape. But with nothing to climb on, and both brothers waiting for him on the embankment, how could he do that?

High called down, "We might work out a deal with you if you tell us who sent you, stranger. Was it the narcs or the Holsombacks?"

"Nobody sent me." Blin continued feeling along the walls. "I'm just traveling through, like I told you. But you will have cops swarming in on you if you don't let me go."

"We're the authority this wilderness, cop," High replied. "We proved that to the local law dogs and everybody else a long time ago. Nobody messes with us Fanchers in these woods. Any strangers Uncle Emmett's pets can't stop belong to me."

"Throw me a rope, and I'll tell you who sent me."

"You just said nobody sent you. That proves you're lyin'. You're talkin' to us like we're as stupid as you are. If you want a rope, tell me what we want to know before I start throwin' in brush."

Blin couldn't see the floor of his prison, but his boots hadn't bumped into any sticks or rocks to use for weapons. He heard one or both men move away from the pit.

Grimacing at the prospect of being burned alive, Blin stopped looking for a foot support and pulled out his hunting knife to begin digging into the earth at knee level. Satisfied with the first toehold, he reached up about two feet and dug another. He had just finished it when an armload of sticks was thrown into the opposite end of the pit. He whirled and looked up, but didn't see a face.

"Help me, Hulie," High said. "We've got to get done with this and finish that batch of meth before dark. We've got a delivery to make in the mornin'."

"Don't do it, High. Wait for Uncle Emmett. Papa will go along with what he decides."

"Am I gonna have to knock some sense into your head like I've done before? Help me fill up the damn hole. You were here when I caught him, and you're a partner in our business. That means you have as much to lose as I have if we let this cop go."

"What about the horse you said he had? What'll happen if the cops find its corpse?"

"Since Uncle Emmett wouldn't let me kill the cop and get his horse last night, we'll leave him over there to starve. The buzzards and coyotes will take care of the evidence."

"But what if somebody finds the saddle? The buzzards and coyotes won't eat it. Whoever finds it will know for sure something fishy went down and call the law. They'd bust up our operation and arrest us all."

"Okay, we'll go back and get the damn horse in the mornin', as soon as we're through with that delivery. Now, stop whinin' and help me before I have to work on you with my Beretta."

More sticks fell into the pit, and Blin heard the two men walk away again in search for more. He was working on a third step at shoulder level when High returned and said, "Bring me the kerosene, little brother. We'll add bigger stuff after we get the fire goin' good."

"I must be crazy, lettin' you talk me into doing this."

His back and hands pressed against the earthen wall behind him, Blin placed his right toe in the first step and pushed himself upward. When he put his toe in the second crevice, more sticks crashed down on him, causing him to lose his footing and fall.

Jumping up, he set his toe in the first step again as liquid splashed into the pit, giving off a strong odor of kerosene. He had run out of time. A match would follow, and he would be burned alive.

Chapter VII

*B*lin placed his left toe in the second step as burning papers were dropped into the hole. Flames leaped upward, and thick, black smoke filled the pit, blocking all light from above. Within seconds, it would be impossible to breathe.

Flames warming his backside, Blin pressed hard against the second step and slid his body up far enough to put his right toe in the third step. Fighting his need to breathe, he pushed up again, plunged his hunting knife into the rim, and pulled himself out of the fiery pit. His face against the earth, he inhaled and rolled through the thick smoke until stopped by a tree at the edge of the trail.

He looked back, but the smoke was still too thick to see through, so he jumped up and ran into the woods, gasping for more fresh air. Falling to his knees moments later, he looked back and listened for sounds at the pit that would tell him if his escape had been noted. He doubted he had enough strength to outrun them if they had.

When he heard one of his captors speak in a normal tone of voice, he began breathing again, convinced they were not yet aware of his escape. He heard High say, "Throw in more kerosene, and help me bring up some bigger limbs. We'll finish the job and refill the pit. Uncle Emmett and Papa will never know unless you tell 'em. I know you won't do that, because you like livin'." He laughed.

Blin took another deep breath, and resumed running, too relieved to think about how he would survive without his supplies and the compass. He told himself he'd have plenty of time to think about that after he put some miles between him and the killer-thieves.

When he could run no further, he stopped to rest and get his bearings. The stream was to his right, and following it would take him to where the drag marks crossed it. They would follow them to his campsite if it didn't start raining.

It wasn't until he found and began following the drag marks that he was convinced he had really escaped, but his relief was spoiled when the impact of what had happened at the pit struck him. It left him shaken, not only for almost being burned to death, but because he had always been deathly afraid of fire after having been badly burned as a boy when his trouser leg caught fire in front of their fireplace. If Mama had not snuffed out the flames with her bare hands, he would have been so badly burned he could have died. He was reminded of that incident when he looked at his grandmother's scarred hands crossed over her bosom in her casket. It had brought tears to his eyes, but this was no time for tears. He had to put more distance between him and the two thieves.

Walking briskly, he recalled the traumatic events immediately before and after Mama's funeral and wondered if his efforts to escape poverty had been an exercise in futility. He looked at his surroundings in view of the day's events, more skeptical than ever about the big woods offering the refuge he had hoped. With no food, he had no choice but to set out immediately for the reservation with Catcher and his metal box, which contained his only remaining connection to meaningful life. Before he could do that, however, he had to determine in which direction he should move.

He didn't know how many days would be required to reach his destination, even if he could move in a reasonably straight line to it. Since he most likely would not be able to do that without his compass or a visible sun, the time required would be much longer. How long could a man walk without eating? Would he find water on the way?

He had to keep moving, because the drug dealers would give chase when they discovered him gone, and when they caught up with him, High wouldn't be so particular about how he killed him.

His entire body ached, his lungs burned, and his back felt as if it had been blistered by the flames. His discomfort was made more severe by mounting hunger and a driving thirst. He would feel better if the sun would only appear. Just the thought of seeing it again improved his spirits.

He reached Catcher at quarter to two, and after making sure the horse's wounds still had salve on them, he picked up his canteen and went to the stream at the foot of the hill. Dropping to his knees, he rested his hands on the sandy bottom near the opposite bank, lowered his face, and began drinking the cool, clear water. He was so thirsty.

A rustling sound in the wet leaves near his head made him turn his eyes toward the water's edge, and he froze. Not more than a foot from his face was a coiled, black snake, its dark, shiny eyes fixed on him. Its forked tongue darted in and out so fast he could barely see it.

Knowing the snake would strike if he moved, he remained motionless, afraid to breathe. Judging by the size of its coil, the snake was long enough to reach his face or shoulder if it struck, and the shape of its head told him it was a pit viper. It was a water moccasin, so close he could see the two pits near the tip of its nose.

Blin kept his eyes locked on the snake's head. His arm muscles began to ache and tremble. In spite of his discomfort, he made himself remain absolutely still, barely breathing. Perspiration began popping from his forehead. He kept telling himself his only hope lay in his ability to wait out the snake and hope it didn't strike before crawling away.

His arms trembled and ached more fiercely now, and the perspiration dripped off his nose, but the snake did not move. Struggling to hold his position, Blin kept his eyes focused on the moccasin's head and tongue as his hands sank deeper into the soft, sandy streambed. A voice within screamed, *Dammit, snake, leave!*

Finally, after what seemed hours, the snake very slowly uncoiled itself and crawled away, and when it was out of striking distance, Blin's arms collapsed, plunging his face and upper body into the water.

Lacking the strength to rise, he rolled to one side to keep from drowning, and moments later slowly searched the leaves and white sand along the other side of the stream for signs of the intruder. Not seeing it, he filled his canteen, stumbled back to the horse, and led him down the embankment. When they returned to the campsite, he was too exhausted to leave, so he re-tethered Catcher and sat down in the leaves to rest.

Continuing his flight in the direction he followed upon escaping the pit would be the fastest way to put miles between him and the killers, regardless of where that took him. The reservation's southern boundary could be found by moving northeast from his campsite. If it was, which way was northeast?

Most streams in level country flowed roughly north to south, or southeast, but the hills in the forest could alter that rule. The stream at the foot of the hill could just as easily be running east or west.

He remembered going to the top of the hill whose base he was on now before pitching camp. He had moved down one side and found northeast on the compass before selecting a campsite, but so much had happened since, he couldn't recall which side. The blacktop ran north to south, and he had ridden east by his compass when he left it, but he recalled changing directions often to avoid heavy brush and hills. That prevented him from determining the direction of the highway in relationship to his present location. He recalled avoiding riding too far to the southeast to stay out of the Big Thicket, and too far east to avoid the little town of Dooly, but that didn't help him now.

He could think more clearly if he weren't exhausted, hungry, and shaken over his narrow escape. The only thing still clear in his mind was that, regardless of his course of flight, he must take it before High and his brother came looking for him. When the thieves arrived and found Catcher gone, they would know he had come back this way following his escape. If the hybrids were with them, they would have no problems following his scent. Even without the hybrids, they would have no problem following horse tracks. If Catcher were still there, they would be convinced he had fled in another direction, giving him more time as they searched for his trail.

An overwhelming sense of guilt swept over him as he studied the gentle red horse peacefully munching grass. He couldn't bear the thought of leaving such a faithful companion to starve, fall into the hands of three desperate men, or be eaten by wolves or buzzards. Perhaps his revulsion was born of his memory of what he was taught as a boy about man's responsibility to the dumb creatures of the earth. It could be the subconscious stirrings of values handed down from frontier families and friends. In Texas, a horse had always been considered more like a cousin than a dumb beast.

He looked at the mule's carcass, but felt a touch of nausea upon thinking of eating any part of him. It would be like eating a friend. Besides, the meat was perhaps already spoiled, and if it weren't, it would soon be. He would continue on the course he took upon escaping the pit. If he were lucky, it would turn out to be a northeast course he could follow for a day or so before turning toward the reservation.

He retrieved his first aid kit, flashlight, and pistol from the buried tent and threw the gun into the hollow log, not wanting to be shot by his own weapon. If his pursuers didn't have ammunition to fit it, they'd get some.

Shoving the flashlight into his back pocket and swinging the kit's strap over his left shoulder, he hung the canteen on his belt and approached Catcher with the saddle and blanket. He placed both far enough forward to keep them from rubbing the largest cut. Tying one end of the halter rope to the saddle horn, he ran it around Catcher's neck a couple of times and pulled it back to the pommel, tying it with a double knot. It would prevent low branches from knocking off the saddle or pushing it back onto the cut.

Reins in hand, he led Catcher away, but he had gone less than a hundred yards when he heard something stir in the leaves to his left. He whirled, expecting to see one of the thieves with his gun pointed at him, but saw only brush. He resumed walking, but immediately heard the sound again. This time, it was followed by what sounded like the whining of a dog.

He looked back at the dead hybrids and wondered if one of them had recovered enough to follow, then again studied the brush. Had one of the drug trafficker's hybrids moved out ahead of the thieves? If so, it meant the killers weren't far behind.

Tying Catcher's reins to a bush, he reached for his hunting knife. He had left it stuck in the dirt at the pit. He moved cautiously toward the rustling sound and froze when he saw its source.

Standing not more than ten feet away was a large white wolf or hybrid, and its slanted eyes were fixed on him. If it weren't such a terrifying sight, it would be a most magnificent one. In its eyes, Blin detected the ominous gleam of a master hunter.

Impressed, but still puzzled and afraid, Blin was uncertain about what he should do as he continued holding the animal's gaze. He saw something red on the animal's right front leg and concluded it was blood. The foot on that leg barely touched the ground, telling him the animal was one of the hybrids he'd shot. Blin looked for more predators and turned his eyes back to the one before him. It had remained as still as a statue.

Blin called aloud to the animal, "Are we going to stand here all day and do the staring thing, or what? If that's all you have in mind, I'll just turn around and be on my way."

The hybrid's tail wagged slightly, and the animal whined, reminding Blin of his own dog a long time ago when it was hurt. Blin said, "Sorry you're wounded, but since you tried to eat me last night, don't be surprised if I don't shed any tears."

The animal wagged its tail again and sat down, picking up its wounded right foot. Its sagging teats told him it was a female at least ten years old, quite old for a dog. She had suckled many pups in her day.

He was told as a boy that if a dog wagged its tail when it looked at you, it wasn't going to bite, but in view of his experiences the night before, that thought brought him little comfort. It occurred to him, however, that if this old animal had been one of the thieves' trackers, she was trained and therefore accustomed to being around humans. Maybe she wanted to be his friend, too.

Wanting to leave, but not daring to turn his back on the predator, Blin continued to study the white animal, whose magnificent coat was marred only by three small black spots: one on each front foot, the other on her left hip. He was impressed by the difference between her appearance and the coats of the hybrids he killed. Theirs were dull and unkempt, hers smoother and shinier.

His protective instincts told him he should find a limb and kill the hybrid, but something made him hold back. Perhaps it was the way the animal calmly watched him, wagging its tail when he spoke. Maybe it was one of the Biblical inhibitions instilled in him during childhood that required him to be kind to all dumb animals. After all, a dog was man's best friend. She was at least one-half dog.

The animal attempted to get to her feet, but fell back and lay down instead, not taking her eyes off him. She again whined softly, as if trying to communicate with him. Blin found himself feeling sorry for her. Picking up a short limb, he moved toward her. The animal didn't attempt to get up or take its eyes off him. She again wagged her tail against the leaves and whined.

With the club drawn back, ready to strike, he stepped forward, and upon getting a closer look at the animal's sad eyes, lowered the club. "I must be the dumbest man in the world for not bashing in your skull after what you and your pals tried to do to me last night."

The hybrid whined and wagged her tail. Her pleading manner brought to mind the way his dog had looked at him a long time ago when it wanted sympathy. Blin looked at her belly and her sagging, wrinkled teats. Evidence of her motherhood and age was reason enough to be sympathetic, he reasoned.

The wolf dog rolled over on her belly and began dragging herself toward him, prompting Blin to raise the stick to strike; but as she came closer with ears laid back, pleading, head lowered as a humble person might bow before a superior, he realized he could not kill the animal. He dropped the club.

He leaned down and held out his hand. "Go ahead, bite it off. Show me what a fool I am."

She jerked her head back, but kept her eyes fixed on him. He moved closer to allow her to sniff his fingertips, then his hand, and when she still didn't try to bite him, he attempted to pat her head. She jerked her head back, but didn't snap.

Blin moved forward enough to gently pat her neck and saw dried blood along her ribs where her white coat had matted. He moved his hand along her neck and down her shoulder to the injured leg, which appeared to be broken just above the foot. The hair in the area was torn and wet with saliva.

He told the animal, "Stay put for a minute. I'll be right back."

He got his first aid kit, and on his way back cut off a small, straight limb with his pocket knife and broke it into three pieces about six inches long. He half-expected to find the predator gone, but she was still there, calmly watching him.

Kneeling beside her, he slowly reached for her injured leg. When she didn't pull back, he stroked her head and gently raised her injured limb, alert to the possibility that she might snap at him at any moment. With such a monstrous head and jaws, she could crush his hand in an instant. She watched his hand, but did not grab it.

"Good girl," he said. "I'm going to fix your leg before I leave if you'll let me." He thought, *what a fool I am, helping an animal that tried to kill me while two killers bear down on me.*

He reached up to pat her head again, but she jerked back, growling softly. He became still, again wondering if he should proceed or walk away. He also wondered if the fire in the pit had burned down enough yet for the thieves to determine his body wasn't in the ashes.

"It's okay," he said to the hybrid. "I'm not going to hurt you."

She whined and wagged her tail, and he extended his hand to gently pat her head and shoulder. He took a role of tape from the first-aid kit and reached for her broken leg, but she jerked it back and attempted to get up. He spoke to her and stroked her side and she lay back down.

She jumped when he touched the leg, but made no move to bite him. He placed her broken limb between the three sticks and quickly wrapped them with tape. At least one bone appeared to be fractured, but from a crushing blow rather than a bullet.

She continued watching him as he examined her side wound, but did not attempt to get up. The matted hair made it impossible to closely examine the spot, but the wound did not appear to be made by a bullet.

He stood up. "I've got to go now, ol' girl," he said. "Don't bother to get up. And if we meet again, try to be a little friendlier than you were last night, okay?"

He stopped once to look back, and found the old hybrid on her feet watching him. He untied Catcher, and began circling the crest of the hill.

Upon reaching its opposite slope, he took a course in line with the one chosen when he left the campsite. He would lead Catcher in that direction the rest of the day. If it were too dark to travel through the brush and trees after nightfall, he would get some much-needed sleep and follow the same course the next morning. If he weren't overtaken by the end of the second day, he would swing left in hopes the sun would break through and allow him to verify that he was traveling in the right direction.

A light rain began to fall, but it stopped in less than a half-hour. He welcomed its coolness, and if it had been harder, would have stripped and bathed in it.

The road map he'd bought indicated that the little town of Dooly was on a county road some forty miles northeast of where he entered the big woods. If he were going in the right direction, he would pass north of it if he missed the reservation.

The dark clouds showed no signs of a break. About an hour later, concerned about his lack of money should he reach the reservation supply store, he stopped to rest and examine the contents of his billfold.

He had less than a hundred dollars. If he had a thousand, it would have no value in his present surroundings, but if he was lucky and reached his destination alive, it was enough for food and clean clothes. After a brief visit with the chief and his grandmothers' surviving relatives, he would return to the big woods until he considered it safe to return for a longer stay. His pursuers would have given up their search by then.

He resumed walking, moving in a straight line as best he could, but he had to change course many times to avoid thick underbrush and vines. It troubled him that making so many turns kept him from putting as much distance between him and the thieves as he could have.

At mid-afternoon, thick underbrush and briars blocked their way, requiring him to make an even more drastic change of course. After another hour, he stopped to rest and check Catcher's wounds. Afterwards, he lay down in the leaves, but he was too hungry to take nap. He sat up to look around for something edible. Even if he did spot grapes or berries, they would be green that time of year. Seeing a hickory tree nearby, he searched the ground under it for last year's yield.

Finding a handful of nuts as big as quarters, he searched for rocks to use to break them open. Finding none, he held one against a tree and hit it with his pocketknife. It wouldn't crack. He needed something heavier.

He looked about in the leaves for pine knots, finally finding one. After brushing off the dirt and decayed wood around its hard center, he tried cracking a nut against the trunk of a large tree. He hit his finger.

"Ouch!" He said it loud enough to cause Catcher to flip his ears forward.

Blin lifted the saddle from Catcher's back and set it on the ground. Holding a nut against the pommel, he struck it with the pine knot, and after the third try, the shell cracked. The meat of the nut was delicious, but eating all of them did not satisfy his hunger. He had to find something more filling.

Seeing a butterfly, he remembered something else his grandmother told him. "If a person gets lost in those big woods without food, he must watch the butterflies. A man can eat the flowers they take nectar from."

He followed the yellow butterfly into a small opening full of blooming plants of different sizes and colors. Since several large butterflies were resting on them, he pulled white blooms from a plant with arrow-shaped leaves and placed them in his mouth. Chewing cautiously for a moment, he found them to have a strong, weedy taste, much like that of uncooked turnip greens, but they were more filling than the nuts. He stripped off more blooms and ate them, then looked around for blooms with a better taste.

He pulled a handful of blooms from a plant covered with purple flowers and ate them. When he stooped to pull more, he spotted a prickly pear. He pulled several pear-shaped growths off the ends of its flat green blades, peeled off their outer shells, and ate them. They were bitter and tough, but not too bad for a starving man. He ate another handful of purple blooms and glanced at his watch. He had to move on.

He was returning to the horse, saddle in hand, when he heard something rustling in the leaves nearby. He froze, convinced he had dallied too long. He saw a slight movement among the weeds beneath a flowering dogwood, but couldn't make out what it was. Then he saw a spot of white fur and the silhouette of a wolf or dog standing on three legs. Relieved, he said to the animal, "Why are you following me, Crip? Are you planning on eating me for supper?" He had become more inclined each day to talk to things that couldn't talk back.

The predator whined and lowered her head in a gesture of submissiveness.

Blin stamped his feet and slapped his hands against his thighs. "Get away from me," he said. "I don't want you. I've got enough troubles already."

She turned as if to leave, but stopped, sat down, and again fixed her eyes on him. Concluding the animal was in no condition to harm him.

Blin put the saddle on Catcher's back, placed the carrying strap of his first aid kit over his shoulder, and walked away.

Because of the continuing cloud cover and his many turns since leaving his campsite, Blin was more confused than ever about directions. If the thieves didn't overtake him, he would walk another couple of hours and turn toward the southern border of the reservation a day earlier than planned. If his directions were correct, he should arrive at a point somewhere south of his destination by the end of the following day.

Hearing something in the underbrush the next time he paused to drink water, he turned and saw the wounded hybrid limping through the brush behind him. Impressed that she had been able to keep up with them with only three good legs, he studied her a moment. She also stopped and gave him another soulful look.

"What's with you, old girl?" he said. "Go away! Shoo!"

She didn't move.

He resumed walking, but the hybrid continued to keep pace with him and Catcher, slightly behind and some twenty feet to his left. Since there was no way to find out before dark if the animal was friend or foe, he decided to ignore her, but he remained concerned about what she might do to him after he went to sleep.

He continued in as straight a course as the terrain and underbrush would allow, and the predator kept pace with them. About two hours later, he turned left as planned and moved in that direction until stopping to give Catcher a drink from his hand. He offered a handful of water to the hybrid, but instead of approaching him to get it, she sat down. She licked her lips, but made no move to come closer.

"Come on, girl," he said, holding out his dripping hand. "Come over and show me you're friendly before I go to sleep."

The hybrid still did not move or take her eyes off him. Blin gave what water remained in his hand to Catcher and turned to study the hybrid. He wished he had food to offer her, because he believed that to be the best way to guarantee her friendship before nightfall. Thinking of food made him remember how long it had been since he'd eaten something besides blooms and nuts. He was still very hungry.

A sudden motion in the tall grass near the old predator caused her to whirl suddenly and leap at a cottontail scampering for his life. With a speed that amazed Blin, the wounded animal caught the rabbit with its mouth and clamped down hard. There was one brief cry from the cottontail before it went limp.

The hybrid gently laid the rabbit at her feet and looked at Blin, as if awaiting his command on what to do with it. Blin stepped toward her, holding out his hand with more water in it. "Come on, girl," he pleaded. "I'll trade you some water for some of that rabbit."

The animal remained still for a moment before turning her eyes to his hand and leaning forward. When she started lapping up the water, he picked up the rabbit. Dropping it behind him, he poured more water into his extended hand. "Good girl," he said.

Calling upon skills acquired as a boy when jackrabbits were plentiful, Blin skinned and cleaned the cottontail, tossing its insides and skin to his new friend, who had moved up to within ten feet of him. She snapped up the scraps and moved back a few steps to gulp them down.

After cleaning his hands with leaves and sand, Blin laid the dressed rabbit on a dead limb and set about building a roasting device with two forked sticks and one straight one. Pushing the straight one through the carcass, he rested his meal between the forks of the two supports and began looking for dead twigs for kindling. By the time he'd found enough to start a fire, the old wolf dog had finished eating and settled down to watch him.

The matches in his shirt pocket were still damp from the morning's fall into the stream, so he spread them out on a bed of pine needles and searched for the driest one. He rubbed it briskly against his trouser leg, and its head promptly fell off. He looked for another near-dry one, but when he tried to strike it, the same thing happened. He tried another, with the same results. He sat down with a long sigh to stare at the uncooked rabbit and listen to his intestines growl. Shaking his head, he mumbled, "There's no way I'm going to eat raw meat."

His new friend whined, and Blin turned to find her staring at the rabbit and licking her lips. "Stop complaining, Crip. You've been fed. The rest of it is mine as soon as I figure out how to build a fire."

Not wanting to waste more matches, he decided to move on until it got too dark to travel and hope the matches would be dry enough to strike by then. He placed the end of the stick with the rabbit on it into the opening behind the saddle horn and picked up a handful of pine needles. He pushed the needles into the opening around the stick and laid the matches on them.

Later, when darkness began closing in, he fought the urge to stop and cook the rabbit to continued walking as long as there was enough light. When night came, he stopped and tethered Catcher. His energy level was near zero. Believing he would feel better after resting, he pulled his flashlight from his back pocket and pushed the switch. It didn't move.

"What the—" Examining the device, he found the switch in the "on" position already. He pushed it off, then on again, but there was no light. The batteries were dead. The switch must have been turned to the on position when he shoved it into his pocket. "That's just dandy," he muttered, tossing it into the brush.

Moving slowly in the near-darkness, he gave Catcher three handfuls of water and removed the straw holding the matches, laying it in a spot raked clear of leaves with his boot. Selecting a match by feel, he rubbed its tip back and forth against the leg of his trousers then gave it a quick, hard jerk. It flared up.

He held the match against the straw until a tiny flame appeared, and then leaned down to blow gently on it until it grew higher. He laced more dead straw and small sticks on top of it.

Although it needed salt and was tough, the meat was tasty. After eating all except what was buried in the backbone, he found his injured companion silently watching him from the outer circle of light.

"If I give this bone to you, will you leave my bones alone tonight?" he said.

When he heard her tail beat against the leaves, he held out the morsel. She limped over and slowly took it from his hand, and he tossed the smaller bones to her as well. She quickly crushed them all with her mighty jaws.

Her presence still made him uneasy, but since he couldn't run her off, it appeared she would accompany him until she decided to leave. He was still hungry, and very tired.

The fire made the surrounding wilderness seem less ominous, especially now, after one of its creatures had become his travel companion. He hoped Crip remained friendly after he closed his eyes. She must still be hungry.

He could barely see the old wolf dog in the outer fringes of the fire's light, watching him as if she might be looking forward to when the fire went out. He said, "Time to go to sleep, Crip."

Crawling around in the leaves until he found a stick about three feet long, he lay down near the dying fire with a cautious glance at the hybrid. The flames became smaller, until they were nothing more than a dim glow. Made more anxious by the darkness, Blin watched the coals slowly turn to ashes and disappear. He could no longer see his four-legged companion or hear her breathing.

"My God, it's dark," he said aloud. "And so quiet. Where are you, Crip? What is that sound I hear? Are you smacking your lips?"

He puckered his own lips and whistled as he had when calling his spotted terrier long ago, and immediately heard Crip's tail beat against the leaves. It sounded friendly enough.

He had to get some sleep! It had been a long, hard day, and he ached all over. He wondered if the two outlaws and their uncle had already probed the pit's ashes. If they had, and the light rain had not wiped out his trail, how long would it be before High overtook him? Maybe all three were looking for him now. If they were, he hoped darkness would stop them, too.

Turning on his side to avoid aggravating his sensitive back, he finally dozed off, but was awakened shortly thereafter by the far-off cry of a wolf. Or was it one of the thieves' hybrids?

He sat up, fully awake. If full-bred timber wolves were out there, he couldn't stop them in total darkness. Another distant wail from his back trail was followed by a second high-pitched cry closer by. Then he heard barking from what sounded like an entire pack.

Disturbed by the animals' presence so near, he got up and felt his way over to his horse. Catcher whinnied softly when he reached out to pat him. "Everything's okay, boy," Blin told him. "Those devils aren't going to bother you tonight." He hoped the horse couldn't sense his master's attempt to cover up his own fears.

Blin stretched out in the leaves nearer the horse in case the predators attacked. If they did, he would jump up, yell like a banshee, and stamp his feet in hopes of frightening them away. If he didn't succeed, he'd suffer the fate of the cottontail.

Where was his crippled friend? He didn't hear her following him, and he couldn't hear her stirring about now, so he figured she had gone to sleep or left. He still was not sure what had moved him to splint the hybrid's leg or feed her. Perhaps a mysterious, subconscious tie with all people and creatures closely connected to nature motivated him. Maybe it was his long-held sense of pity for creatures with handicaps. His mama had had a handicap. He found that out early on, witnessing the rude treatment she suffered at the hands of the white majority in West Texas. School bullies beating up on him because he was of her blood confirmed it.

Crip most likely was rejected by her animal friends because of her age and inability to have more pups or go on long hunts. He and Crip were two of a kind, in a sense; both were outsiders, losers, maybe.

He had just begun to doze off again when he received another start. His heart pumping like a jackhammer, he listened as an ominous sound came again. He found the club and beat it against the ground, and from the tree came the flapping of large wings as a big bird flew away. A harmless owl. He relaxed.

He settled back on the pine needles as his surroundings quieted again, so still he could hear something rooting around nearby. An armadillo, perhaps, or a raccoon. He wished he had a light so he could club whatever it was for the next day's food. He had formerly believed man's highest priorities were money and sex. Funny what hunger and fear will do to a man.

He yawned as the hard seat of the saddle and the ground made him think again of the king-sized bed in his air-conditioned home. He hoped the mortgage company would allow him to make missed payments and re-occupy it. He wished the same thing about his car, abandoned in the thicket. When he considered it safe, he would retrieve it, if somebody didn't steal it first. He missed the good life he'd become accustomed to, and the company of interesting people. Such things seemed a part of another world.

He wondered if Veronica was sleeping alone tonight. Perhaps she was spending the night with one of Zaavedra's men, Victor "the Cat" Catori, perhaps. He had a way with women. Some women, at least.

He looked around him in the dark, as if he would see a friendly sight. He couldn't even see his watch when he held it near his face, but he figured it must be near midnight. Where were the dope-dealing thieves now? Thinking of them made him want to get up and move on, but that was impossible.

He finally felt himself getting sleepy, and as he drifted off, one question kept hammering his tired brain. *Will I still be alive this time tomorrow night?*

Chapter VIII

Still half asleep, Blin slid his hand across his face to brush something cool and moist from his cheek. That's when he became aware of the breathing near his face.

He rose with a start, and the crippled hybrid jumped back, frightened by his sudden move. Blin glanced around him in the new day for signs of other predators, but saw none. "Good morning, Crip," he said. "A nuzzle beats a bite any morning, any place."

The clouds were still depressingly dark and heavy, but he was relieved the thieves had not overtaken him. He was also pleased that his travel companion had proven harmless. She stood on her three good legs, watching him, as if waiting to see what his next move would be.

He stood and held out his hand. "Hungry? Why don't you use your sniffer to locate another rabbit instead of cold-nosing me and scaring me half to death?" The animal didn't move or blink. Welcoming the sound of his voice, he continued, "Well, since you insist on hanging around, I've got to think of a suitable name for you. I'm sure you've got one already, but since you can't tell me what it is, I'll pick another one." On his knees, he held out his hand. "Come on; take another sniff, now that we're real friends."

The old wolf dog stared at his hand, licked her lips, and wagged her tail, but didn't move towards him. He said, "I don't want you to eat it. Just smell it."

The animal took a cautious step toward him, then another, and stopped. Her eyes remained fixed on his hand.

"Let's see," he said. "What can I call a crippled, reformed killer whose former friends tried to eat me?"

She moved a step closer.

"Can't keep calling you Crip. Too disrespectful for an animal that's been a mother as many times as you have and caught my supper last night. I knew a girl in high school who had one short leg. She was a nice girl, real smart. Her name was Cleota, but I can't call you that. That would be too disrespectful of her. How about Friend? Looks like you qualify, and you're the only one I have right now. Do you want to be my friend, Friend?"

The animal slowly extended her head to sniff his fingertips, and he said, "That's a good start. Do I smell respectable?"

The animal licked his fingertips, but jumped back when he wiggled his fingers.

"Sorry," he said. "Are you going to let me touch you now?"

When he reached out, she took a step back, but stood still when he moved close enough to touch her nose and rub her head beneath her left ear. She wagged her tail.

"Good girl," he said. "Now, let's move away from here before your previous owner catches up with us. Keep your eyes open for another rabbit, or that armadillo I heard rooting around last night."

After emptying his bladder, Blin checked Catcher's wounds. Finding them still clean and moist from the salve, he settled the blanket and saddle astride his withers and secured them as before. He hung the kit on his shoulder but carried the canteen in hand, intent on quenching his thirst while walking. He set out in line with the course he selected the previous day.

Friend being so close caused Catcher to pull back and roll his eyes, but after some coaxing and firm tugging on the reins, the horse settled down.

They had walked only a few yards when Blin was startled by the sound of a bush scraping across something, or somebody. He stopped and pulled out his pocketknife, dropping the canteen. Footsteps in the leaves told him something or somebody was very close. A bush shook as the intruder approached. *Is it one of the thieves?*

A whitetail buck with a wide rack moved into a narrow clearing twenty feet away and stopped to stare at him with big, innocent eyes, completely unafraid. Blin was amazed that such a beautiful creature could have survived so long in an area teaming with predators, but his mind quickly turned to a more practical line of thought. How many venison steaks could he get off the buck if he had a rifle?

When Blin turned to see what Friend was doing, the buck whirled and ran back into the brush. Friend gave chase, but soon returned, breathing hard and holding up her injured foot. She whined softly.

"Good try, girl," he said, reaching out to pat her head.

When he picked up his canteen, he found water running from a loose cap. There was barely enough left to splash when he shook it.

He hooked the canteen on his belt, telling Friend, "I don't know about you, but I think I'm going to get very thirsty before this day is over."

The trees grew larger and the underbrush less dense, allowing them to make better time. By four o'clock, however, he was too exhausted and hungry to keep up the pace. He tethered Catcher and looked for something edible, finally finding some green berries on a tall vine. He put a couple in his mouth, but spat them out because they were too bitter. He allowed himself one swallow of water and poured the rest in his hand, first allowing Catcher to wet his lips, then Friend.

He told the animals. "Unless we come to a stream soon, we're in deep trouble."

He sat down next to a tall pine to rest, estimating they had moved at least twenty miles from the campsite. Because of the continuing cloud cover and the many turns he had made, however, he wasn't sure he was still walking toward the southern boundary of the reservation. He remembered Mama telling him how to determine which way was north by something growing on trees. What was on the tree, and what kind of tree was it on? Then he remembered. Moss.

He walked around the big pine, but saw nothing unusual. He moved to an oak and examined it. Same results. Several trees later, he returned to the big pine and sat down.

In spite of growing hunger pains, he believed his muscles had become stronger since arriving in the big woods, his mental facilities keener. That, however, did not make him like the forest any better. The back-to-nature advocates could have all the storms, wolves, trees, vines, and snakes. He wanted city lights, air-conditioning, bathrooms, and the company of interesting, exciting people, preferably women.

The latter caused him to think less about food for a moment. He had never enjoyed a woman's company in such a rustic setting, but he believed it would be an unforgettable experience. It might have something to do with primitive urges being in tune with primitive places.

Kicking the ground, he said aloud, "What I need more than that is a plate of hamburgers, a tall Coke, and a cold shower."

Friend looked at him as if sensing his troubled state. He said, "Spot a rabbit, and I'll stop it with a big stick."

He led Catcher from the spot, and Friend fell in beside him. He watched for signs of a stream or a stump hole with rainwater in it, realizing he needed a bath almost as much as drinking water. After three days of perspiration and the stench acquired in the pit, his scent had become very unpleasant.

The dense growth around and over him prompted him to recall something else his dear mama told him about survival in such a place. "Remember this, Bright Light in Night, my grandson. Nature is neither your friend nor your enemy. It *is*." She added, "It doesn't need you and will provide only what you are wise and strong enough to take."

Her remarks held little meaning to him at the time, but his experiences in the forest made him appreciate that bit of advice. They also made him realize how trifling his personal troubles were by comparison to the power of his surroundings.

He heard something humming nearby, and he turned to see honeybees going in and out of a hole in a dead oak tree about ten feet from the ground. Six inches wide, the hole was covered with working insects.

Tying Catcher a safe distance from the bee tree, he approached it with Friend at his heels. "What we need, ol' girl, is a handful of fresh honey."

He remembered a farmer in West Texas wearing long gloves and netting over his face as he robbed his beehive. He also had smoke coming from a bucket at his feet. Without those things, he would probably get stung, but a good meal was worth a few red bumps.

Placing a pine knot against the tree, he stepped up on it, turned his face away from the insects, and slowly slid his hand up the tree. By the time it reached the hole, he felt many bees crawling on it, but no stings.

He remained motionless as other bees began flying about his face and shoulders before settling in his hair. Slowly turning his head to look at his hand, he found it completely covered. Other bees crawled around it on their way to and from the hole. Looking down, he saw Friend calmly watching him.

He turned his eyes back to the hole, telling himself he was going to have honey for supper, regardless of the cost. Closing his eyes and turning his head, he moved his hand slowly through and over the mass of bees around the opening, but jerked it back when the insects began crawling down his arm. Grimacing, he slid his hand back into the hole. Many more agitated bees began buzzing around his head.

The moment his fingers touched the top of the honeycomb, he grabbed a handful of it and jerked his arm out of the hole, but bees trapped by his fingers began stinging him. He lost his balance and fell, but held onto the sticky prize.

Buzzing became louder as the insects began stinging his arms, face, and neck. Dropping the honey to fight them off, he began rolling wildly through the leaves and over bushes. He must have rolled thirty feet before all the bees left.

Dizzy from rolling, he lay still for a moment before sitting up to take stock of his situation. That's when he became aware of an intense aching and throbbing in his arms, neck, and face. His left hip hurt from the fall. He was relieved when he saw no new blood around the thigh wound.

He lay still until his heartbeat slowed to near normal and looked for the honey. He couldn't see it, but he did see many bees flying about. When none of them came his way, he examined the red welts on his forearms. A heavy price to pay for such a small piece of honey, and Friend might have already eaten that.

Near the hollow tree, he found his prize, no larger than his fist, oozing clear, rich honey. Several bees buzzed around it still, and some were crawling on it, but he brushed them away with a small branch, scooped up the delicacy, and moved to a spot near Catcher. Friend joined him. She looked at the honey and licked her lips.

"Didn't know half-breed mongrels ate honey," he said. "If that's the case, you should've kept those pests off me. Some friend you are."

Sensing displeasure in his voice, she lowered her head, as if apologizing, and lay down, resting her head between her extended front legs. The splint was askew, but still attached to her broken leg.

The crushed honey had a considerable number of dead leaves stuck to it, but he picked them off and took a large bite of the gooey, sticky mass. It was very rich and sweet. After eating most of it, he offered the rest to Friend, and she got up and gently took it from his hand, gulping it down.

"Never saw a four-legged vacuum before," he told her.

Blin licked his fingers clean, pulled off his shirt, and rubbed alcohol from his first aid kit on the red welts he could reach. The red spots had become bumps and were throbbing fiercely. Putting his shirt back on, he glanced at his watch. It was six-thirty, still early enough for him to travel another hour or so before sundown.

He led Catcher away, vowing not to let his new aches prevent him from completing his mission. After a night's rest, he would continue in the same general direction if the thieves and their hybrids didn't overtake him.

He had never heard of anyone dying from bee stings unless they were extremely allergic to the venom, but if the pain got any worse, he might be unable to travel. The honey had energized him, but he was still hungry and very thirsty.

Blin maintained a steady pace, Friend close at his heels, and when darkness began to fall, he looked for a suitable place to lie down. He had come to dread night more each day, and with the added discomforts, dreaded this one even more. The only thing that could that would make his situation worse would be for the thieves to overtake him while he was sleeping.

Chapter IX

*A*s expected, Blin did not sleep well because of the constant itching and aching, and each time he woke, thirst and hunger made going back to sleep impossible. Convinced finally that he could sleep no more, he got up and spent the remainder of the night sitting against a pine tree, hoping the new day would be free of clouds.

When he relieved his bladder, the output told him his body was running dangerously low on fluids. Catcher and Friend needed water, too. In spite of the shortage of food and water, however, he considered himself fortunate that he had not been overtaken. He suspected the thieves' delay was due to their waiting for their uncle, or not having discovered that his remains were not in the pit. Maybe their uncle had returned sooner than expected and convinced High to allow his father to make the final judgment. Not being overtaken had given him precious time, but he wondered how long it took a man to arrive at the point that he didn't care what happened to him as long as it brought relief from his misery.

About two hours later, with barely enough light to see beneath the trees and heavy clouds, he led Catcher away on a course he believed to be a continuation of the one chosen the previous day. He was determined to find water and catch a few perch or frogs to eat before the day was over. He would bathe, too. Cold water would do wonders for his aching, burning bumps.

By late afternoon, he was so exhausted he could barely walk, so he began looking for a spot in a grove of young pines where he could bed down. He doubted his pains and hunger would allow him to sleep, but he could at least rest. In spite of a steady lookout for water and something edible all day, he'd found nothing.

Friend and Catcher continued to plod along, apparently not as disturbed as he by their plight. He did not realize how exhausted Friend was until she limped over to lie down near him with a whimper. He put part of the straw he'd gathered for his bed in a small pile near her, but she didn't get on it.

After much turning and tossing, his fatigue overcame his misery, and he went to sleep, but his itching wounds and hunger often woke him. Each time, he listened for sounds that announced the approach of his would-be killers. He heard nothing, not even the gentle rush of wind through the pines or a night bird.

The humidity was stifling. He would never have believed there was a place in an otherwise crowded world where a person could be so uncomfortable in mind and body. More and more of late, during sleepless nights, his thoughts turned back to his boyhood when Mama talked to him about how best to live his life. At the time, he thought such talk to be merely something that old folks did, so it was nothing for him to be concerned about. Up to about three years ago, Mama's advice had remained dormant in his memory. It came flooding back now, stronger than ever.

Perhaps some mysterious force within a person experiencing hard times prompted him to think of spiritual matters. Except for brief intervals following disappointment in a romantic affair, he made no serious efforts to explore matters of a non-material nature, because such undertakings seemed unimportant in the overall scheme of a modern world. But during those infrequent periods when he did find his mind wondering about such things, the only reward he received in his search for answers was the draining impact that accompanied emotional dead-ends. That caused him to suspect that there were no clear, defining answers to some questions, certainly no guaranteed worldly rewards for those who belabored the issue.

He was fully awake when the dim light of a new day began seeping into his humid, quiet world. It was as dark as it was the previous two days, which meant he would have to move without a clear sense of direction. He climbed stiffly to his feet and heard Friend move on her pile of straw. Convinced that he must find food and a stream or die, he secured the saddle to Catcher's back, picked up the first aid kit and empty canteen, and headed out with Friend limping along beside him.

They had been walking about an hour when Friend suddenly yelped and lunged at a cottontail that jumped out of the bushes ahead of her. She immediately stopped and raised her broken foot.

He checked the splint. "Does it hurt that bad, old girl? It's okay if you can't catch us fresh meat. We'll make it."

By mid-afternoon, they still had not come upon a stream. Disappointed, he pushed on, in spite of his mounting discomforts and waning energy.

By the time darkness arrived, he was convinced there were no streams in the forest besides the one they left. Disgusted, he found a spot under some large pines to spend the night, but was too tired to gather straw for his bed. He also did not have enough energy remaining to remove Catcher's burdens.

In spite of his physical discomfort and disturbed state of mind, he fell asleep immediately, but after what seemed like only minutes, he was awakened by severe aching of his bumps and itching about his wrists and ankles. Unable to go back to sleep, he spent the remainder of the night propped against a tree, dejected and confused, alternately scratching and listening for unfriendly sounds.

The option of appealing to a higher power for help came to mind, but he shrugged it off, convinced a man had to overcome his problems by his own efforts. If a supreme being had the power to solve problems, why hadn't he stopped the killers and dope dealers from putting him in his present predicament?

Near the point of collapse, he wondered if anything could give him the strength to survive more setbacks. Wanting to escape his painful present, he began re-thinking his past. Could he have found a better way to improve his life besides going into business? Would he have been better off had he not agreed to work as a government agent? Instead of finding ready answers, however, he was confronted by yet more questions. More questions demanded more answers, leading to another emotional dead-end.

The ominous cry of animals in the distance sent a rush through him, pushing aside considerations about anything other than the danger it represented. It appeared the hybrids had struck his trail and would close in by daybreak. He had to move on.

In the dim light of the new day, he looked at his wrists and ankles to find a fresh rash, caused apparently by poison ivy. He must have gotten into the stuff when he escaped the bees. The affected areas needed cleaning with soap and water and treatment with lotion. His scratching had already caused the red spots to swell and burn fiercely.

It began thundering in three directions. Maybe Mother Nature would give him a bath; she hadn't done him any other favors so far. Rain might also create puddles from which they could drink. If he didn't find water and something to eat soon, he might have to eat his shirt.

Mid-morning arrived, and he still hadn't found a stream, wild grapes, or berries. He had likewise seen no butterflies to lead him to their food source. He was at the point that he believed he could eat grass like his animals; a bellyache could not be more uncomfortable than hunger pains.

He stopped to rest at noon. He had to decide whether to hold their present course or change and hope to find a spring or a stream. Nothing in his surroundings gave him any indication of direction, and there was still no sign of a break in the clouds. It was so dark he kept looking at his watch to make sure he had not misread the time. There was no wind, so there was no breeze to help him decide directions.

Out of desperation, he altered course, swinging more to his left, and by early afternoon was encouraged when he spotted a familiar sight on an incline ahead. It was a tall, dead tree, its top bent as if weeping. But how could he remember it if he hadn't seen it already?

The answer jolted him: he saw the dead oak the morning of the previous day. *I've been walking in a circle for two days.*

His blunder brought a fresh wave of despair rushing over him, and he sat down hard. Only the realization that he would die unless he found food and water gave him the strength to return his mind to his sacred promise to Mama. He told himself that in spite of his setbacks, there was one thing for which he should be thankful: he could have been killed in that pit, and even if his remains were found, no one would ever know why he died or by whose hands. He got back on his feet and left in the opposite direction.

Grimacing from hunger pains and so dehydrated he could not urinate, he stopped and stripped a branch of a bush of its leaves. Catcher could eat grass. Why couldn't a man do the same?

Stuffing them in his mouth, he chewed the bitter mass and swallowed. Pulling off another handful, he chewed and swallowed again, but when he reached for more, he began vomiting, losing all he consumed.

Made weaker by retching, he sank to his knees, still clutching Catcher's reins, then stretched out on his back and closed his eyes in hopes sleep would come and give him relief. Moments later, sensing the presence of some*thing* or somebody, he opened his eyes to find Friend standing over him on her three good legs. He sat up and reached out to gently pat her head.

"Tired of eating grass, too?" he said. "Hold on. We'll find something soon. Water, too." He wished he believed that.

He could hardly feel the bumps on his face under his heavy beard stubble, but they were large enough to keep him from shaving if he had a razor. It would be a relief to be rid of the hairy mass, but he needed a bath more than a shave. He smelled bad.

He led Catcher away in a direction he hoped would take them well to the right of the course he'd followed to that point. Surely, they would cross a stream going that way. He had never eaten live frogs, tadpoles, or fish, but he believed he had reached that point. The weather would surely clear up soon.

He saw only one squirrel all afternoon and very few birds, which suggested that the creatures of the forest were as unhappy with the weather as he was. His hunger pains became sharper with each passing hour, and his mouth and throat had become so parched he doubted he could talk. He continued to be amazed by how hot it was under heavy clouds. The humidity was so high he felt it might smother him.

He moved on as fast as he could, not bothering to rest all afternoon. When nightfall began to settle in around them, he stopped on the side of a hill, under the cover of some small trees, and tied Catcher close by, where he could feed on native grasses.

Moving back from the horse a few steps, he lay down, too exhausted to remove the saddle or prepare a bed of leaves. He began to have serious misgivings about having the strength to walk to the reservation, even if the sun did come out and allow him to get his directions straight.

The thought of failing to fulfill his sacred promise to Mama caused him to become more depressed. It would mean he had failed her in much the same way he had failed to live by her rules. The mere thought of failure at anything had always sickened him.

Friend lay down in the near darkness, her eyes fixed on him, as if her animal instincts had sensed his disturbed state of mind. He knew she was as hungry as he was, so he wondered why she remained with him rather than finding something to eat or rejoining her pack. Studying her now in the growing shadows, he sensed the growing tie between them that, in turn, evoked thoughts of his blood ties to Mama. That thought provoked an even more puzzling question. Was it possible for the spirit of a departed loved one to reappear in the form of an animal? He thought not. And thinking about such a thing was a sure sign of mental deterioration. He had heard of people suffering delusions while starving or under extreme pressure.

He shook his head, saying aloud, "I'm hallucinating. I can't trust my thinking any more."

He tried to direct his thoughts to a more rational line of thinking, but couldn't dismiss the close relationship that had developed between him and

Friend. Nor could he forget the circumstances under which they met. Was it possible that she was not a member of the pack that attacked him, after all? Perhaps she was a member of another pack that had just happened by when he fled the drug traffickers. Regardless of Friend's origins, he could think of nothing that explained why she would take up with him so quickly and make special efforts to help him in spite of her wounds.

Mama believed strongly in the spirit life, and he remembered her telling him, "I'll be dead when you go back there, but I'll be with you in spirit to help you if you need me. You won't see me as I am now, but I will be there."

Recalling her statement made an eerie sensation sweep over him, and he sat up. Looking at Friend, now no more than a dark shadow, he waved his hand and said, "That's impossible. I've been in this God-forsaken place so long I'm going nuts."

He lay down and tried to remember more things said by Mama, his only connection to meaningful life, and as his thoughts dwelled on those and other pleasant experiences of his formative years, he drifted off into a deep sleep. Some time later, he was awakened by a sound much like that of a human voice somewhere in the woods nearby. Shocked into wakefulness, he sat up in the light of the new day, his heart pounding. He turned his head, waiting anxiously for the sound to come again. If it was one of the voices from the pit, he had to know which direction to take when he fled.

Catcher was calmly munching grass, and Friend was sitting up, ears and eyes turned toward the woods down the slope, as if she had also heard the sound. Looking in that direction, he saw nothing, but suddenly realized how much brighter it had become. The clouds had broken, allowing the sun to peek through. It was a wondering sight, but seeing the sun so high prompted him to look at his watch. Ten to ten. He should have been at least five miles deeper into the woods by now.

In spite of his disappointment at having overslept, the sight of the sun caused his morale to soar, and had it not been for the mysterious sound he heard, he believed he would have had the strength to jump and shout with joy.

He climbed stiffly to his feet and listened, again searching the area in the direction of Friend's gaze. Seeing nothing to indicate the presence of another human or animal, he told himself the sound must have been made by some kind of bird. It was his fear of what it *could* have been that worried him.

He stepped toward Catcher but stopped when a pleasant sound drifted up the hill, so comforting he suspected he might be hallucinating again. Perhaps he wasn't yet fully awake. Maybe he was still asleep and dreaming. A sharp stomach pain and his foul body odor told him he was fully awake in a real world.

Turning toward the sound, he identified it as that of a woman singing. Her voice was soft and melodious, like that of a child singing while alone and occupied with other things. The words of the song drifted up to him like gentle waves along a seashore, some strong, some weak and inaudible. He finally made out some of the words: "I believe in angels. I believe in everything—"

The song stopped, and a deep sense of disappointment swept over him. He remained very still, hoping the beautiful sound would begin again. When it did not, he thought it was an illusion after all. Something that pleasant could not exist in such a place. He had read of cases of men experiencing apparitions when faced with death.

But the singing began again, same song, same verse, fading and drifting back again, mellow and sweet. Where did she live? Had he drifted in too close to Dooly? He had to know, and he had to ask her for food and water. She must live somewhere close by, as no woman would venture far from home in such a wilderness.

Adrenaline pumping new strength into his legs, he walked briskly down the slope to find the singer, whom he guessed was at least two hundred feet away.

The singing stopped, but began again. "I have a dream. I have a dream—" *Nobody in his or her right mind could have dreams in such a place.*

The singing stopped again, causing him to believe he had made too much noise and frightened the woman away. Standing still, he listened for sounds of running feet, but heard nothing except the pounding of his pulse. Moments later, the words of the song drifted up to him again.

Moving more cautiously, he soon found himself looking at a clump of small green bushes at the end of what appeared to be a narrow footpath coming up the slope from the opposite direction. The voice came from the other side of the bushes.

Moving to the side to see around the obstruction, he found himself looking at a most unusual sight. A young woman with brown hair pulled up into a bun behind her head was sitting in a blue folding lawn chair under a pink beach umbrella, a flat board across her lap. Her head leaned forward, as if she might be studying something on the board.

He couldn't see her face, but judged her to be young because she had a trim figure, and the skin on the back of her neck and arms was smooth and unblemished. Her neat, fresh appearance also told him she was a woman who took pride in her appearance. She was wearing blue jeans, and her striped, wide-collared white blouse appeared to have been freshly ironed. His mind immediately conjured up grand visions of how pretty she must be.

Should he call out and risk frightening her away, or continue walking toward her and hope he could get close enough to speak before she detected his presence? While he tried to decide, he studied her surroundings and saw a barbed wire between them. Near her, in a dip in the ground's surface, he saw large ferns, blooming flowers of some kind, and a spreading willow tree. Near a winding trail that disappeared into underbrush down the slope, he saw a large vine with blue blooms.

Keeping the bushes between him and the woman, he moved closer as she began singing another song, and upon reaching the fence, he disregarded his sore back and bee stings to lie down and roll under the bottom wire. Back on his feet, he moved toward the young woman but stopped when a dead twig snapped beneath his boot.

The ashen face of the woman appeared, dark eyes wide with fright. "Who are you?" she demanded. "And what are you doing back here in these woods?"

"I'm sorry I frightened you," he said, holding up his hands. "Please, don't be afraid of me. I'm lost, and I need food and water. Will you please help me?"

"You didn't answer my question." Her eyes swept over him, and he thought he noted a hint of sympathy, but she remained poised to flee.

"My name is Blin Burge, and I'm passing through on my way to the Alabama-Coushatta Reservation." Feeling something against his leg, he looked down to find Friend leaning against his leg. "Some men stole my supplies and killed my pack mule four days ago, and I've had nothing to eat or drink since but blooms and a wild rabbit." He touched the aching bumps. "And a handful of honey."

She appeared to relax a bit as she glanced into the woods behind him, then down the foot trail, as if trying to decide whether to stay or flee. She gave him a skeptical look. "Which way were you traveling?"

He pointed behind him. "The thieves stole my compass, too."

She pointed to her right. "You can't be on your way to the reservation because it's *that* way."

"It is?" He looked to his left. "Found out yesterday I'd been traveling in a circle."

"You're no more than five miles from Dooly in *that* direction." She pointed up the hill.

"This your property?"

"Jim Fancher's, on this side of that fence. He's my stepfather. If you wanted to go to the reservation, why didn't you just drive through the front entrance? There's a highway running by the place."

He hesitated, not wanting to reveal too much to a stranger. "I had good reasons for not doing that."

She held his gaze without replying, clearly skeptical. He added, "I know I'm a mess. I'm dirty, I have poison ivy sores, bumps from bee stings, and I need a shave, clean clothes, and a bath. But if you'll trust me enough to spare a little food and water, I won't harm you, and I'd be very appreciative. I don't think I can go any further without something to eat and drink."

"You said thieves stole your supplies?" She looked at his arms and ragged clothes. "Where were you when that happened? Who were they, and what did they look like?"

"I didn't get a look at them because I fell into a pit trap they set for me. I heard one of them call the other one High, and—"

"High? Are you sure?"

"That's what it sounded like, and I think I heard one call the other 'brother.' I was a little busy at the time trying to get out of that hole. I've been so turned around since I can't tell you exactly which direction is which."

"Was the other one called Hulie?"

He hesitated, suddenly made wary by her questions and the fear she was related to the thieves. If she was, she could be a co-conspirator, or the girlfriend or wife of one of them. He said, "Maybe. Who are they to you?"

"That's a long, sad story that I'm ashamed of sharing with a stranger. And I'm not sure you'd want to hear it if I did."

"I want to know if you belong to one of them. I got away from them once, after they almost burned me to death. I don't want to meet up with them again."

"*Belong* to one of them? No way in this world! I'm not even related to them by blood."

"Since I'm on your Stepfather Fancher's land and you're not blood kin to them that must mean they're your stepbrothers."

"Unfortunately." She appeared to relax finally, and her eyes told him she wasn't frightened any more. "You *are* a mess," she said. "Come closer so I can take a look at you. If you're High Fancher's enemy, you can't be all bad."

Something about the way she said it made him want to trust her. It was a great relief to run into someone he could trust for a change.

She pointed at Friend. "What about your dog? Will he bite me?"

"He's a she, and she's only part dog. The other half is wolf. I call her Friend, and she won't hurt you. At least, she hasn't taken a bite out of me since she took up with me."

An expression of fresh concern appeared, as if she might be having second thoughts about helping him. "She wasn't with a pack of hybrids?"

She was slim but full-figured, about five feet seven inches tall and had a proud and pretty face in spite of a touch of melancholy in her dark eyes. Her face was blemish free, her hair so dark it appeared black in places. He said, "She wasn't with a pack, but a pack did attack me and my animals the night before. They were with those thieves."

Her expression of concern made her eyes appear darker. "I'll look at those bumps and that rash."

He approached her, and she slowly moved around him, studying the sorry condition of his face, neck, and arms. She said, "You need to clean those places and apply lotion." Her voice was kind, possessing a hint of sadness.

"I need a bath, first," he said, crinkling his nose. "Sorry about the way I smell and look. The thieves took my razor, too."

"How do you feel?"

"Like a Mack truck ran over me."

"Sit down—Blin, is it?" She pointed toward the chair.

Passing her, he caught the fragrance of sweet smelling cologne. "And yours?"

"Eva. Eva DeBerry."

He gave her the spiral notebook from the chair and sat down with a long sigh. "I very much appreciate you helping me. I'll go on to the reservation as soon as I rest a while."

"You're in no condition to go anywhere. It's a two-day walk from where we are."

"I can at least start."

She appeared to be in her mid twenties, and he saw no wedding band on her finger. Her hands appeared smooth and soft, and there was no makeup on her pretty face. Picking up a thermos, she poured water into a metal cup and gave it to him.

He drank it, and she gave him another. "Thanks. Is there a stream around here where I can take a bath later?"

"There's a spring over there." She pointed to the ferns. "I scooped out a hole big enough to dip a cup in, but it's not large enough to bath in."

His eyes swept over her face and hair. "Sounds like you might come here often. You live nearby?"

"With my mother and stepfather on the top of the next hill." She pointed down the slope. "My stepbrothers and my stepfather's brother are there part-time, too. I take care of my mother, who is ill, and I slip off to come over here every chance I get. Mostly when mother and stepfather are having one of their better days or sleeping."

"Slip off?" His eyes met hers.

"This is my secret place. If my stepbrothers and step-uncle knew about it, they'd badmouth me for doing such silly things."

"What *do* you do here?"

She turned her eyes toward the path, as if she might be concerned about how he reacted to her answer. "I write stuff. Short stories, essays. I even started a novel, but I doubt I'll ever finish it."

"Very interesting," he said. He studied her some more and detected a certain sensitivity about her eyes and mouth he had not noticed before. "I've never known a writer. Anything published?"

"Haven't tried. Now, that's enough about me. If you'll stay put, I'll go to the house and get you some food, soap, and lotion."

"Half-dead people have a way of staying put. I just hope I'm still alive when you get back. Your step-brothers are hot on my trail, unless they're waiting for their uncle to tell them what to do."

"Their Uncle Emmett was still with Papa when I left."

"High wanted to shoot me on the spot. Do you think he did what Emmett told him to do if his uncle got to the pit before he took out after me?"

"Probably not. If High found out you got away before Uncle Emmett got back, he didn't wait for him. High's crazy."

She pointed. "That's an air mattress if you want to lie down while I'm gone. I use it sometimes to take a nap."

She propped her lapboard against a tree and leaned down to set the notepad behind it. The front of her loose blouse fell forward and he found himself looking at her exposed breasts past a small golden cross hanging from her neck. She was not wearing a bra. He quickly averted his gaze, feeling guilty for having invaded the privacy of someone so helpful.

"No peeking," she said, straightening up.

"Sorry," he said sheepishly.

"I don't allow anybody to sneak a look at what I've written in that notebook."

"Oh, that." He sighed. "I promise not to peek."

"I'll be back in about an hour."

"Great. And thanks again." He held her gaze a moment, wanting to trust her without reservation. "I wish I could bath while you're gone. That wouldn't improve my looks, but it would make me smell better."

"The runoff from the spring collects in a hole at the bottom of the hill. You can bath there when I get back with a washcloth and soap. I can't slip out of the house with much more than that and the sandwiches without being noticed. I don't want my stepfather and Uncle Emmett to find out you're back here. I'd explain why if it weren't such a long story. See you."

"Without your stepbrothers, I hope."

"Guess you'll have to trust me, won't you?" she said over her shoulder.

He watched until she disappeared down the trail, thankful for the opportunity to gaze upon someone whose presence reminded him of the beauty and kind attentiveness he admired in women.

His better judgment told him he should be moving on, but he lacked the strength. He had to have food, but waiting for it was very risky. As a precaution, he would wait in hiding by the trail down the hill. He had to make sure Eva returned alone.

Walking toward the spring behind the ferns, he whistled at Friend. "Come on, girl!" he said. "Get some water."

The hybrid limped down the incline and followed him through the ferns to the spring flowing out of the embankment into a hole as large as a man's hat. While Friend drank her fill, he got Eva's thermos and refilled it. When Friend finished drinking, Blin took the thermos up to Catcher, pouring the water into his hat. Catcher drank it empty two times.

His exertions left him so weak he had to rest before going back down the hill. A few moments later, he crawled through the fence, picked up the air mattress, and continued down the hill, behind heavy underbrush beside the footpath, from which he would have a good view of anybody arriving from the woods below. Turning to Friend, he said, "No barking, heavy scratching, or sniffing. I don't want that pretty woman to know I'm down here 'til I'm sure she's alone."

He stretched out to wait and wondered if he might have allowed Eva's beauty and winning manner to influence him into doing something foolish, but hunger pains told him he had no choice. Would he have stayed if he didn't need food? In view of his long-standing naiveté regarding pretty women, he suspected he would. In spite of disappointing experiences, something made him continue looking upon feminine beauty and charm as a symbol of perfection in an otherwise ugly world.

He was in much the same position as when the narcotic officers offered him the opportunity to save his businesses and find his sister's murderer: he needed her. Responding to real needs in that undertaking resulted in tragedy. Would trusting this pretty woman also bring disastrous results? There was no way of finding out without waiting. The only thing more disastrous than her returning with the thieves would be coming back without food and soap.

The clouds continued to clear, making it a good day for traveling. It also made it a good day for tracking. If Uncle Emmett had returned to the cabin and given his approval, High could be making up for lost time.

Chapter X

*B*lin was dozing about an hour later when he heard footsteps coming up the trail. Sitting up, he watched Eva pass holding a brown paper bag. When he was convinced she was alone, he followed her.

His legs were still so weak he could barely walk up the incline, so he had to stop twice and rest. He found her looking for him beyond the wire fence. "I'm here."

She whirled. "I didn't expect you to be down there."

"Thanks for coming back." He dropped the air mattress by the chair and sat down on it. Giving the bag a hungry look, he asked, "Any problems?"

"Not yet. Papa was awake, but shut in his room with his brother. Mother said Uncle Emmett left on his four-wheeler to go talk to High and Hulie when I came over here the first time. Said he came back very angry and rushed in to talk to Papa just before I got back. I couldn't make out what he and Papa were arguing about, but it must have been important, because both of them were very excited. Papa is a gentle man. He seldom raises his voice." She gave him the sack. "Hope you like ham and cheese."

"I'm hungry enough to eat hide and hair. Thanks." He pulled out a sandwich and took a big bite. "Excuse my manners."

"You'd be more comfortable in the chair."

He continued to be impressed by her concern for his welfare. "Thanks. This is fine."

She took the chair as he continued eating.

Swallowing, he gave her a cautious look. "I was hoping Emmett would persuade High not to track me down when his nephew realized he hadn't roasted me."

"One can never predict what Uncle Emmett will do. He's known as the Wolf Man in this part of the state because he breeds and trains hybrids—half German shepherd, half wolf."

He took another bite. "Does your stepfather ever suspect that he and your brothers—excuse me, your *step*brothers—run a business other than a kennel?" He regretted not trusting her completely. He had to know how much she knew about her relatives' dope business. Too much could mean she was taking part in it.

She said, "My mother told me shortly after she married Papa that Emmett was a moonshiner. I always figured he was hiding his operation deep in the woods because he was afraid of being sent back to prison. Mother said he was arrested several times for moonshining, public intoxication, and fighting, and had served one term in state prison for assault. Later, when Papa talked to me about this moonshining, I concluded High and Hulie were helping him."

Her reply seemed sincere enough. "Is that what Papa believes?"

"I assume so. He's never talked to me about what Emmett and my stepbrothers did for a living after they went broke in the broiler and pulpwood business he set them up in. I haven't talked to Mother about them lately because she's too ill to be bothered. But until you get out of these woods, there are some things you should know that are a bigger threat to you than what they do to make money."

He took another bite. "They're gonna set the woods on fire?"

"High is insane, and Uncle Emmett is mean and vicious and can't be trusted. Hulie is too afraid of them to do anything but what he's told. And as for me knowing what else they might be doing back here, I'm not sure I want to know after finding out what they did to you."

"Thanks for trusting me enough to tell me that."

"There's only so much I can do. I don't dare do anything that'll make High and Uncle Emmett distrust me, because I've got to share the house with them from time to time until my mother gets well or passes away."

"Would knowing what they do be any more dangerous than helping me, if they found out?"

"I don't think so."

"They're raising pot and making meth—methamphetamine. Crack, too, probably."

Her expression of surprise looked genuine. "Then they've been lying to Papa all along. Papa has been confined to a wheelchair for several years, so he can't go back there. He didn't care about the moonshining because where he came from a long time ago, that was an honorable profession. And he's convinced that helping Emmett keeps High occupied and out of trouble. Papa is a well-educated, honorable man. He was a lay preacher a long time ago. In spite of him seeing nothing wrong with making good whiskey, he's law abiding and deeply religious. He would never approve of anybody in his family selling illegal drugs."

"Maybe you should enlighten him before his brother and sons get the entire family into trouble."

"And get killed by High? I told you he's crazy. I'm living here because I love my mother. When I'm no longer needed, I'm leaving."

Blin pulled out a second sandwich. "If you lived somewhere else, how come you know so much about High?"

"I lived with my mother and Papa long enough after they married to find out all I wanted to know about that mental case." She shuddered. "After I left, when I came back to visit Mother, Papa and I had long talks about High when he was down. He told me High had been in trouble since he was old enough to walk. Always hurting children he played with, stealing, tearing things up, and pulling the heads off chickens and lizards. Papa said when High was very young, before his mother died, he was sent to a state institution for juveniles for assault and stealing. Later, Papa took a teaching job in Dooly, where he thought it would be easier to keep High out of trouble." She gave him a concerned look. "I don't want to burden you with Fancher problems."

"Why not? I'm not going anywhere for a while, and there's nothing better for a worn-out, bee-stung man in need of a bath than a pretty face and a voice that's music to the ears."

"What a nice thing to say." She smiled.

He took another bite. "So how did your crazy stepbrother behave in Dooly?"

"High had been in Dooly less than a year when he abducted a fifteen-year-old girl, took her into the big woods back there, and raped and killed her. An investigation revealed that before she died, he did unspeakable things to her with bottles and wires from a car battery. The jury found him not guilty by reason of insanity, and committed him to a mental institution. They released him after ten years, saying he was sane enough to live at home. The girl's family was outraged."

"So he's been home since?"

"Yes. When High was discharged, the prosecutor couldn't try him again on the murder charge because of the insanity thing. By then, Papa's first wife had died, and he was married to my mother. It got so bad for them in Dooly that Papa bought this farm and moved everybody out here. He retired not long after that."

"But living out here didn't change High, I gather."

"High had been free about a year when another little girl came up missing in Dooly. The authorities, the girl's family—everybody— believed High murdered her in those woods back there like he did the other one, but they never found her body. High was never charged, but for a long time, the sheriff sent his deputies out here and back in the big woods looking for the little girl's remains and other evidence. When he failed, the girl's family took up the search."

"Over at that pit trap, they told me they knew I was either a cop or somebody sent by somebody. I don't remember that somebody's name."

"The last little girl was a Holsomback."

"That's the name." He shook his head. "And I came in here thinking I was getting *away* from trouble."

"That's the reason you're hiding in the woods?"

"That's a keg of worms you don't want to add to your list of things to worry about." He swallowed, taking a drink of water.

"Both of us have a long list." She sighed. "I felt so helpless back when I was living with Mother, knowing about all the bad things that happened in Papa's first family. My long list got longer when you told me what High and Hulie did to you. I've been praying Papa and Mother don't have to take on another burden on account of High. I'm afraid for them because Papa has been slowly losing control of High and Uncle Emmett since he got sick. I wanted to take Mother to Beaumont, but she wouldn't leave Papa, and Papa won't abandon High. Seems he made a deathbed promise to High's mother to look after their troubled son as long as he lived, no matter what he did. Poor thing. He's had to depend more and more on Emmett. Uncle Emmett was willing and able to help, but of late has become afraid of High, too. He told Mother he's tired of worrying with High and wants to leave, but Papa won't release him from *his* promise."

When he gave her an inquisitive look, she added, "Uncle Emmett has no other living relatives and no family of his own. Papa promised him a place to live if he'd promise to help him control High."

"Emmett might've found out what High did to me and realized he'll have to serve more hard time with his nephews if I file on them, or tell the authorities about their dope operation. He probably believes I'm a cop, too."

When he saw the questioning look in her eyes, he added, "I didn't come in here to do police work."

"I don't care if you are a policeman, because I have no sympathy for my stepbrothers or Emmett, after finding out what they did to you and their dope business. I just don't want anything bad to happen to Papa because of this. If he has to go through another bad experience with High, it will kill him."

He reached for the third sandwich, but decided to save it for later.

She said, "A person would have to have a compelling reason to travel alone through the big woods."

Feeling better, he decided it was safe to tell her more because she had trusted him enough to talk about her family. He told her about Mama and his promise to her. "I got so tied up making money I never got around to bringing her home before she got too ill to travel. She made me promise I'd visit her surviving relatives at the reservation some day, even if she died first."

She looked at his black hair, brown eyes, and face. "Your skin is almost as fair as mine. I wouldn't have suspected you were part Indian."

"One-eighth. Too much for some of the people I've known." Looking around them, he asked, "How long a walk is it through your step-dad's place?" He took a drink of water.

"I'll show you a way to get to the reservation quicker."

"Hope that shortcut doesn't have as much timber and brush on it as the land I've been on so far." He glanced at the sun. "I've got to get moving."

"You've come a long way, and if it rained enough to keep Emmett's hounds or those hybrids from tracking you, you'll be safe here 'til morning. You rest; otherwise, you may pass out."

Seeing Friend lick her lips, he asked Eva, "Would you mind if I gave half of the last sandwich to my friend there?"

She glanced at the hybrid. "I admire a man who cares about the welfare of his animals, but knowing she could be one of Emmett's pets gives me the creeps. It's okay, I guess."

He pulled off half of the sandwich and tossed it toward Friend, and she jumped forward to catch it before it hit the ground. He placed the other half in the sack.

She said, "I'll bring more food in the morning if you stay overnight. You'll need more to make it to the reservation." Reaching over to pull a jar of white lotion from the sack, she said, "Ready for me to treat that rash and those bumps?"

"I smell too bad. Couldn't I wash off, first? I could run down the hill and do that in a few minutes. I promise I won't come back naked."

93

She smothered a laugh. "If you'll take off your shirt and move closer, I'll wash off your face, neck, and back so I can treat the welts now. I really have to get back to the house before I'm missed. You can finish bathing later."

"If you think you can stand me." He took off his dirty shirt and moved closer, amazed at how much he had come to depend on a woman he'd just met.

Pouring water on the washcloth and rubbing it against the soap, she leaned forward and began to gently clean his face. The soap made the bumps and abrasions burn, but her presence made the pain bearable. She applied more soap and cleaned his neck, chest, and belly.

Close to her face, he saw shallow circles under her eyes and tiny crow's feet at their corners that he had not seen before. There were also dim lines across her forehead. Instead of distracting from her more appealing features, the minor flaws added a certain mystique. He also spotted a small scar on her chin and wondered if her crazy stepbrother had struck her there.

She had returned wearing the same blouse and jeans, but had put on a bra. He could see the straps through her thin blouse. Although she wore no makeup, her skin showed no blemishes other than the scar and the shallow wrinkles. Her soft, well-manicured hands told him she didn't do outside chores on her stepfather's farm. Her hair was still pulled into a bun, but several silken strands of it were free to float about her ears in an occasional breeze. One strand had dropped down over her right eye, causing her to brush it away with the back of her hand from time to time, as she finished cleaning his face and neck and applied lotion.

He winced when she moved behind him and began rubbing the soapy cloth across his back and sides.

"Sorry," she said. "I'll try to be gentler. Hold up your arms."

"Okay, but I won't guarantee your eyes won't water when I do." He held them up and she washed under them, and then continued cleaning his back, neck, and sides. He lowered his arms. "Thanks."

Her calm demeanor during their initial meeting and her manner while discussing family problems convinced him she had immense inner strength and insight. He had not found such admirable traits in any of his woman friends. Seeing them now caused him to recall the devotion he received in his early years from his beloved mama.

He dreaded the moment when Eva left, and wondered if he would ever see her, or another woman like her, again.

As she began wiping off the soap with the rinsed-out cloth, he said, "I never knew how lonesome it could be in a place like the big woods with nobody to talk to." His statement just came out, as if possessing strength of its own. It was, he thought, something a man thinks about, but doesn't put into words before strangers.

She began applying lotion, as if she had not heard him. "A person can be lonesome in a crowd. I guess it depends on your state of mind. That's why I like my special place. Life is what my imagination tells me it is."

The lotion made the bumps and rash burn less, but they still throbbed. "It would take something besides a strong imagination to make me think good thoughts about the people I've known lately."

She glanced at him, as if something in the way he said it concerned her. "You'll probably overcome your cynicism with time. Allowing my imagination to conjure up beautiful thoughts about imaginary characters helps me control mine."

"But that's not true to life. Maybe you should write about *real* people and happenings."

"You're saying you don't believe there's still beauty in the world, or that there are still lots of kind people in it with good intentions?"

"I stopped being a dreamer the first time my nose was split by a school bully that hated me because I wasn't like him. It's been split lots of times since in different ways, and for different reasons."

Her brown eyes met his, making him wish he had not been so blunt. He added, "My dear old grandmother was a good person who had good thoughts and ideas about lots of things, but she was an exception to the rule, and she belonged to another world that's dead now."

Having someone to talk to with the capacity to understand and appreciate his troubles was as beneficial as the food and water she gave him. Up 'til now, Mama was the only one in his life to offer that kind of support.

"You were lucky to have your grandmother to turn to. My only real refuge has been my books and the stories I've written." Her words had a sad ring.

"What about love? Isn't living it much better than reading or writing about it? A pretty woman like you must've had plenty of chances for that." He immediately realized he'd been too bold. "Sorry. Didn't mean to get personal."

She met his gaze momentarily, then moved around him examining his bumps and rash.

95

Wanting to break the strained silence, he said, "Being with you perked me up, so I started thinking about things that aren't any of my business. Am I forgiven?"

"There's plenty of soap left for your bath," she replied. "I'll pick it up the next time I come over here."

"You've decided not to come back in the morning?"

"Depends on how Mother is feeling and who is there. There's an apple and a candy bar in the sack if I don't make it.

"If I'm perked up enough after taking a nap, I'll miss you if you come back. In case I do, I want to tell you again how much I appreciate what you've done for me."

"Enough to tell me why you were hiding in the big woods?" Her eyes met his.

He'd hoped she wouldn't press him on that matter, because he still wasn't convinced it was safe to reveal that he was an undercover agent, but cold reasoning told him she wouldn't have put herself at risk helping him if she meant to turn him over to High and Hulie. And she did share her family secrets with him.

She said, "You were in some kind of trouble, weren't you? I mean, back before you had that run-in with my stepbrothers and Emmett. I'm a good listener if you'd care to talk about it, and it might put me in a better position to know how best to help you when my stepbrothers come back to the house."

"Sit down. This will take a while."

He told her about his fight to build a successful business, the developments at his clubs that compelled him to work as an undercover agent, and the events at the aborted trial. "I had to have a place to hide, so I came to the woods, where I could also keep the promise I made to my grandmother."

She was silent several moments, causing him to wonder if she was sympathetic or just indifferent. Finally, she met his gaze and she said, "I don't understand how things like that can happen. We have laws, and we pay people to enforce them. They're supposed to protect us from bad people."

"Particularly organized crime, killers, and crazy stepbrothers."

"I don't suppose I'll find the answers in books and made-up stories, will I?"

"Not unless you find lots of money between the pages. Love of that is what makes things happen."

"You can't believe that." She gave him an admonishing look. "Was it love of money that moved your grandmother to care for you as she did?"

He shook his head. "For a dreamy writer, you throw a mean reality punch. Of course not. But all that proves is that there are occasional exceptions to general rules. Mama was more like you, always believing in the good of people. Always kind and helpful. She warned me about greed."

She picked up her tablet. "The more I learn about the real world, the more I want to get back to my teaching job in Beaumont and bury myself in my books and made-up stories. I've always hoped that if a person believes in something strongly enough, it becomes reality."

"Believing I'd be safe in these woods didn't help me."

"I've got to go," she said, getting up. "I'll wish you good luck now, in case I don't get back before you leave. Are you sure you have your directions straight?"

Glancing toward the sun, he pointed left. "That's north. Going that way will get me to the reservation, and to the highway that runs by it, if I don't get caught and miss it."

"Right. But you're so far east and south of the southern boundary it would be best to head northwest for a day before turning north." She pointed down the trail. "Papa's house over there is only a mile off a dirt road that leads to the blacktop running by Dooly." Looking up the grade, she pointed to the fence. "That's Papa's back boundary, but it doesn't run straight with the next section that runs north. Keep going in a straight line in the direction the fence is running before it makes that first turn. You'll pass a cutover on your left. Hold your course past that well into the afternoon tomorrow, then with the sun on your left shoulder, walk north as straight as the brush will allow until dark. After a good night's sleep, keep going north until you reach the reservation boundary. It's a good day and a half walk from here."

"Will that take me across the trail your stepbrothers take to town or where they make their dope?"

"I've never been to their camp, but the trail to it leaves the house in that direction." She pointed to her left.

"Then all I have to worry about is High catching up with me before I get out of these woods."

"If that happens, I pray Emmett is with him to keep him to keep him from killing you. Papa gave Uncle Emmett orders a long time ago that

High was never to be allowed to have a gun, but Hulie told me he got one some way. Both Emmett and Hulie are too afraid of him to try to take it away from him."

Her eyes held his a moment, making him want to hold her in his arms before she left, but he was in no condition to embrace anyone so pretty and well groomed. He couldn't risk offending his only human friend. Her eyes seemed to say she wouldn't object.

Behind him, he heard Friend whine softly. Her eyes were fixed on him, as if her primitive instincts had told her what he was contemplating.

He told Eva, "In case I miss you in the morning, I'd like to visit with you sometime so we can become better acquainted."

"I'd like that, too. If you don't find me here, I'll be in Beaumont."

When she turned to leave, he caught her arm. "I hope your mother gets better soon so you can get away from your crazy stepbrother and get back to those books and stories full-time."

"Thanks. You'd best give yourself a full night's rest before leaving. That skin irritation will feel better by then. You don't want to risk getting an infection. And you need more time to recover from heat exhaustion and lack of food."

He watched as she walked down the trail, tablet in hand. At the first turn, she turned and waved, and he waved back then watched the spot where she disappeared for several moments, pondering his good fortune at having met such a splendid example of womanhood in such a place.

Picking up the cloth and soap, he set off down the trail with Friend following on her three good legs, close at his heels. It appeared she had finally overcome all fear of him.

Picking up a used paper towel he found crumpled up o the ground near the chair, he moved into the bushes and relieved his bowels before going down the trail to finish bathing. In his dehydrated state, it took a while.

On the left side of the trail at the bottom of the slope, he found a place in the stream where the downhill flow had cut a cavity about three feet wide and a foot deep between shallow banks. Crinkling his nose, he undressed and stepped into it, washed his hands, and examined the gauze taped against his thigh wound. Finding it loose on one side, he slowly pulled it off for further examination. He was relieved when he found a tight scab formed over the lesion and fresh bleeding.

Scooping up the cold water, he splashed it on his privates. "Oooh! That's cold, Friend!"

Taking care not to get water on his upper body or the wound, he lathered his private area, legs, and feet. It was a slow, tedious undertaking, and when finished, he tossed the cloth into the bushes, got down on his knees, and splashed water over his washed areas until all the suds were gone. He was relieved when he found the thigh wound still intact.

The water was cloudy from all the splashing about, but he was clean and his wound had not been disturbed. Stepping out on the bank to dry, he was chilled by a gentle breeze, proof that he still had a slight fever.

Looking at Friend calmly watching him, he noticed she had pulled off the splint but was still holding her injured foot off the ground. "Does it still hurt, ol' girl?"

He held out his hand, and she sniffed it and lay down.

Not wanting dirty clothes on his clean body, he took his billfold and knife from his trousers, tossed the clothes into the water, and picked up the soap. Washing and rinsing them, he returned his billfold and knife to his pockets, hung them over his shoulders, and walked naked up the trail. It was like stepping back in time, for he hadn't walked naked around a swimming hole since he was a boy.

With so much daylight left, he wished he had the strength to move on, but he had barely enough to walk up to the fence after stopping twice to rest. When Friend sat down near him during his second stop, he said to her, "Didn't you know nice ladies aren't supposed to stare at naked men?"

Approaching the fence, he told Friend, "I'll bet you never saw an uglier sight than a naked man walking around with his appendages swinging in the breeze. Just make sure you don't confuse them with something to eat when I crawl through the fence." *What a horrible thought.*

Hanging his shorts, socks, shirt, and trousers on the top wire, he leaned over to press down the second strand to make a space wide enough for his body to pass through, but when he attempted it, a barb on the top strand stuck in his right buttock. He froze in a stooped position. "Ouch!"

His hands pushing down on the wire beneath him, he unhooked himself and pulled his right leg back, intending to roll under the bottom wire, but changed his mind when he thought about all the leaves and dirt that would stick to his sore spots.

Pushing his right leg back through the opening, he lowered his backside and began to slowly move his body between the rusty wires, but stopped when his penis bumped against the wire in his hands. Shuddering at the thought of what a barb could do, he gently raised his privates with his left hand. With less pressure on the wire under him, it raised up, giving him less space to pass through.

Straining under the pressure of having to stand in such an awkward position, he lowered his hips until the back of his left hand touched the lower wire and he began to very slowly move through. When all body parts had cleared the wires, he fell to his hands and knees, exhausted, but thankful he had no new wounds.

Friend had moved ahead to watch him from the uphill side of the fence. She wagged her tail when he looked at her and said, "Lucky dog. Your hanging parts are shorter than mine. Why did you crawl under the fence instead of going through it like I did?"

Removing his pocketknife from his trouser pocket, he hung his clothes and boots on low limbs near a tethered Catcher and opened his first-aid kit. He cut off a piece of gauze and taped it over the scab with a large Band-Aid.

He lay down on the air mattress, completely spent. The warm air had dried his body on his way up the hill, but he was still chilly. In spite of the fever and his remaining aches, the bath made him feel human again, but nothing improved his morale as much as being with Eva. It gave him a hint of how good life could be if his world ever became safe again and he found a companion with her qualities.

Perhaps a nap would raise his energy even more and he could leave after all. Afterwards, there would be several hours of daylight left. It was two-thirty by his watch, and the sun was still shining brightly.

He awoke at four-fifteen feeling a bit refreshed, but upon standing found his legs still too weak for walking through rough terrain. He also felt chilly still, and he ached all over, as if he might have fever. His skin lesions were not as painful, but still bothersome.

Thinking a few more minutes of rest would make him fit to leave, he lay back down and felt himself drifting between semi-wakefulness and light sleep, snapping back to full awareness at the slightest sound. One time, it was Catcher pawing the ground. The next time, it was Friend scratching herself. Going back to sleep following one such disturbance, he dreamed he was running naked through the woods ahead of a pack of large, vicious wolves snapping at his bare behind. He woke with a grunt and found it almost dark. Standing, he looked around him at the lengthening shadows and moaned. *Too late to go now, no matter how good I feel.*

His clothes were dry except for their seams. The garments gave him a sense of re-joining the civilized world. Nudity was appropriate during a man's private moments, but nakedness in public was primitive.

Staying the night would mean more food and another visit with Eva, but at what price? He had done foolish things in the past to be with a particular woman, but never something so risky. All his experiences in the big woods had been nothing less than a series of disasters.

He looked for Friend in the growing darkness. Perhaps she had left to find food, or decided to rejoin her animal friends. Maybe she had gone somewhere to get well faster or die. Animals knew when their time was at hand. He would miss her. He had come to think of her as family.

Looking through the trees in the fading light, he decided it best to at least gather his things and put the blanket and saddle on Catcher before it became completely dark. Saving time in the morning would allow him to put more distance between him and the drug traffickers before he had to stop and rest.

It was dark by the time he had secured the saddle on Catcher, refilled his canteen, and put the apple and candy bar inside the first-aid kit. After eating the remaining half of the sandwich, he sat in the dark listening to the night sounds then laid down on the air mattress.

He was dozing off when he was aroused by a sound down the slope. He sat up and searched the black void around him, but saw and heard nothing. The new moon didn't give enough light see anything but the dim outline of the trees.

He fumbled for his socks and boots as he looked and listened. Moments later, he was startled by more sounds from the trail below the fence. Suspecting that High and his hounds had caught up with him, he jumped to his feet and headed for Catcher, but stopped when a light appeared near the fence. The flashlight's beam moved over the area, then flashed his way.

Without a weapon, High would kill him for sure this time.

Chapter XI

"Blin?" a voice called. "Are you there, Blin?"

The voice was high-pitched, much like the first one he heard at the pit. He remained quiet.

"Blin, it's me, Eva. Where are you?"

He began breathing again. "Up here, past the fence. Why are you out in the dark?"

"I came to warn you and tell you what happened at the house." The light swung to the ground as she approached the fence.

He walked toward her, but hung his foot on something and fell hard with a loud grunt.

"Are you all right?" she asked. "Don't move 'til I get to the fence with my light."

Getting to his feet, he shielded his eyes from the glare as she moved toward him. "What happened? Are your stepbrothers coming?"

"Yes, but thank God they didn't get here before I did. You remember me telling you about that closed-door meeting Papa and Emmett were having when I left to come back over here?"

Stopping at the fence, she snapped off her light and took a deep breath. "I found out what that was all about when I gave Papa something for his angina after his run-in with his brother. Papa said Emmett told him that when he went to his still after stopping at the house, a very excited Hulie was waiting for him. Hulie told him that High made him help him burn a cop in the pit and that High left with his hounds to find him when he didn't find his corpse. Hulie told Emmett High had his pistol and swore he would kill you when he caught up with you."

He glanced around them for an approaching light. "Did Emmett tell Papa why High was so scared I would report what I saw over there?"

"Emmett must not've told Papa about the dope or anything else, because Papa didn't mention anything to me. Anyway, after Hulie told Emmett that, Emmett rushed to the house to tell Papa he was leaving so he wouldn't have to go back to prison because of what High was about to do."

"And what did Papa do?"

"Papa was so disgusted with High this time that he asked Emmett to go to town and get a state trooper, but changed his mind when Emmett convinced him he and Mother would also be arrested if he did that."

"Because of the dope?"

"Emmett didn't explain. Just said he was leaving town with his Dooly lady friend. Papa begged him to stay and help him with High one more time, and Emmett finally promised he would if Papa wouldn't call the authorities."

"So where are Emmett and your stepbrothers now?"

"Looking for you. Emmett promised Papa he'd try to find you before High does."

Blin glanced around them again. "I've got to get moving, dark or not."

"Not 'til I finish. Papa had Emmett promise him that if you're still alive when he finds you, he'll bring you to the house and let him decide what to do with you. Emmett said he would if he could keep High from shooting him when he tries. So if they do catch you, you have to go with Emmett to stay alive."

"And get shot if Emmett finds out I was a federal agent."

"Maybe not, but Emmett is a cunning, scheming individual, and he can be vicious. He'll do what best serves his best interests."

"What time tonight did all this happen?"

"It wasn't tonight. It was about four o'clock this afternoon."

"What time is it now?"

"It was quarter to nine when I left the house."

"Where's Emmett now?"

"Don't know. He left right away to go back to their camp to tell Hulie he's to watch the front road while he searches for High further back in the woods."

"Unless dark stopped them, they can't be far way by now."

"They'll all have lights, and if you don't show up along the front road, Hulie has orders to join Emmett. All three have walkie-talkies, so Uncle Emmett and Hulie will let the other know if they spot you. Their first priority is to catch up with High before he finds you."

"Any hybrids with them?"

"Don't know about Emmett and Hulie. As far as I know, just the two hounds with High."

How far could he get in the dark without a flashlight? "Why didn't Papa raise High on his walkie-talkie and order him back to the house?"

"Papa's radio isn't working, and High wouldn't answer Emmett's call."

He was so close he could hear her breathing and smell her sweet fragrance. "Thanks for coming. I've go to move out."

"I did it for Papa and Mother, too. Neither have much longer to live, I'm afraid, but as long as Papa is able to, he'll do what he can to save his crazy son. He'll try to keep him from hurting anyone else, as long as doing that won't jeopardize his family."

"So, if I'm caught and can't convince him I didn't come to kill High, I'll still be in trouble."

"If Emmett and his nephews convince him you're another killer sent by the Holsombacks, I don't know what he will do, the poor dear. Here, take my flashlight."

"And leave you alone in the dark? You'd be stuck here 'til daylight, and in as much danger as I am if High finds you."

"Then follow me down the trail, and I'll show you where to turn north through some cutover timber. It won't be quite so dark there."

"How will I get my horse through the fence?"

"You have a horse? Then ride him! You can move faster, and the hounds can't track you."

"Dogs can track a horse, and I'm not sure he'll let me ride him because he's got some cuts on his back."

"Those hounds will be trailing your scent. It would at least throw them off for a while. They'll follow you for sure if you walk away from here." She patted his arm. "Got to go now. I don't want High's dogs to lead that imbecile to me. And Papa might need me. Remember how I told you to go?"

He pointed to his left. "Keep going in the direction that fence is running up to the first turn."

"Good luck." She snapped on the light and walked down the trail, and as she moved away, her body's silhouette against the circle of light ahead of her slowly became smaller, disappearing when she took the turn at the bottom of the hill.

He rushed up the grade to his horse, realizing that if Catcher wouldn't allow him ride, he might not have sufficient strength to stay ahead of the hounds.

Fumbling in the darkness, he loosened the rope holding the saddle and moved it and the blanket forward, drawing the cinch tight. Blin talked to the horse as he tied the water jug and first aid kit to the saddle horn and climbed cautiously into the saddle.

Catcher pranced about a bit, but didn't try to throw him off. Blin nudged the horse's sides with his heels and turned him toward the fence. Finding the fence by the dim light of the new moon was nearly impossible under the trees. He held his right hand out and up in case Catcher took him under a low limb as he searched the darkened area. He spotted one post, then another. Holding Catcher to a slow walk, he followed them, but moments later, it became so dark under the heavy cover that he had to stop.

Feeling around him, he touched a small limb, which he broke off. Stripping it of its smaller branches, he held it out until he found the top wire and urged Catcher forward.

It was very slow going, but about an hour later, they arrived at a small opening where the fence turned. He continued riding in line with the wires he had followed, in accordance with Eva's directions. The trees and brush became thicker, and in less than an hour, his way was blocked. Getting a fix on the stars, he changed course, and soon arrived at a clearer area that allowed him more light. Glancing at the stars again, he continued riding in what he believed was in the right direction, watching for the cutover Eva told him about.

After slowly weaving in, out, and around patches of heavy ground cover and thick timber for what seemed like another hour, he was thrown forward when Catcher stopped suddenly. Pushing the limb forward, he moved it up and down and heard it strike a wire that Catcher must have seen or bumped with his nose.

He moaned, shaking his head. He had circled back to the east boundary of the Fancher place. He would have to reverse course and hope to get back on track.

He followed the road until they arrived at another opening and stopped. He searched the sky for the Big Dipper, hoping to find the North Star, but couldn't find it through the surrounding tree cover. Turning to what he believed was a more northerly direction, he nudged Catcher into a fast walk, soon arriving at a wider clearing on his left, which he assumed was the one Eva had told him about. Spotting the North Star, he turned to place it off his left shoulder. He rode for what he guessed to about a half-hour, dodging branches he saw, ignoring slaps in the face from those he could not see, until he found himself under heavy cover again. He pulled Catcher to a slow walk as he strained to spot clearings ahead.

He maintained the slow pace for what seemed like another hour, finally stopping when it became impossible to see well enough to ride in any direction. He looked for openings that would let him locate the Big Dipper again, but didn't see one. He climbed to the ground to relieve his bladder and take his weight off Catcher's wounds.

Without the sound of Catcher's hooves thumping against the earth and the scraping of passing branches and bushes, the stillness of his black surroundings became more eerie and threatening. What should he do, risk injury from riding into low limbs and Catcher stepping in a hole and breaking a leg, or wait for daybreak and risk being overtaken? He couldn't hear High's hounds approaching. Maybe they hadn't found his trail yet. High could have stopped to rest. Where were Emmett and Hulie?

His thoughts were interrupted by a rustling in the leaves nearby. "Who's there?" Receiving no reply, he tried again. "Friend, is that you?"

The rustling in the leaves told him that whatever it was, it was moving away from him. It was most likely a raccoon or an armadillo. He wondered where Friend was. He missed her.

Reins in hand, he led Catcher deeper into the dense undergrowth, intent on feeling his way as far as he could. He hadn't gone more than a dozen steps when he caught his foot on something and fell hard, almost dropping the reins.

Getting up, he moved his foot to make sure he hadn't broken it, and then looked around again for an opening. The dense trees and underbrush were spread out in all directions like a black umbrella.

Disgusted, he sat down in the leaves to think about what to do, finally deciding he had no choice but to wait for daylight. He didn't know how long that would be because he couldn't see his watch or locate the moon, but he believed it was no more than a couple of hours away. He was very hungry again, so he ate the apple and lay down to rest.

In spite of the hour, it was warm, humid, and still as death. With nothing to do but wait, he thought about Eva and her family troubles. He wondered what she was doing at that moment. Sleeping, most likely, if she wasn't attending her ill stepfather or mother. He wished he could help her with her family problems, but he couldn't even help himself. All he could do was wait and hope High's hounds were either sleeping as their master slept, or had not picked up Catcher's trail.

His mind turned to what could happen when he arrived at his grandmother's ancestral home. How would those in charge receive him?

Eva's remarks about what *might* happen troubled him because it caused him to recall reading about Indian unrest up in the Dakota country and other places. It was impossible to believe that any relative of someone as kind and loving as Mama could hate anybody, white or otherwise.

He had too much Indian blood to be accepted in West Texas. Perhaps he was he too white to be accepted by Mama's people. The tribe could very well have a young chief who didn't like any man three-quarters white, but that shouldn't prevent him from allowing the tribal rights and privileges of the mixed-blood grandson of Laura Bartee, who was of full blood.

With social values as liberal as they were in today's world, it was inconceivable that any chief could allow his grandmother's leaving to marry a white man stand in her grandson's way of fulfilling his sacred promise. But what if his grandmother had been banished because of what she had done? He had read of such things. In that case, he might not be allowed to fulfill his obligation to Mama's living relatives. If turned away, he would leave her ancestral home in disgrace.

He wished he could remember his grandmother's Indian name, but it had been pushed to the back of his mind too long, like lots of other things from his boyhood. Confront and compromise. Win some; lose some. The last few years of his life were too hectic, had passed too quickly. And if he were overtaken by High Fancher, it would come to an abrupt end.

He jumped when he heard the far-off wail of a coyote or a wolf. He thought it not as sharp as a coyote's. Then there came a deeper, longer cry that sounded more like a wolf. It could've been the hound leading Eva's crazy half-brother to his master's next victim.

The sound came again, and this time, he could tell it was coming from the general direction of his back trail. That sent a rush through him. How far away was it? It was impossible to judge distance in the timber, but any distance was too close.

He remounted and tried to ride on, but riding was impossible in the heavy brush and vines. He dismounted and tried to find an opening on foot, but after a half hour of trying, had to stop. If the animals he heard were High's hounds, he was trapped. Finally succumbing to his feverish body's urges to rest, he tied the reins to a bush and lay down. Moments later, he felt himself drifting into a semi-conscious state as an inner voice told him he must move on. Perhaps it wasn't High's hounds; maybe he'd be lucky this time. If so, he'd have the strength to move on as soon as the sun came up to give him light.

107

He was aroused from a deep sleep by a sniffing sound, followed by the touch of something cold and moist against his face. He brought his hand up to push it away. "Go away, Friend," he mumbled, without opening his eyes. "We can make up later."

He was jolted to full wakefulness by a hard blow to his side and an angry, high-pitched voice that screamed, "Get up, cop!"

He sat up with a startled grunt in full daylight to find himself looking over the top of a pistol into the fierce, dark eyes of a tall man with a beard wearing a dirty, camouflage jump suit.

The pistol still pointed at his face, the man stepped back, baring large, uneven teeth in a sick smile. His crazed expression told Blin he would be shot immediately.

Chapter XII

A large black and tan hound jumped back into the wall of brush and vines when Blin attempted to sit up, and a tall, slim man leaned closer to shove his pistol against his forehead, forcing him back to the ground.

Laughing like a child, the man said in a high-pitched voice, "Man, there ain't nothin' prettier than the look on a man's face that's been woke up by the business end of my pistol. It's a pure joy."

"Back off, High," another voice said from the thicket behind the man.

Dazed by the sudden turn of events, Blin turned his eyes to the other man walking toward them with a shotgun in his hands. He was younger and shorter than the man with the pistol, but he had the same dark eyes. A look about his eyes told Blin he was afraid of the man standing over him. Blin guessed him to be Hulie, and the older, tall one was High.

Blin moved to get to his feet, but High shoved him back again with his foot, telling him, "Try that again, cop, and neither my brother nor God himself can keep me from shootin' you." Glancing at Hulie, he added, "Did you see that, Hulie? He tried to jump me. I told you and Uncle Emmett he was dangerous, but nobody listens to me. But his snoopin' days are over because I'm gonna splatter his brains all over the place."

"No, don't!" Hulie said. "If you do that, you'll get all of us sent to the pen, includin' Papa. You don't want to do that, do you? Papa gave me and Uncle Emmett strict orders to bring this man to the house. He also told me to get your pistol as soon as I caught up with you. He doesn't want you to hurt anybody ever again."

Blin turned his eyes back to the thin, slope-shouldered brother wearing a dirty baseball cap and a wrinkled, camouflage jump suit, judging him to be well over six feet tall, but not weighing more than one hundred fifty pounds. He had a crazed look about his dark, close-set eyes. A black beard covered his face, and the long black hair protruding from beneath his cap was pulled back and tied in a ponytail.

Blin said, "I told you at the pit I'm not a cop. Are you hard of hearing or just stupid?"

"Don't push me, runt," High snapped. "If you ain't a cop, you're a Holsomback man, and there ain't nobody I'd rather kill than one of them."

Blin saw the other brother give the gun in High's hand a cautious look as he pushed a vine to the side to come nearer. He had both hands on his shotgun now. Blin told him, "You look like a reasonably intelligent person. Surely you must know by now that if I'd been looking for you or your brother, I wouldn't be this far away from where I found you."

"Don't let him slick-talk you, Hulie. He's dangerous, I tell you."

"Put down the gun, High," Hulie said. "Papa said you're not to hurt this man. We'll let him decide what's best to do with him."

"But don't you see?" High protested. "He was on his way to get more help after he found out he couldn't take us alone. You saw all his supplies. No man that's just passin' through by himself would have that much stuff. And before my hound struck his trail comin' over here, he tracked him to a place inside our back fence where he and his cop pals were camped. There was a chair and an air mattress by our spring. My hound followed his scent to the bottom of the hill, which means he most likely went all the way to the back yard fence to see if I was home. You know the Holsomback killers have done that before."

Hulie turned accusing eyes on Blin, apparently unwilling to challenge his brother.

High continued his harangue. "He and his pals have been using that spot by our spring as their meetin' place for a long time, judging by the way the brush was beat down." He stepped closer, his pistol still leveled at Blin's head. "I say let's kill him now and show the Holsombacks and the law they can't keep sending men in here after me. You don't have to tell Papa. We'll bury him and tell Papa he got away, like he did over at the pit."

"And make me a party to murder? You're not pullin' me into one of your crazy killin' sprees. We'd both spend the rest of our lives behind bars. Uncle Emmett, too, because he's on his way here."

"But don't you see? You, me, and Uncle Emmett will go to the pen anyway if we don't stop this man from reportin' what he saw at our camp."

"Papa'll think of a way to keep that from happening. If you do anything to this man before you bring him to the house, Papa said he'd call the law himself."

"Papa said that?" High gave his brother a puzzled look, allowing his gun hand to drop to his side. "How in hell did he know the cop was back here, anyway? I sure as hell didn't tell him. I didn't answer any of his calls before his radio went dead."

"Uncle Emmett told him. And he told Papa what you tried to do to him at the pit."

The baffled look on High's face told Blin he was having difficulty grasping the significance of his brother's statement. When he did, his dark eyes flashed angrily. "Uncle Emmett did that when he wasn't even there? How come he'd do a dumb thing like that when I was doin' it as much for his benefit as ours? Looks like I can't trust him anymore, neither. I'll make him pay for tellin' on me."

"You can take that up with him when he and Jimmy get here."

"He's bringin' Jimmy? He knows not to let our little brother find out about anything we do. He'd blab it all over the county." He shook his head. "Uncle Emmett has got the gall, comin' here after squealin' on me."

"Well, since he is and Jimmy's with him, you don't want him sent to reform school like you were, do you?"

Taking advantage of the distraction, Blin stood as the sound of an approaching motor drifted through the trees.

Hulie told High, "You could've saved us all lots of trouble if you'd answered Papa's calls. Uncle Emmett said you wouldn't answer him, either."

"Papa wouldn't turn me in to the law," High said. "He knows he's a Holsomback man." His voice was that of a disappointed child. Suddenly remembering his prisoner, he leveled his pistol at Blin. "Who told you to stand up, cop?"

Hulie said, "Move him out of this thicket to where we can all stand up and talk. I'll bring his horse. Emmett can't drive his four-wheeler into this mess."

High motioned with his gun and Blin walked out of the thick underbrush and vines ahead of High. About fifty steps later, High pointed to his right. "Over there, cop."

Hulie had followed them with the horse to a small clearing. High jumped in front of Blin, shoved his pistol into his belly, and snarled, "Far enough, runt."

Hulie tethered Catcher to a small sapling. "Be careful with that pistol, High. If you kill that man, you'll have to kill me, Uncle Emmett, and your little brother to save yourself. You don't want to do that, do you?"

They all watched a mud-spattered four-wheeler weave toward them through the trees carrying a large, bareheaded man and a young boy. The passenger appeared no more than twelve years old, and when he spotted High, Blin saw an expression of dread sweep over his face.

The large man stopped and shut off the motor with a cautious glance at High and Blin. He looked at the gun in High's hand and climbed off. The driver's hair was long and red. Dressed in faded jeans and a short-sleeved black shirt, he appeared to be at least six feet tall and weigh at least two hundred and fifty pounds. His face was deeply tanned and weather-beaten, and his wide shoulders, muscular arms, and prominent chin gave him the appearance of a professional wrestler or a pugilist. His nose was large and red.

The uncle placed his right hand on the butt of a pistol pushed under his belt and cautiously approached High. Both his feet turned inward, confirming him to be the man whose tracks Blin had found at the stream. He said gruffly, "Your daddy gave me strict orders to get your pistol the minute I found you. Hand it over." He held out a beefy hand.

"Like hell, I will," High said, stepping back. "Do you realize how long it took me to get my hands on this Beretta? Even if it was just a Saturday Night Special, I wouldn't give it up, because I get no respect at all without a gun."

Emmett hesitated, looking at Hulie for support. Hulie shrugged, saying, "He's hell bent on shootin' the guy."

Emmett looked at High. "You've done some dumb-ass things in the past, nephew. How come you want to do the dumbest thing ever by throwin' away the quick cash we can get for this man?"

"Huh?" High appeared more confused than ever.

"Don't you know that regardless of who sent this man, they'll be willin' to pay a tidy sum to get him back in one piece? There ain't no better way to stop cops and hired killers from comin' for you than to make 'em pay every time they do it. Why get ourselves into hot water when we can catch their triggermen and hold 'em for ransom?"

"Huh?" High was still confused.

"My plan will let us make a bundle without going against your daddy and gettin' ourselves sent to the pen," Emmett explained, more confident now. "All we've got to do is take this man to the house, where we have a place to hold him 'til we get our money. We can't get nothin' for a dead man."

"Uncle Emmett is right," Hulie said, apparently buoyed by his uncle's unexpected proposal. He gave his uncle a questioning look. "But what if you can't convince Papa to let us hold him?"

"I'll think of a way if you and High'll help me." He looked at High. "But you have to promise you'll at least keep your pistol in your pocket out of sight. Will you do that?"

High gave Emmett a puzzled look. "I know in my gut he's a cop, and I oughta kill him. What happens to your plan if Papa decides he ain't a cop or a Holsomback?"

"Trust me," Emmett said. "He'll at least let us hold him 'til he finds out for sure."

"Either way I'd still get to keep my pistol?"

Emmett nodded.

High smiled. "With that money I can buy me another girl in Beaumont. But if your plan don't work, I can still shoot him. It don't seem right, me catchin' a man that was gonna kill me and not shoot him."

Emmett nodded. "Just don't get all riled up if I have to tell your daddy something you don't like in order to make my plan work, Search the stranger for some I.D. He'll have something on him that'll tell us who to call."

"I guess this proves you ain't against me, after all, Uncle Emmett," High said, smiling. He shoved his pistol in his right front pocket and told Blin, "Stand still and don't run, unless you want me to shoot our prize." He began patting down Blin's pockets, telling Emmett, "You shoulda left Jimmy at the house. I don't want a kid mixed up in our business."

"Your daddy told me to bring him," Emmett said, taking his hand from his pistol. "Maybe he thought you'd be more likely to behave yourself if I did."

Overcome suddenly by a sudden mood swing, High stepped back and kicked at Blin's groin, barely missing when Blin jumped aside. Blin crouched to rush High, but stopped when the crazy brother shoved his hand into his front pocket and snarled, "Just because I agreed not to kill you now don't give you no special privileges, runt. I'm gonna have lots of fun with you, plan or no plan. You're gonna wish you were dead by the time I get through with you."

Fighting to restore his self-control, Blin said, "Getting shot by you wouldn't be any worse than being eaten up by those wolf dogs of your uncle's." He looked at Emmett.

Too late, Blin realized he had said too much. He watched as the three exchanged anxious glances. Emmett turned accusing eyes on him. "Wolf dogs? Who told you I had wolf dogs? And how would you know these boys are my nephews unless you really are a cop or another one of the Holsombacks' paid killers?"

"I told you! I told you!" High exclaimed, jumping about like a child. "Does that mean you don't want to hold him for ransom now? If you don't, can I kill him?"

"Simmer down, High," Emmett snapped. "It only makes my plan better. Even if it didn't, I wouldn't let you do something stupid that would send all of us to the slammer. Can't you see you've nearly killed your daddy already?"

"Papa's too old and sick to run things any more," High moaned.

Hulie said, "We'll have to go into town to make them calls. We don't want anybody to trace 'em back to Papa's place."

"We'll do that as soon as Jim talks with him, if we can find out who to call." Emmett turned to Blin. "Give me your billfold and tell me your name."

Blin pulled out his billfold, deciding it best not to give him his real name. "Max Potrella."

"What kind of a damn name is that?" High said, laughing. "Are you a Mescan, or did your skin get that brown from stayin' out in the sun too long? And what's them bumps all over your face? That's not leprosy, is it?"

His demands brought back memories of the bullies from his early school days, so for a moment, Blin was almost overwhelmed by an urge to hit High in his ugly mouth. Instead, he said, "Do you act stupid because you've been out in the sun too long, or were you were born without a brain?"

Hulie laughed, but stopped when High shot him a warning glance and shoved his right hand into his pocket. Just as Blin thought he would be shot for sure, a flash of color fluttered between him and High, causing the crazy brother to jump back and swing his gun hand at the object. "Damned wasp!" he snarled.

Hulie laughed openly this time. "You're so jumpy you don't know the difference between a little ol' yellow butterfly and a yellow jacket. You'd better calm down before you bust a head gasket."

Blin watched as the yellow butterfly lit on a nearby flower. What a wonder it was, he thought, to be saved by something so small and fragile.

"Smart mouth," High whined. "You've never been stung by one of them devils. You're not allergic to wasp stings like I am."

A movement in the brush in line with the butterfly caught Blin's eye. High saw it, too, and pulled his pistol and fired. "A white wolf!"

"Have you ever seen a white wolf, harebrain?" Hulie asked, laughing again. "It's just one of Uncle Emmett's hybrid bitches on the loose. Put your pistol back in your pocket."

Blin saw a flash of white as the animal disappeared into heavy cover. Friend had not abandoned him after all.

High fired again, and Blin heard a painful yelp. "Stop it! What possible harm can she do you?"

"Go ahead; kill her," Emmett said. "She's the bitch that got away from me a couple of years back. She can't do me any good because she's too old to have more pups." He looked at Blin. "How did you know she was a she?"

"Just a lucky guess," Blin said, shrugging.

The crazy brother pushed his pistol back into his pocket and jerked the billfold out of Blin's hands. "I'll find out who he is. Tell us, runt. What kind of a damn name is Max Potrella, anyway?" He rubbed his beard as if in deep thought. "Let's see. What does Max stand for? Maximum?" He laughed. "I knew a judge once called Maximum John. He wound up dead after he got too tough with some friends of ours over in San Antoine. Empty your pockets, runt."

Glancing at the spot where Friend disappeared, Blin dropped his loose change, pocketknife, and handkerchief at High's feet. He was thankful he had thought to remove everything from the billfold that revealed his true identity or Houston address.

Ordering him to step back, High got down on his knees to pour through the contents of the wallet, and when he saw the money, he shoved it into his back pocket. He rummaged through the other items as Emmett moved closer to watch.

A sense of urgency swept over Blin when he saw a small card among the items, the card the federal prosecutor George Madsen gave him following the aborted trial. He remembered tearing off and saving the end where he'd written the prosecutor's name and title.

Blin was relieved when High stopped his search upon finding the photo of Veronica. Holding it at arm's length, he grinned and said, "You're not so dumb when it comes to pickin' women, runt." He gave the picture to Emmett.

A fresh wave of anxiety swept over Blin when he glimpsed writing on the back of the photo. Was that Veronica's name and address? He admonished himself for not throwing the photo away. It was another example of how he sometimes allowed sentimentality to overrule practicality.

He glanced at the first aid kit containing Mama's letters hanging on the saddle, hoping they didn't open it.

Emmett turned the photo over and read the inscription. "To my arresting friend, B.B."

"What more proof do you need?" High demanded. "That proves he's a cop. Why else would he lie?"

Emmett nodded. "Maybe. B.B. sure as hell don't stand for Max Potrella." He returned the photo to High. "Check it for telephone numbers or an address."

High studied the photo with glowing eyes before turning it over. "Here's a street address and a telephone number." He grinned.

A fresh wave of dread swept over Blin.

"Which town?" Emmett asked, moving closer. "We'll call our friends there and have 'em check him out."

"It don't say, but if it did, I'd check him out myself. I ain't sharin' my share of the ransom money with nobody."

Hulie said, "All we've got to do is call that number."

Blin watched anxiously as High picked up the torn-off card. Examining it, he said, "Here's some more numbers, Uncle Emmett."

"Great." Emmett extended his hand. "Give 'em to me. I'll call 'em as soon as I get to a phone where I can talk in private."

"But I found 'em," High protested, pushing the items behind him.

"But it's my plan," Emmett said bluntly. "Hand 'em over."

"But you'll give 'em to Papa." High's dark eyes were cold and angry. "That'll ruin our plan, and I won't get money for another woman."

"I won't give 'em to your dad. So what's it gonna be, the photo and card, or your pistol?"

High gave him the card and photo.

Hulie said, "I'll check out the stranger's horse." He leaned his shotgun against a bush and took the first aid kit from the saddle. Opening it, he ran his hand through its contents.

Concerned about him destroying the letters, Blin said, "That's personal stuff. There's nothing in it you'd be interested in."

Ignoring him, Hulie pulled out the first aid kit, the envelope containing the other letters, and the brown sack with the apple and candy bar in it. Dropping all except the brown sack, he said, "Look here, Uncle Emmett. This sack is from Drucker's Grocery in Dooly, where Eva buys groceries." He looked at Blin. "If you're just passing through, who gave you this sack?"

High said heatedly, "Nobody. He bought the groceries in it before he and his cop friends rode into these wood. I told you he was a cop."

"Well?" Emmett said, moving closer.

Blin looked at the sack, then Hulie. "I stopped at lots of places when I was driving around looking for a place to leave my car and trailer. Drucker's must've been one of them." If they didn't believe him, Eva could be in serious trouble.

Hulie dropped the candy into his pocket and tossed the apple to High. "Thanks for buying my favorite candy." He opened the large envelope. "Looks like letters."

High approached his brother. "Any pictures of naked women?"

Hulie opened a letter and scanned it then dropped it to go to another. When Blin walked over to pick them up, High put his hand in his front pocket "Stay put, runt." He looked at Hulie. "Well?"

Coming to the last page of the last letter, Hulie studied the writing a moment and said, "Looks like he wasn't lying about this stuff being personal. Looks like they're all from his grandmother. I didn't see any numbers or addresses on 'em."

The three exchanged glances, and High laughed, "What kind of a guy goes around with letters from his grandma in a box?" He kicked one of the pages and walked over to say something his little brother on the ATV.

Blin gathered up the pages as Hulie examined the first aid supplies in the metal box. Sorting out the pages as best he could, Blin returned them to the envelopes, and when Hulie closed and dropped box, he put the letters in it. He heard Emmett mumble something to Hulie, but all he understood was "Had to come up with something. The more I find out, the better I like it."

Jimmy gave High a frightened look, as if he was afraid High was about to strike him, but when High saw Hulie approaching Catcher, he called out, "That's my horse." He moved away from Jimmy. "I've always wanted a fine horse like that. You and Uncle Emmett watch the runt while I look at him. Get over here, runt."

Hulie picked up his shotgun and pointed it at the wallet, nodding to Blin. Blin scooped it up as High approached Catcher.

The crazy brother's face lit up when he saw the cuts behind the saddle. "Uncle Emmett, your pets cut him up real good." He offered the apple to Catcher, and when the hungry horse reached for it, he tossed it into the weeds and laughed. He mounted, and Catcher moved from side to side with a toss of his head then settled down, disappointing Blin, who'd hoped the horse would buck him off.

"Let's go to the house," Emmett said. "Hulie, make sure our hostage follows close behind me and Jimmy. High will ride behind you." He told Blin, "Don't get stupid and do something that'll give High an excuse to shoot you, and don't get your hopes up about my brother showing you any sympathy. He's old and sick, but he's tough. Just because he's trying to keep High from dragging the family into another killing don't mean he'll be any kinder to you than you'd be to High if he decides you are a Holsomback man." Blin decided further protests would be futile, and that by following orders, he would at least stay alive a few more hours. If the elder Fancher believed him, he might order his release.

He looked for Friend but didn't see her. Her appearance was a pleasant surprise and made him wonder if there was any significance in her appearing at such a critical moment. Her yelping meant High's bullet had either frightened or wounded her. If she was hit, she might be dead already. Perhaps he would be, too, by the end of the next day.

He had been put to the test many times since arriving in the big woods, and each time had come out the loser. It was enough to make him doubt he would ever regain control of his life and enjoy a safe, clean environment in the presence of law abiding, respectful people.

Chapter XIII

*B*lin walked at a brisk pace behind the all-terrain vehicle as Emmett led them through the woods toward the Fancher farm. Holy followed him with the hounds. High brought up the rear on Catcher, constantly taunting Blin and Hulie at having to walk while he had such a fine horse to ride.

Jimmy didn't speak to Blin before he left, but his eyes appeared to reflect sympathy. In his boyish face, Blin saw a resemblance to his half-sister, in spite of his blue eyes and lighter hair.

Blin fell back to avoid being slapped in the face by low-hanging branches that Emmett rode through, but each time he did, Hulie poked him in the back with his shotgun, and High said things like, "Watch him, Hulie. Don't let him jump you," and "If he makes a break, step aside, and let me blow him away. I've got a better view from up here." He laughed.

Uncle Emmett didn't turn or speak, but Jimmy occasionally glanced at Blin. Each time, he quickly turned forward again, as if he might be afraid of a rebuke from his half-brothers. He held tightly to his uncle or the luggage rack as Emmett drove under, around, and through the trees and bushes. Although still early, it was hot, and the fumes from the vehicle's exhaust burned Blin's eyes and made breathing more difficult.

About half an hour later, Blin detected another odor, and when he turned, he saw High smoking what appeared to be a hand-rolled marijuana joint. Moments later, the crazy brother's remarks became more abusive, his threats more frequent. He ordered his uncle to ride on ahead to tell Papa they were on their way, but Emmett ignored him.

They maintained a slow but steady pace for what seemed like another hour as they traveled up, down, and around hills covered with dense undergrowth and large trees before Uncle Emmett stopped the vehicle and got off, telling Hulie, "I'll let y'all rest a while."

"It's about time," Hulie said, falling down on the leaves to fan his flushed face with his soiled camouflaged cap.

119

As Emmett and Jimmy sat down, High dismounted, mumbling protests about his uncle not going on to the house and allowing him and Hulie to take the prisoner the rest of the way. Sitting down, Blin gave Catcher concerned look as High tied the reins to a bush. The horse needed water.

Emmett wiped his brow with the back of hand. "It's too hot to be ridin' a-straddle that motor."

"It's cooler on top of my new horse," High said. "But that's what happens sometimes. The best end up with the best." He gave his uncle a contemptuous look. "You're just like Papa, too old to follow me and Hulie around in these woods takin' care of business."

Emmett threw High a concerned look. "I'd feel a lot better if I had a cold glass of water and a plate of Eva's biscuits and eggs with ham on the side."

"I expect Mr. Potrella is hungry, too," Jimmy said. His remark was so unexpected his uncle and brothers turned to give him a look of disbelief. Jimmy added, "I noticed he didn't have anything to eat with him but that apple and a candy bar."

"So who cares?" High said "A man that wants to put Hulie, me, and Uncle Emmett in the pen don't deserve to eat nothin' but a bullet."

"How long has it been since you ate a real meal, mister?" Emmett asked.

"Not since you and your nephew stole my supplies," Blin replied, not wanting to include Eva's sandwiches.

"He's lying," High whined. "His friends had food back there. It was in that grocery sack with that apple." He suddenly reached out, grabbed a green lizard scurrying by, bit off its head, and spat it at Blin. Tossing the bloody body into Blin's lap, he sneered, "But in case you're still hungry, that'll help fill your lousy gut." He laughed, beating the ground with both hands.

The others gave High sober looks, obviously concerned by his gruesome act, but neither spoke as High lay down in the leaves and said, "Being out here like this always makes me think about something besides food. What I need right now is a tumble from that stuck-up Eva."

"Better be careful what you do to Eva," Hulie said. "You hurt her and Papa finds out, he'd do something to you worse than callin' the law. He and Lily have always believed the sun rose and set on Eva. More so since she came back to take care of 'em."

High raised his head to give his brother a contemptuous look. "Her comin' back ain't got nothin' to do with it. Papa has always thought a lot more of her and Jimmy than he has you and me. How come he's like that?"

Hulie shrugged.

"Well, it makes me mad," High said. "And it makes me madder when Eva treats me like trash."

"She'll never let you touch her, that's for sure."

"That's too bad, because I could save her a lot of travelin' between here and Beaumont when she needs a man." High sat up.

"You had your chance with her early this year out at the barn, remember? You struck out bad, big brother." The gleam in his eyes told Blin the subject made him as excited as his brother.

"That's because Jimmy showed up, the little brat," High said, throwing an angry look at Jimmy. "That time don't count."

"I'll have to hold her for you if you ever do any good with her," Hulie said, pleased he'd found a way to rattle his brother.

"I don't need help takin' *any* woman, smart aleck. That ain't no trick at all these days."

"How would you know? You haven't been allowed to go to town in years."

"You talk like you believe I've never done any good with our snooty step-sister, Mr. Smarty-Pants."

"It's not because you haven't tried. Everybody in the family except Papa knows you've been pawin' around on her ever since Papa married her mama. And the more she filled out, the more you tried to make her put out." He laughed. "What a loser."

High threw a handful of leaves at his brother. "How many women have you had lately?"

Hulie waved a hand at his brother, not answering.

Upset by his refusal, High turned his fury on Blin. Throwing a stick at him, he said, "I'm really gonna have fun with you, runt cop. Your kind is always makin' life miserable for people like me. Cops are just like Papa, never lettin' me do what I want to do."

Emmett said, getting up, "If all you two are gonna do is fuss and argue, we'd better get goin'."

High rammed his heels against Catcher's sides and jerked the reins hard when the horse whirled, as if about to throw him off. "I'll teach you who's boss, you dumb horse."

121

They resumed moving at a steady pace, and within a half-hour arrived at a wire gate in the fence that crossed what appeared to be an old logging road. Blin assumed it was the boundary of the Fancher farm. Jimmy opened the gap, and they all filed through as Blin tried to decide the best way to approach the father. Should he tell him everything, including the part about his undercover work, in hopes he would be sympathetic, or nothing but his assumed name? The truth would confirm his crazy son's suspicions, causing him to defy them all and kill him. If he didn't, Emmett might want to forget the ransom plan as too dangerous. Blin needed the time the plan would buy him.

Blin decided it was safer to tell the father what he told his captors already and hope Eva hadn't already passed on to him what he told her. He couldn't risk telling Jim Fancher his real name. It wasn't easy to think clearly because of High's constant harassment and his own mounting resentment at being treated like a sub-human creature. He looked forward to his meeting with the father.

They walked into a clearing, and Blin saw a white frame house with a steep tin roof surrounded by large sycamore trees. Although it resembled farmhouses of an earlier time with its wide front porch and dogtrot center hall, it appeared to be in good repair with gleaming white walls, a concrete porch, and a brick foundation. There was a satellite dish in its side yard and electric power lines running from a utility pole near a gate out front.

"It's about time," Hulie said. "This walking is for the birds."

Beyond the fence on the far side of the house, Blin saw three long, metal structures in an opening grown over with weeds and tall grass and concluded they were the old broiler houses Eva told him about. Between the broiler houses and the residence was a cluster of saplings and more weeds, which he believed to surround a small pond. To the right of it, he saw a large open field that apparently had been under cultivation at one time, but was now covered by more weeds and pine saplings.

Stopping near a flat-roofed metal shed with a mud-spattered sports car and a Dodge pickup parked under it, Emmett said something to Jimmy and the boy jumped off to run to the house, calling, "Papa, we're back!"

High rode up alongside Blin. "Wait right here, runt. We've got to make sure your friends didn't beat us here." He looked at the running Jimmy. "Dumb kid. There's no tellin' what he'll tell Papa before I get in there. I wanted to tell him about the prize pig we caught."

The hounds trotted past two four-wheelers near the back porch to begin drinking water out of a metal pan beneath a faucet. Blin saw other improvements now. The house's outside walls were covered with vinyl, and behind a bed of flowers near a side window, he saw an air compressor.

Nodding toward Blin, High told Hulie, "Keep your eye on him. He may make a run for it any second now. Me and Emmett will watch the house for signs of other strangers."

Hulie placed both hands on his shotgun and stepped back as Emmett said, "You know what your daddy thinks of having guns around for anything besides huntin'. You may have to leave your shotgun outside when you go in." Turning to High, he added, "Now that we've got our prisoner to the house, why don't you give me your Beretta and save your daddy from gettin' upset about it when we go inside? I know he'll ask us if we took it from you. He's more likely to let me hold the stranger 'til his friends can come get him if he knows you don't have a gun."

"I already told you I'm not givin' my gun to anybody," High said.

"Well, if you're gonna keep it, you'll have to keep it out of sight, and you'll have to tell your papa a lie."

"I wonder what's keepin' the dumb kid," High said.

Blin looked around the edge of the clearing for signs of Friend and studied the black sports car and the red Dodge pickup under the carport. Both appeared to be recent models. Both had heavy coats of dried mud. Their windows were darkly tinted, and telephone or radio antennas protruded from their tops.

Blin saw two small buildings behind the main house, one a relatively new utility shed made of painted metal. The other was very old, its walls built of unpainted vertical boards and bats that extended from the gabled roof to the ground. It appeared to have no windows, and its front door was closed. Further back, near the towering pines, he saw an old barn with a rusting metal roof. A fence extended around three sides, and the space it enclosed was full of tall weeds.

Inside the outer fence out front, Blin saw an iron gate in a chain link fence extending across the front and side yards that blocked access to a dirt road leading to the wire gate and tank. Several hundred feet past the fence, the lane disappeared into tall timber.

Excited voices came from the house, but Jimmy did not reappear. The expressions on the faces of High and Emmett indicated their concern for what might be going on in the house, but neither moved to find out what it was.

"I don't like it, Uncle Emmett," High said, pulling his Beretta from his pocket. "I'm afraid the cop's friends circled around and came in through the front while we were chasin' him. Yeah, that's it. That's why I didn't find 'em at their camp. The runt took off by himself to pull us off."

"Could be, I guess," Uncle Emmett said. "But we sure as hell ain't gonna find out for sure standin' out here like gobblers in a rain storm."

"If they're in there, I'm gonna kill the runt cop with my first shot," High whined. "Call Papa, Hulie. He'll tell us if somebody's waitin' for us in there."

"Hey, Papa!" Hulie yelled. "Everything all right in there?"

It became very quiet again, and when Hulie got no response after his second call, High became more nervous and frightened. "They sent in somebody by the front road, I tell you," he said. "They've already took Papa and the rest of 'em to jail, or killed 'em. And now they're gonna shoot us down like dogs as soon as we get close enough."

"Calm down," Uncle Emmett cautioned. Looking around the clearing, he said, "I don't see any cars except yours and Hulie's. And the gate's still locked. Your daddy is just having another one of his sinking spells, most likely."

Blin saw hope in their fears. If law enforcement officials had taken the father into custody, some were probably still inside.

High said, "If the law didn't come in the front way, a Holsomback came in the back." He raised his pistol. "You know how sneaky they are. They don't need a car or a gate. They just barge through the woods out back as they did before. And if that's who it is, they've killed Papa and the women for sure, and are sittin' in there waitin' for me to get close enough. I'm gettin' the hell away from here!"

Both brothers were poised to run when Jimmy reappeared and signaled to them from the front door. "It's Eva!" he yelled. "Something's wrong with Eva!"

"Is that all?" High sneered, pushing his pistol back into his pocket. "Uncle Emmett, put my new horse in the barn while me and Hulie go in and find out what's wrong with Miss Stuck-Up."

Emmett said, "I'll put your horse in the lot if you'll promise to keep your pistol in your pocket and not do anything else real stupid before I get back."

"Only if the cop don't make a run for it," High replied.

Hulie prodded Blin with the barrel of his shotgun, and they walked toward the front steps. High had run inside, where he was greeted by more excited talk. One of the voices belonged to a woman, who apparently was very tired or ill. She said, "High, talk to your daddy. Tell him Eva needs to go to a doctor."

"What's wrong with her?" High demanded.

"She's been snake bit," the woman said. "It happened out at the tank. I told her she should stop bathing out there, because it's all grown up with weeds and snakes, but she wouldn't listen."

"Hell, I've been bit before, and it didn't kill me," High said.

"But you're a man," the woman pleaded. "Where's Emmett? Come in here, Emmett. You're a reasonable man. Come talk to your brother."

Blin heard another voice, deep and commanding, but wavering, like that of an old man. "Do like I told you, Lily," it said, "Suck out the venom and keep her quiet. The poison will be all over her before Emmett could get her halfway to town."

"I don't know how to suck out venom, and I'm too sick. Please, Jim?"

Blin hoped Emmett would go inside and that Hulie would become distracted enough for him to run to the woods before being shot. Instead, Emmett headed to the barn with Catcher, as if he hadn't heard the mother's plea.

"Don't even think about it, cop," Hulie said, apparently reading his thoughts.

In the house, Jimmy said, "Eva wouldn't let High and Hulie take her to town even if you wanted them to, but that stranger we found in the woods has a first aid kit. Maybe he knows what to do."

"Then bring him in," the quavering voice said.

"But, Papa," High protested. "He's the enemy."

"Then bring in the enemy," the man ordered. "First things first."

High appeared in the doorway. "Hulie, bring in the bumpy runt."

Hulie prodded Blin with his gun, and they walked up the steps and across the porch, entering an air-conditioned living room where Blin found himself facing a frail old man in a wheelchair. Dressed in a long-sleeved white shirt and khaki trousers, he had white hair and intense blue eyes. In them, Blin saw the look of a very tired or a very ill person under great stress.

A slender, pale, elderly woman stood in a doorway leading to a second room, as if she might be there to block High's entry. She turned frightened eyes to Blin.

The father's expression was cold when Blin stopped in front of him. He said, "Stranger, the boy told me about his brothers and uncle finding

125

you in the big woods like I told them to. We'll discuss your case later. Right now, we have a more pressing problem on our hands. Do you have anything in your kit for snake bites?"

Blin nodded and gave High a cautious look when the crazy son put his hand in his front pocket. The father said, "I assure you, sir, that we are not all savages here. I had you brought here to save your life, not harm you, unless I determine you've come to harm us. Until I do that, I'd appreciate it if you'd lay aside your anger long enough to save my stepdaughter."

"But, Papa," High whined. "It ought to be done by family, not somebody sent here to kill me."

"Shut up, High," the father said. "I'll talk to you later about this latest mess you've gotten us into and about that gun you're carrying that you're not supposed to have."

"I haven't done anything bad, Papa," High said. "The cop's alive, and we brought him in like you told us to. We're not gonna hurt him even after you talk to him, because we've got a plan."

"Shut up, High," Hulie snapped.

High added, "And I already gave my gun to Uncle Emmett, and he threw it away," He gave his brother a warning look.

Papa looked behind Hulie. "Where is Emmett, anyway? I'd like to hear more about your plan."

"Puttin' the cop's horse in the barn," High said. "He's comin'."

The father said to Blin, "What about it, mister? Are you willing to forget for a moment what High tried to do to you and help my stepdaughter? If so, she's in the next room."

Blin nodded. "I'll do my best, but I'm no expert on snake bites." He approached the door leading to the joining room, but the frail woman didn't step aside.

The woman looked at her husband. "It wouldn't be proper, Jim. The bites are near her privates."

"Our doctor's a man. You wouldn't object to him treating her, would you?" It was clear that the father's patience was wearing thin. "Now, show him in and give him what he needs. You can watch him if it'll make you feel any better. Stand back, High."

"But, Papa," Hulie said. "I need to stand guard."

"You can watch the window and the back hall from the yard," Papa said.

The woman stepped aside, and Blin entered an orderly room that smelled of fresh flowers and clean linens. The flowers were in colorful vases on a chest of drawers. Between him and a window, he saw a dark-haired woman with a sheet pulled up to her chin. It was Eva,

Their eyes met when he stopped by the bed, and in hers, he saw fear and embarrassment. She whispered, "I'm sorry you didn't get to go on to—"

He signaled her to silence. "I'm sure you heard what your stepfather asked me to do. Show me where you were bitten so I can pull out the venom before it's too late."

She clutched the sheet tightly against her neck, apparently puzzled by his acting as though they had not met already.

"If I can help you, maybe your stepfather will be more inclined to help me."

The mother stepped to the end of the bed. "Eva, honey, I begged Jim to send you to the doctor. I'm too sick to do what needs to be done. This is the only way you're going to get any help."

Eva tightened the sheet against her neck, saying nothing.

Blin set the metal box on the bed and pulled out the package of first aid supplies. "You could let High do it, if you prefer to keep it in the family."

"I don't even want that creep in my room. Please close the door, Mother."

Blin said to the mother, "Give me a clean white cloth and some alcohol, please. And a box of facial tissue."

Eva pointed to a box of Kleenex on the bedside table and turned anxious eyes back to her mother, who said, "It'll be all right, honey. I'll be here."

Hearing footsteps, Blin glanced behind him and saw High leering at Eva from the living room doorway. His presence caused Eva to shout, "Get out of here, pervert! Mother, get him out of here and close that door."

Her mother gave High a disapproving look as Hulie appeared outside the window. "Don't you know Eva shouldn't be getting upset? Go back in the front room." Turning, she told Hulie, "Get away from that window. Jim, call your boys."

The mother disappeared down the hallway as the old man called from the front room, "High, come back in here. You've got lots of explaining to do. Hulie, move back. You can watch the window without causing such a ruckus."

"But Papa," High protested. "The cop might run out the back door."

"Hulie will see him if he does. And your stepmother will call me if he tries that. Now, get back in here and close the door."

"I can do what has to be done, Eva baby," High said with a sick smile. "All a man's got to do is cut and suck. Just cut and suck." He laughed.

Eva's eyes flashed. "Get out of here, moron!"

"Don't you try to run off, runt," High warned. "I'll be watchin' this door from the front room, and Hulie will blast you if run his way." He looked at Eva again and grinned. "I'm a good sucker." He laughed and slammed the door shut.

The mother returned with the cloth and a bottle of alcohol as a heated exchange began between the father and High. Trying not to allow their argument to distract him, Blin wiped his hands with the alcohol-soaked cloth and told the mother, "Please bring me some ice, another piece of clean, white cloth, and a pan of water."

Eva's eyes were fixed on him as he leaned down. They seemed larger and darker than before, telling him she was afraid, in addition to being embarrassed.

"How long has it been since the snake bit you?"

"About ten minutes."

"This kit might not help if it's been that long, but I'm willing to try if you are."

"Am I going to die?"

"That depends on whether you're too modest to show me the fang marks."

She gave the living room door a cautious look. "Did Uncle Emmett come back with you and the boys?"

Her unexpected question caused him to suspect she might already be suffering from shock. "Yes. Now, cooperate with me so I can do as I was told."

"The bites are on the inside of my right thigh and my stomach," she said, relaxing. "But I didn't have time to put on all my clothes before I was bitten."

He placed a pillow over her chest and pulled the sheet beneath it. "I'll try not to embarrass you. We've got to get on with this if I'm to do you any good at all."

He felt her eyes on him as he pulled the sheet down to a point just below her navel. Seeing no fang marks, he reached for the sheet over her legs, pulling it up until he saw two tiny red dots on the inside of her right thigh about six inches above her knee.

There was a tourniquet above the fang marks, and the flesh below it was turning blue. Making sure not to press too high, he pushed the sheet down between her thighs and untied the tourniquet as the heated exchange continued in the front room.

He told Eva, "I'll tighten it again as soon as the color returns to normal."

When he didn't find the bite marks on her stomach the second time, she whispered, "Further down."

He found the bite marks midway between her naval and privates and removed a razor blade from its cardboard container. "This is going to sting a little, but try not to jump and make me overdo it."

He nicked her skin and she jumped anyway. "Sorry," he said. "I'm going to do it again, so try to relax."

She continued to jump as he crossed both fang marks. Swabbing away the blood, he placed a suction cup on each wound and moved down to repeat the cuts on her thigh. She jumped with each nick of the blade.

Eva's flesh was soft and white, made more provocative by the sweet odor of perfumed soap and bath oil. Under more favorable circumstances, it would have been so distracting he could not have concentrated on the task at hand.

"Where did the snake bite you first?"

"My leg."

"That's good, because that's where it left the most poison, furthest from your heart. Did you run to the house?"

"Yes." The pillow muffled her voice.

"Naughty girl. That's the worst thing you could've done." He hesitated. "I don't have any more cups, so I'll have to improvise. Try to relax."

When his lips touched her skin, he heard a quick intake of breath and felt her muscles tighten. The sweet smell of soap and warm feminine flesh was much more compelling now. He wished the mother would hurry with the ice.

Finished, he wiped blood from his tongue and lips with tissues and felt her forehead. "How do you feel?" he asked. "Are you chilly?"

"A little."

"Where are your blankets?"

"In that trunk over there." She pointed.

Blin pulled a blanket from the metal trunk, laid it over Eva's hips, and pulled one end of it up over the pillow. He pulled the pillow out and placed it under her head, rolling out the other end of the blanket to cover her legs, pushing it aside to reveal all fang marks.

He removed the suction cups, cleaned them, and replaced them. He had just sucked out some more blood from the thigh wounds when the mother returned with ice and a large white cloth.

He heard High's voice again, louder and bolder than before, suggesting he was not backing down to his father's demands. Blin hoped the crazy brother would at least give up his pistol.

Blin tore off two pieces of cloth, wrapped each around ice cubes, and removed the suction cups, placing them on the wounds. He repeated the process on her thigh and pulled the blanket over her exposed limb. He leaned down to check her eyes and found her pupils slightly dilated, but thought that might be due to the darkened room.

The intimate nature of the procedure and the heavy responsibility it represented had made him very tense. If Eva got well, the father might be more inclined to challenge Emmett's plan to hold him, but if she died, he would be furious, killing any chance he had of being set free.

Removing a small glass bottle from the kit, he told the mother, "I need a spoon and a cup, please."

He found Eva's eyes fixed on him as they had when they first met. He said, "I'm going to give you a solution of water and snake root, an old folk remedy that my grandmother told me about. It'll make you sweat out some of the poison. How did this happen?"

"I'd just bathed in the stock pond out there as I've done lots of times when the boys were gone. When I picked up the towel, the moccasin was in it."

"Can't say I blame the snake."

Her expression brightened a bit, but immediately became somber again. "I need to talk to Emmett."

"That's the second time you've mentioned Emmett since I came in here. Why are you so worried about him? He doesn't strike me as the kind of man that has great concerns about anybody's welfare but his own and his nephews'."

She beckoned him closer. "You're in grave danger here," she whispered.

"You're telling *me*?" He almost laughed. "High's been frothing at the mouth to shoot me ever since he caught up with me. He would have if Hulie and Emmett hadn't shown up. Even then, my chances didn't look good before Emmett convinced High they should hold me for ransom."

"What happens to you might be determined by what happens to Emmett. But don't underestimate him. He can be ruthless and scheming. He's as afraid of High as Hulie, but that doesn't keep him from doing what he thinks will benefit him. If he wants to hold you prisoner, he'll do it in spite of what Papa says."

"He told your half-brothers your stepfather would have the final say."

"Not if Emmett has a plan be believes will serve him better and he can get High and Hulie to go along with him. My stepfather—"

The door swung open. "What's all the whispering about in there?" High demanded.

"Get out of here, creep!" Eva ordered. "Papa, call your retarded son!"

"Get away from the door, High," Papa said in a weak voice.

High remained in the door, his eyes fixed on Eva. "How come you let a stranger touch you when you won't even give me the time of day, Miss Uppity?"

The mother returned with a cup and a spoon, and Blin poured snake oil into the cup, filling it with water and stirring it. Leaning down, he raised Eva's head.

She swallowed it with a shudder. "I hope it works better than it tastes." Her eyes followed him as he checked the ice packs.

"I want your mother to keep ice on the bites until it all melts," he told her. "It'll slow down the spread of the poison. Don't be afraid if those places hurt and swell."

Placing a wet cloth on her forehead, Blin turned to give more instructions to the mother but found her sitting down with her eyes closed, as if asleep.

High moved into the room. "Get out of here, runt. I'll take over now. I can suck on her pretty belly some more."

"I told you to get out of here!" Eva said angrily. "Get him out of here. Papa!"

"Come back in here, High." The father's voice was weaker now.

Mumbling his protests, High left the room and closed the door.

Blin closed the kit, telling Eva, "If you get nauseated, have your mother get you something for it. If you lose the medicine, call me if I'm still around, and I'll fix you another dose. I'll check on you if allowed."

"I'd appreciate it. And thank you for what you've done already."

"You treated my bumps. I treated your snakebites. The trade is more than fair for me."

"Don't forget what I told you. Get away from here before it's too late."

Chapter XIV

Jim Fancher fixed cold blue eyes on Blin, but didn't speak. The scowl on his face indicated his fight with High had left him angry and exhausted.

Blin didn't see Emmett, but High was watching him from a wooden chair leaned against a side wall. Blin saw the bulge of the Beretta in his pocket. He stopped in front of the old man and surveyed the room. On a standing ashtray next to the father's recliner, Blin saw a black pipe. There was also a brown sofa, a television set on a mahogany table, and a stereo system with two standup speakers. Against the wall, behind Jim Fancher, stood a bookcase filled with books, on top of which he saw a fading photo of a pretty, young woman dressed in clothes from an earlier time. Beside it was a picture of two little boys next to a large Bible with a frayed black cover. On the opposite end of the bookcase stood a picture of another young woman who bore a marked resemblance to the father's present wife. Beside it was the picture of a little boy who he guessed to be Jimmy.

Blin looked at the father, wondering why he had not spoken already. Finally, the old man pointed to a wooden chair facing his recliner. After Blin sat down, the old man continued to study him without speaking.

Anxious to make his case, Blin said, "Mr. Fancher, your sons committed a serious crime by leading me into a trap and trying to kill me. They made another big mistake when they took me prisoner. I'm asking you to please tell them to let me go."

High moved his hand into front pocket and dragged his chair into a position that placed him between Blin and the front door. Emmett was still nowhere to be seen.

"How did you know my name was Fancher?" Papa asked.

"He knows because he's a law man or a Holsomback killer, Papa," High said. "I've been tellin' everybody that ever since me and Uncle Emmett found him snoopin' around in the woods back there. Maybe you'll believe me now."

Blin glanced at Eva's bedroom door. "Your daughter with the snake bite told me."

The father's eyes indicated neither belief nor disbelief. "Regardless of who you are, or why you were in the big woods, I want you to know how much I appreciate your mercy just now. But I can't allow sentiment to make me forget my responsibility to all members of my family."

"I understand. But since I'm not a threat to any of them, I see no reason for you to become a party to what's already been done."

"What's been done this time and all the times before is the reason you're here. I can't undo what's been done to you so far, but I can try to prevent something much worse from happening."

Blin was impressed by the father's manner, and wondered how he could have two sons and a brother so malicious.

"It's like me and Hulie told you already, Papa," High said. "We didn't do anything to this meddler we didn't have to do to keep him from killin' me. And after he got away, I took out after him because I wanted to bring him to you."

Blin was amazed that someone so mentally impaired could be so clever when threatened.

Papa said, "And like I've already told you, that doesn't ring true with what Hulie told Emmett when he returned to your work camp."

High stamped his foot, waving his arms. "Then Hulie lied! Everybody tells lies on me because everybody's against me. Bring Uncle Emmett in here and ask him if he saw me do anything to this killer."

"He can ask *me*," Blin said. "I was the one in the pit."

"You fell in my animal trap while you were sneakin' around our bootleg operation lookin' for me. So what? Big deal. I use it all the time to burn trash in and catch wild hogs that tear up our camp. I didn't make you take a job with the law or them murderin' Holsombacks."

"I was sneaking around your *bootleg* operation?" Turning to the father, he said, "Is that what you think they're doing over there?"

"That's what they tell me," the father said. "And I've never seen anything to indicate otherwise. There's nothing wrong with a man making good whiskey. My father did it up in West Virginia, as did his forefathers before him. I'd rather have my boys raise broilers, but that didn't work out. So they went to work for the timber company part time and make homebrew. I won't allow High to work in town."

Blin feared any attempt to change the father's mind about something he firmly believed would be seen as yet another attack on his family, but if he didn't try, the father might be more inclined to abide by the wishes of his lying son and scheming brother. He said, "Will you at least talk to your brother again about what happened at their so-called work camp?"

"Bring Emmett in here, High. And call Hulie."

"Come in the house, Hulie, Uncle Emmett," High said from the door.

Emmett must have been sitting on the porch, because he immediately entered the room with his shirttail out to hide his pistol. He glanced at High's right hand, apparently worried about his own safety. He could not have helped overhearing what his nephew told his brother already.

Moments later, Hulie appeared in the door, shotgun in hand. "Yeah, Papa?"

"You and Emmett sit down on the couch and tell me again exactly what each of you saw or did over at your still." He looked at the shotgun. "Do you need that in here?"

"Maybe. Our prisoner could be a dangerous man like the last one that came bustin' in here tryin' to kill High." He glanced at High's bulging pocket.

Hulie and Emmett sat down, and the brother said, "I didn't do anything to this trespasser, Papa. He slipped into our camp and fell into a pit we use for burning trash and catchin' hogs. I believe he was looking for High or evidence to use to put us in jail for makin' moonshine. While we were tryin' to figure out how to get him out, he climbed out and ran off." He looked at his uncle, as if hoping he wouldn't contradict him.

Emmett said nothing, and didn't look at Hulie or High.

Blin leaned forward. "Tell him the truth, Hulie. Tell him how your brother and uncle stole my supplies, and how I came to get them back. Tell him about the fire you and your brother built in that pit after I fell in it."

"He's lyin', Papa," High said, jumping up again.

"He sure is," Hulie said.

"Sit down, High," the father ordered. Turning to his brother, he said, "Tell me again what you saw when you got back to your camp."

Emmett glanced at High's right hand. "I didn't see High, because he'd already left to look for this trespasser. Hulie was cleanin' up around the place, waitin' for me."

The two brothers smiled.

"But you said Hulie told you High tried to kill this man by building a fire in that pit."

"There'd been a fire in the pit all right," Emmett said. "But there wasn't anything in it but ashes when I got there. And thinkin' back now,

I remember Hulie tellin' me he was just pullin' my chain when he told me about burnin' a man in the pit. He knows how scared I am of him pullin' me into more trouble with the law. He said they built the fire to burn trash."

High said, "Ask him if he actually saw us do anything to this runt."

"I didn't see them do anything to this man or anybody else," Emmett said. "In fact, I never saw this man until I caught up with him and High this mornin'."

"What about the pistol you said High had? Was that nothing but another little joke?"

"No, he had a pistol." He glanced at High.

"But like I told you already, Papa," High said, "I gave it to Uncle Emmett when he caught up with me."

"What about that, Emmett?" the father asked.

Emmett shifted nervously with a glance at High's front pocket. "No, but I, uh, I know where it's at. The gun ain't a problem no more, Jim."

High smiled in triumph and the father leaned back in his recliner, exhausted and confused.

Blin said, "I was passing through the big timber on my way to the Alabama-Coushatta Reservation when some animals I thought were wolves attacked my tent. While I was shooting some of them, somebody called off the rest and stole my supplies. I had to get them back or starve."

"Ha!" High cried. "If you were just passing through, how come you crossed our back fence and came down the hill toward our house? You was lookin' for me, that's why."

Blin said, "*You* said I did that. Nobody saw me come close to the house because it didn't happen. Tell your dad the truth so I can finish my trip. You can settle your family problems after I leave."

The father's eyes were steady and defiant. "There are lots of coyotes and timber wolves running in those woods. I know, because I saw them from time before I became ill. And for years since, I've heard them. Some of them may have inbred with dogs. Emmett there has raised hybrids for guard animals that he sells or uses to guard his still, but he has assured me that he never lets them run loose."

"They killed my mule, and would've killed me if I hadn't had a light and a rifle."

"Did you see Emmett that night, or either one of my boys?"

"In the dark? No, but—"

Papa looked at his brother. "Were you and your hybrids wandering around in the woods like he claims?"

Emmett shook his head. "If anybody bothered this man, it must've been a coon hunter and his hounds."

"So you had nothing to do with stealing his supplies?"

Emmett shook his head.

The father turned to Blin. "To my knowledge, Emmett has never lied to me. That means the animals that attacked you were most likely some of those wolves I've been hearing, or a hunter's dogs. If they were timber wolves, I'm not surprised they attacked you; they used to break into our broiler houses at night and drag out our birds."

Blin said, "I saw your brother's footprint, large and pigeon-toed."

"You're saying my brother is lying?"

Blin nodded.

Papa held his gaze. "And he and my boys say you're lying. I'm more inclined to believe family than I am a man whose statement about why he's in the big woods lacks credibility. Any man would've gone directly to the place on the highway."

"I had good reason for not doing that," Blin said, sensing he was fighting another losing battle. "But my reason had nothing to do with your family, and since I've done no harm to any of you and have done all I can do for your stepdaughter, there's no reason for you to hold me. So please tell your brother and sons to let me go. I'll promise not to file charges against any of you for what's been done already."

High snickered, but fell silent when his father threw him a warning look. The father's face was flushed when he turned to Blin. "*You* won't file charges on *us*? It's your fate hanging in the balance here, and you're in no position to pass judgment on me or anybody else in this room, because you don't know what we've been through already. Why, it hasn't been six months since another stranger sneaked in here, just like you did, and when he found out High was home, that killer shot my house full of holes trying to kill him. A year before that, another Holsomback man set fire to my house in an attempt to kill us all. I'm not counting the times the sheriff sent out men to snoop around."

"Tell him, Papa," High said, laughing.

Jim Fancher's voice trembled with emotion when he added, "Whether I like it or not, it's *my* responsibility to judge what's best to do with you. It's a sad day when a man can't control what happens to his family."

Emmett said, "Jim, I've always done what I thought best for you and the family, so now I'm gonna tell you what I think you should do with this stranger. I brought him and High to you as I promised I would. So I believe that entitles me. We've got no choice but to hold this man until we find out for sure who he is. He'll be okay in the old smokehouse out back while we're checking him out."

The father gave Emmett a thoughtful look and turned back to Blin. "Give me the name of just one friend we can call. If he or she corroborates what you've said and tells us how we can verify it, I'll tell them where to come to get you."

His statement brought a disturbing thought to mind: *I have no friends.* Friend was his only animal friend, but even she might be dead. He wished the brothers and the uncle weren't present so he could tell the father everything. Surely, George Madsen would send for him. Blin knew he was looking for him. If he could do that, the troubled old man might be more inclined to befriend him. Telling all in High's presence, he would be committing suicide and Emmett would defy his brother and hold him for sure.

He said, "Everything I've told you so far is the truth. The law didn't send me, and I'm not a paid assassin."

The father said, "You must you have friends somewhere. If you are just passing through like you say, give me their names so I can call them, or Emmett can go talk to them."

"Call your local sheriff. He'll check me out and give you a report."

"No!" High said, stamping his foot. "He's a Holsomback man. Do you think the sheriff would tell you if the runt was sent by his best friends?"

"He's right, Jim," Emmett said.

"Can I talk to you alone?" Blin asked.

"No!" High said, jumping up. "Leavin' a young killer in the room with an ol' man like you is too dangerous. And we can't take a chance on him talkin' you into lettin' him go."

Emmett nodded. "If he is a Holsomback killer, it would be too risky, like High said. And even if he's neither a killer nor a lawman, he'd still file on us for runnin' a still if you let him go. That way, High, Hulie, and me will end up behind bars. They might even put High back in the asylum. You don't want none of them things to happen, do you, Jim?"

High and Hulie nodded, and Hulie said, "You need Uncle Emmett, remember? I'm sure he'll keep livin' here if you do what he suggested. " He glanced at High.

Emmett said, "Just turn him over to us and get yourself some rest. We'll see that he's taken care of while we're makin' some calls. Surely, somebody'll know him and tell us why he's here."

The exhausted father responded finally, speaking as if to himself. "It's a sad day when a man comes to the point that he has problems making decisions regarding his family. It all used to come so easy. All right." He looked at Emmett. "I'll allow you to take charge of this man under the following conditions. You'll see to it that no harm comes to him while he's on my property, and you'll release him to his friends when we find them, if we determine he told me the truth and has no intentions of filing a complaint."

Emmett glanced at Hulie. "Good. I'll drive into town and get some answers."

"I have a retired schoolteacher friend in the county seat that has contact with both sides of the Holsomback-Fancher conflict. While you're doing that, I'll find out if this man is working for the Holsombacks or the sheriff."

High smiled, winking at Emmett. "Sounds good to me, Papa."

The father looked at Blin. "For too long now, we haven't been able to live in peace on this place because of the Holsomback matter. I was hoping High had paid enough for the mistakes he made years ago and we had put that problem behind him, but there remain people that are convinced the county would be better off if all Fanchers were killed or run off. Your showing up has opened old sores again, and made me wonder if we'll ever be rid of the sins of the past."

"Don't tell the runt anything, Papa," High whined. "That's none of his business."

"If he's who you think he is, he already knows." The father turned to Blin. "We're on our own out here. Can't count on anybody in Dooly or the county seat to help us."

"Lie down and rest," Emmett advised. "We'll handle this man."

"We know you don't feel good," High said.

Hulie nodded. "We'll take good care of him until we locate his city friends. They can pick him up," He gave Emmett a knowing look.

Jim Fancher didn't appear pleased, but he was obviously too exhausted to pursue the matter further. He told Emmett, "You can make your calls from this phone if you'll wait 'til I call my friend."

Emmett shook his head. "It might take a while to locate your friend, and my calls can't wait. I don't want to tie up the phone or give the ones

139

I call a way to trace me to this number. I'll call from my lady friend's house. Besides, there are some people I have to talk to in person."

Seeing his chances of remaining alive slipping away, Blin said, "But don't you see? If I am an officer, holding me would only make matters worse for you and your entire family."

The old man's face flushed and his voice trembled when he responded to Blin's threat. "I'm fully aware of the consequences of what my boys and I are doing, were I making my decisions under ordinary circumstances, sir. I am also aware that my wife is dying and her daughter's life is uncertain. Also, I have a troubled son and a home to protect, and I'm knocking at death's door myself." He leaned forward. "Now, tell me, young man. Why should I worry about trifling matters like how I might be getting into trouble with the authorities?"

For a moment, Blin was moved to silence by his emotional outburst. He said, "There must be someone in authority in this county you trust. Let him check me out. I'll tell him anything he wants to know in his office. Just don't let your brother and boys hold me prisoner."

The redness in the father's face faded, leaving him shaken and out of breath. "We're all prisoners in a sense. If my friend determines the Holsombacks did send you, I'll have Hulie take me to the district attorney, where I'll file charges on you. If you're with law enforcement, I'll demand to be shown a search warrant. If there isn't one, I'll sue the county and you." To Emmett, he said, "Don't let me down after all we've been through together. And after this matter is settled, I pray you'll change your mind about leaving. That would be a terrible blow to this household."

Papa's shoulders slumped, and it became so quiet in the room that Blin could hear the clicking of the mantle clock and the father's labored breathing. The old man looked at the older of the two pictures on the bookcase, then the dusty old Bible, appearing to lose himself in his own thoughts of the past. He sighed, looking at Emmett and his sons. "After all my best efforts, prayers, and sacred promises, it has come to this. I can no longer adequately handle the affairs of my family." He attempted to say more, but he suddenly placed his hand on his chest and slumped to the side. He would have fallen from his chair if Blin had not jumped up to catch him.

When Emmett and Hulie rushed over to assist, Blin made a dash for the front door, but High was quicker. Jumping in front of him to point his pistol at his face, he snarled, "One more step, runt, and you're dead meat.

The only reason I didn't shoot you for tryin' is because Emmett told me you're worth more to us alive than dead."

Behind him, Blin heard Emmett tell Hulie, "Help me put him in bed, then go tell Lily to give him his medicine. High can guard our prize."

Blin looked at the old man's pale face. "You're not taking him to the hospital?"

"Nope," Emmett said. "We tried to once and got a good chewin' out for our efforts. He'll snap out of it when Lily gives him a tablet and he gets some rest."

Lifting Papa by his shoulders and legs, they took him from the room, calling for Lily to join them as they crossed the dogtrot.

High laughed and danced about like a child. "You belong to us now, runt cop. I'm gonna have lots of fun with you."

Moments later, Emmett and Hulie rejoined them, and Blin was ordered to walk outside. When they passed Jimmy sitting forlornly on the top step, High said, "Go inside and help Lily with Papa." Pulling a large knife from his pocket, he snapped it open and shoved it close to Jimmy's face. "Little brother, if you leave the house without one of us, or call anybody, I'm gonna stick this in your sister's pretty little belly and lots of other places. Do you understand me?"

Jimmy nodded, and High caught up with them at the corner of the house near the telephone line that ran through the outside wall. Emmett said, "Can't take a chance on Eva messin' up our plans, and Jim ain't in no condition to be bothered anymore. Cut that line."

The crazy brother paused long enough to cut the wire then caught up with them in the back yard to jab Blin in the back with his pistol. When Blin turned to protest, High said, "Did I tell you could look back, runt? See that smokehouse out there? That's gonna be your hotel for a while." He laughed.

High continued to poke him in the back with his pistol and shout insults as Emmett and Hulie held tightly to his arms, pulling him toward the little house. In view of the other developments of the day, Blin's anger and resentment had almost pushed him to the point that dying was no worry. His ability to reason was barely intact enough to tell him he didn't want to die, but his rage screamed at him not to allow himself to be caged like a wild animal. Dying would be preferable to suffering more at the hands of a crazy man and his conniving uncle.

Chapter XV

*B*lin was ordered to stop in front of a wooden structure that appeared to be no more than ten feet square. He saw no windows or openings in its walls or roof except the front door and a metal pipe protruding through its composition shingle roof. The front door was made of rough-hewn two-by-sixes hung on large metal hinges, and on the left side was a brick firebox built into the bottom of the wall at ground level. The metal door of the firebox was secured on the outside by a metal clasp held in place by an iron pin dropped through an iron U-bolt.

High swung the heavy door open, but Blin held back, gazing into the darkened interior of the foul-smelling room. His first impulse was to risk being killed rather than allow himself to be locked up in such a place.

High jumped back, out of his reach. "Inside, runt cop," he ordered. "And don't look for a way to break out, 'cause there's not one." He laughed. "I ought to know."

Hulie shoved him inside, and before he could get on his feet, the door was slammed shut and locked.

"Have fun, bumpy runt cop," High said, laughing. "Do it now, 'cause you ain't long for this world. One way or the other, you're dead meat, 'cause I'm about to take charge of things around here."

It was damp and hot inside the little building, and so dark he could barely see its walls. The only light came through cracks in the old vertical siding and a wide crack around the door. The stale air smelled of rancid smoked meat and mold.

Remaining still until his eyes adjusted, he called, "How about some food and water?"

"How about it?" High said, laughing. "It's fine for them that deserve it. We've got too much to do to waste time feedin' a pig. I'm goin' to town with Uncle Emmett to protect my share of our prize money and make sure he don't take off on us. Can't let him do that, 'cause the first time he got busted, he'd cut a deal with the cops and tell all about our business and the cop we caught."

Blin leaned against the wall with a groan of despair. Veronica would give them the names and information they needed to put them in touch with Doss Saavedra and associates. Doss and Frank Deno would pay well for the privilege of having him delivered into their custody.

Blin heard High call Jimmy, and when the boy arrived, High ordered him to sit near the door and stay put until he or Hulie relieved him. "If you don't," High warned, "the cops are gonna take Papa to jail, and you know what I said I'd do to your sister. She ain't in no condition to fight me off or run away now. Understand?"

"Yeah," Jimmy replied.

"The cop can't break out, and you can't let him out because I'm hidin' the key where only Hulie and me can find it. If he gives you any trouble, yell to Hulie, who'll be inside makin' sure Eva don't try to pull somethin'. I'm leaving him in charge while me and Uncle Emmett are gone."

Blin moved around his prison looking and pushing, hoping to find a loose board, but he didn't. He did determine that the structure was anchored to the earth by large square posts beyond the ends of bottom beams sunk into the earth. The roof was constructed of rough-hewn two-by-four rafters on two-foot centers. There was no ceiling, only ceiling joists, so he could see the solid decking, made of one-by-twelve lumber. The tips of some of the roofing nails protruded through the wide boards. He would need a heavy tool to knock a hole through either the wall or the decking, but the noise would alert his captors. Even if he did slip away, Hulie's hound could track him down. It was lying by Jimmy's chair.

Hearing a car start in the carport, he looked for an object to use as a digging tool, but he didn't find anything. He did discover a crack around the edges of the door that gave him a clear view of the house some fifty yards away.

He looked through other cracks in the walls and found the area clear of trees and bushes he would need for cover if he found a way to break out. From the back wall, he saw Catcher eating grass behind a rusty fence. Obviously unused for some time, the area inside the fence was grown up in tall grass and weeds. He didn't see a water trough. He'd hoped to see Friend along the edge of the timber, but didn't spot. He wondered why he kept looking for her when his better judgment told him she was dead.

Returning to the crack by the door, he peered out at Jimmy. The boy's dour expression told him he was unhappy with his assignment.

Blin had sensed from the beginning that the boy was made of better stuff than his half brothers. In that he saw hope. Perhaps he could persuade him to find a crow bar and break the lock. Maybe he would bring him some water and food.

"Jimmy Fancher," he called. "I've got to talk to you."

The boy jumped. "You talkin' to me, mister?"

"Yes, I am. I noticed right away how much you favor your sister Eva. I can tell you are like her in other ways, too. You're not mean, like your brother High."

"Half-brother," he corrected. He threw a cautious look at the house.

"Half-brother, right. And Eva's no kin to him at all. She's very nice. I hope she doesn't get too sick. I know you love her very much."

"She kept me up with my schooling after it got too dangerous for me to go to school in Dooly. Papa was afraid somebody that hates High'd hurt me. He said I could go back to Beaumont with Eva as soon as Mother gets better."

"I know you're excited about that."

"Yeah. I'll finish high school there and get a good job at one of the refineries. Papa had a good job in the schools there a long time ago." He said it as if he was relieved to talk about his interests.

"Your daddy must love you very much to let you leave him to live where you'll be better off. Even though he didn't tell Emmett to release me, I can tell he's a good man. I can see why he's afraid of strangers, but he's got no reason to be afraid of me. You, either."

The boy looked at the house again. "We have to quit talkin' now. If Hulie hears me, he'll tell High when he gets back, and High'll beat me up."

"Hulie can't hear you. Just talk to me as you talk to your daddy. You do talk to your dad, don't you?"

"Papa's so tied up with High's problems he doesn't have time for me," he said sadly. "But he told me one time he wanted me to finish my education, like he did."

"More proof of how much he loves you."

"I wonder sometimes." He sighed. "He never talks to me about how he feels about anything except to say he don't want me to stay here and grow up to be like High and Hulie."

"Too bad your uncle cut the phone line to keep your dad from calling his friend in the county seat. Is there any other way your dad can contact him?"

"Nope. And you heard what High told me about leaving to do anything. And Papa's too sick right now to call his friend if he could."

"I know High is on drugs. I know he doesn't think like everybody else. What do you think he'll do to me if Emmett can't find somebody that'll pay ransom money?"

Jimmy didn't respond for several moments, causing Blin to believe he had decided to say no more. Finally, he said, "Because you helped Eva, I guess it's all right to tell you one more thing. After that, don't ask me any more questions about my family, and you'd better listen good if you want to stay alive."

He glanced at the house and lowered his voice. "You're right. High's not right up here." He tapped his head. "I heard what was said in the house about Uncle Emmett's plan. High will kill you regardless of what Uncle Emmett, Papa, and Hulie say if Uncle Emmett can't find somebody to pay money for you, and he'll kill anybody that tries to stop him. I'm even afraid he'll do something to Uncle Emmett after he heard him tell Papa he's leaving us as soon as they decide what to do with you. He'll think Uncle Emmett will tell the law about what he's done over in the woods the first time Uncle Emmett is arrested and needs a ticket out of jail. Uncle Emmett has been arrested lots of times."

"That's not good. But why is High so determined to kill me? He said it's because he thinks I'm a policeman or one of Holsomback's men. Is that the real reason?"

"Partly, but mostly it's because he enjoys killing things. He doesn't need a reason."

"Thanks for talking to me. I knew you weren't like your brothers."

"I wonder about that sometimes. I seem to always end up doing what High tells me to do. That's the way Hulie got started doing bad things."

Steeling himself for the ultimate question, Blin asked, "So why don't you just get a crowbar and tear off that lock or a board so I can leave? Both of us can run away from High."

"Can't. He would do bad things to Eva. Mother and Papa, even. Besides, he'd find us with his hounds, and there'd be no witnesses to keep him from shootin' us."

"Could you at least bring me some food and water?"

"Not without a key. But I couldn't do it if I could, because High would beat me up and do bad things to me."

"Just one more question, James. It's not about your family, but about you. When you look at me, I see something in your eyes that puzzles me.

Is it because you know something the others don't know or because you want to tell me something but are too afraid?"

"I know who you are."

His statement jolted Blin. Did he really know who he was, or was he prying on High's orders? Blin asked him, "What do you mean, you know who I am?"

"I saw your picture on the late TV news the day of that big trial in Houston. They told all about you working undercover and how you got scared and ran off when the crooks were turned loose."

"Have you been talking to Eva?"

"Not about that. She wasn't watching TV at the time. Only Papa and I stayed up that late that night, and he was asleep. He always goes to sleep."

"Why didn't you tell your brothers and your uncle that when they found me or your father when they brought me to the house?"

"Because I'm sick of killin' and lyin'. I was afraid of what High might do to me for not tellin' him sooner. You'd never be able to convince them or Papa you're not still a cop sent to make a case on High for the feds as you did on those guys they had in court. High would've killed you on the spot back there in the woods, and that would've got all the family in trouble, Emmett for sure. Papa can't get by without Uncle Emmett."

"What happens if High finds out who I really am when Emmett makes those calls?"

"I guess it depends on how much those city crooks are willing to pay for you, and whether Uncle Emmett can stay alive. High likes money almost as much as he does killin' things."

"Why don't you have a gun like High and Hulie?"

"Because they don't trust me with a gun while I'm watchin' you. And if they did, I wouldn't want one. I'm not gonna shoot anybody."

"You've got a lot of spunk, Jimmy. You'll do well in Beaumont."

Blin sat down against the wall, dizzy from hunger, heat, and lack of fresh air. Feeling like he might pass out, he got up and moved around to stir up the stale air. Emmett and High would be back soon, and Jim Fancher couldn't call his friend, the only chance he had at staying alive.

Chapter XVI

*P*ressing his mouth to the crack beside the door, Blin inhaled fresh air to clear his head. With the dizziness gone, he tried to strike up another conversation with Jimmy, but the boy pretended not to hear.

He crawled along the walls, probing the bottoms of the boards for weak spots, giving up when the stale air became unbearably hot in the early afternoon sun. He tried to urinate in a corner, but couldn't. He lay down to conserve his strength.

Approximately three hours later, he was aroused from a heat-induced stupor by a car driving into the yard. Moments later, he heard two sets of footsteps approaching. Standing, hoping the door would open, he put his eye to the crack to peer out.

High and Hulie were approaching at a brisk pace, Hulie holding his shotgun in one hand and what appeared to be a small radio in the other. High's excited expression told Blin he was very pleased about something. He heard him tell Hulie, "I told everybody he was a cop. We'll be rollin' in dough as soon as we deliver him to the guys bein' sent out here from Houston."

"Great. I'm glad Uncle Emmett got it all worked out."

"Uncle Emmett didn't work out nothin'. He was too busy makin' plans to leave town with that Dooly woman. I talked to the runt's ex-girl friend myself. She was a little cagey at first, but after I described the runt and told her how he was over here tryin' to break up our operation, she opened up. After she told me who the runt was and what he'd been up to in Houston, I figured right away them big-shot gangsters would pay top dollar to get him back. I told her to tell her friends they could have the runt for fifty thousand dollars, and if she could get more, she could keep the difference. She really got enthused them. Said she'd call 'em and call me back."

"Fifty thousand? That's a lot of money, High. You might've been too greedy."

"Naah. When she called back, she told me her friends were ready to do business and that I was to hang up and stay by the phone 'til I got another call. A guy called in about five minutes. Told me all I had to do was tell 'em where to meet. I gave him directions to that spot on the ol' Delany place where we've made pick-ups and deliveries before. He said they had to check out the place, so I have to meet there tomorrow at four, and if they like what they see they'll set a time for the pick-up and pay-off."

"Fifty thousand dollars! Split three ways, that's still lots of cash."

"Two ways, with me gettin' the biggest half."

"We can't cut out Uncle Emmett. You might've already screwed up by not lettin' him make those calls. We've got to have a plan that'll keep us from gettin' killed."

"Huh?"

"Don't you ever think of nothin'? How do you know those crooks won't just take the prisoner, shoot us, and keep their money?"

"Huh?"

Maybe I should meet him at the drop zone."

"Hell no! This is my deal. I set it up, and I'm gonna handle the payoff."

"Well, okay. But when you meet the guy, you'll have to tell him only one of us will be with the cop in my car when they come back with our cash. The other one will be hidin' in the bushes with a shotgun to make sure everything goes our way."

"Okay, Hulie."

"Where is Uncle Emmett anyway? How come he let you make those calls?"

"'Cause he stayed in town with the widow woman. You heard him tell Papa he was runnin' out on us. On the way to town, he told me the same thing. Said he didn't want nothin' to do with this deal. Don't worry about him. I'll see that he gets a few dollars out of the deal if he don't leave town before we collect."

Hulie was not convinced. "I don't understand Uncle Emmett runnin' out now. It was his plan. And he promised Papa."

The brothers stopped just outside the door where High said to Jimmy, "We've come to check on our roasted pig, little brother. Has he been a good little cop?"

Ignoring his question, Jimmy asked Hulie, "How's Papa?"

"He's not doing so good. He's still in bed, asleep or passed out."

"Yeah," High said. "Our dear ol' daddy ain't long for this world. Pretty soon, *I'll* be king of the hill around here."

"Papa's not gonna die!" Jimmy said. "He can't die!"

High slapped his little brother on his bottom. "Get in the house and let Eva change your diaper or somethin'. She's been askin' for you. And don't come back out here unless I call you." He kicked the door. "Wake up and say your prayers, Blin Burge. You're not long for this world yourself."

Jimmy left, and the brothers moved back from the door for a quick conference. Moments later, they walked back to the carport, and High climbed into the pickup as Hulie backed his car from under the shed. High backed up to the front bumper of the car. That's when Blin saw the power lift.

Hulie unhitched the hook at the end of the lift cable and attached it to the car's front bumper as his brother played out the line. Moments later, the front wheels of the sports car were lifted off the ground. After a short conference, High drove through the yard to the front gate.

Shotgun in hand, Hulie returned to the smokehouse and sat down in the old wood chair. Snapping on the radio, he tuned in country and western music and said to the door, "Mr. Undercover Man, I'm playing your funeral music. Ha! Don't even think about tryin' to break out while High's gone to spot my car. Even if you could do the impossible, I'd be right here with my gun cocked and ready."

Blin moved away from the door to slide his hand along a shelf near the top of the back wall in hopes of finding something with which to dig. He found an assortment of jars and old bottles, and when his hand bumped into one of the taller containers, it fell against the others with a clatter. Blin froze and turned toward the door.

"What's goin' on in there, cop?" Hulie demanded.

Blin said nothing, and when Hulie didn't come to the door, he took down the large bottle and crouched down next to the back wall to begin digging. When his eyes came close to a crack, he thought he saw something move under the trees at the edge of the clearing.

Placing his right eye against the crack, he scanned the area and saw several clumps of color that appeared to be weeds or blooming bushes. He was about to move away when one of the white objects moved. It was the head and back of a dog.

"Friend!" he whispered. "You're still with me. Good girl."

"What you whisperin' about, cop?" Hulie asked, turning down the radio. "You're not prayin', are you?" He laughed. "It won't do you any good to pray. If you'd wanted to stay alive after you finished that job for the feds in Houston, you should've high-tailed it out of the country."

Hearing Hulie approach the door, Blin dropped the bottle and moved back to the front wall. "I was trying to figure out how much quick cash I could put in your hand, risk free, if you'd unlock that door, and let me walk away."

Hulie peeked inside. "If you had a fistful of money, I couldn't see it in the dark." He kicked the door and went to sit down. "But you haven't got any money. High got it all in the woods." He went back to the chair.

Blin returned to the back wall and resumed digging. The dirt was dry and packed. Turning his head, he told Hulie, "If I could show you the money, would you take it instead of letting your brother set you up for a murder rap?" He pushed the neck of the bottle into the earth and pried out another chunk of dirt.

When Hulie didn't respond, Blin realized he would have to be more convincing. Jumping his jailer was his best hope, but he couldn't do that if he couldn't entice him into opening the door. He said over his shoulder, "If cash is all you want, open the door and I'll give it to you. It's in thousand dollar bills in my boots." Circumstances had finally made lying easy.

Hulie turned up the volume on a country song and remained silent, as if he hadn't heard him.

Blin continued digging, convinced the brother wasn't taking the bait. After another hour or more, he had a hole no more than six inches deep in the hard earth floor. He could have done better if he hadn't had to stop and make sure Hulie wasn't peeking inside.

The odor of something like sweet corn told Blin Hulie was smoking a joint, and it wasn't long before he heard him snap open a can. Moments later, he threw the empty can against the door and laughed. "Damn dumb cop," he said. "Why did you have to come in here and mess things up? We were about to the point where we could make real money in our operation."

Blin heard the snap and fizz of another can being opened. Moments later, the brother said in a slurred voice, "You don't really have money in your boots, do you, cop?"

Weak and feverish from his exertions and sweat-aggravated bee stings and poison ivy rash, Blin was near the point of collapse. He stopped with a sigh and faced the door. The light coming through the crack was much dimmer in the fading light of late afternoon. "High checked everything but my boots, remember?"

"You're really stupid, cop. High always told me cops were dumb, but I didn't know *how* dumb." He approached the door. "If you were even half-smart, you'd know I'd just take the money away from you and lock you up again."

Blin stepped to the door as Hulie began fumbling with the lock. Jerking the door open, the brother said, "Throw out your boots, stupid."

Blin remained in the shadows, waiting for Hulie to move closer. The tip of his shotgun appeared, but Hulie stopped, too wary to come further. "It sure is dark in here," he mumbled.

Blin steeled himself for the moment he could jerk the gun from Hulie's hands.

"Where are you, cop?" Hulie said, moving forward a step. "Throw out your boots unless you want to get shot. Throw 'em out, and I'll see to it you get some food and water."

When the tip of the gun's barrel came to within three feet of Blin, he sprang forward and grabbed it, jerking it out of Hulie's hands.

Hulie fell forward into the smokehouse with a loud grunt. "Damn you, cop!" he moaned. "You tricked me. Gimme that shotgun."

Blin pointed the gun at the brother and backed through the door. "Stay put, and you won't get hurt."

"You can't get away from us, cop," Hulie said, rising to his knees. "My hound can trail you in the dark as good as he can in the daylight. He'll be grabbin' you in the butt before you get out of the clearin'."

"Not with you locked up, he won't." He breathed deeply and reached for the door to close it, anxious to be free of the stinking place, but a heavy blow to his head stopped him.

Dazed, he fell forward, hitting the ground so hard it blinded him. As from a great distance, he heard Hulie say, "I think you might've killed him, High. He won't be worth much to us if you did."

Chapter XVII

A kick to his groin jerked Blin back to full awareness, and he heard a woman scream and shout, "Stop it!"

"Go back in the house, Eva!" High ordered. "This ain't none of your business."

"I'm making it my business, moron."

Groaning and rubbing his head, Blin felt himself being dragged back into the smokehouse. Dropped on his face, he turned over, sat up just inside the doorway, and tried to focus on Eva, who was looking down at him with dark, angry eyes.

She pushed Hulie to the side. "Get out of here, both of you. What were you trying to do to him, anyway?"

Ignoring her, Hulie pulled off Blin's boots. Turning them upside down, he shook them and ran his hand into each one. "Lyin' cop," he moaned, dropping the boots.

High said from just outside the door, "You mean you fell for another one of his lies? It's a good thing I decided to check on things here as soon as I dropped off your car."

Hulie kicked Blin in the side. "That'll teach you not to lie to me, cop."

"Stop acting like your dim-witted brother," Eva said. "Now, get out. I brought Blin some supper."

The brothers exchanged glances. It was very quiet without the radio. High asked, "How did you know his name was Blin?"

A frightened look swept over Eva's face, and she said quickly, "I overheard one of you morons using the name out here. How would I have known otherwise?"

High and Hulie exchanged glances, and High asked Hulie, "Do you remember us sayin' his name loud enough for her to hear us?"

"No, but we could've, I reckon."

Grimacing from the pain in his groin and side, Blin crawled over to a side wall. Leaning against it, he looked anxiously at the mound of dirt in the shadows. He would be in even more trouble if the brothers spotted that.

152

High told Eva, "You can't stay in there. He outsmarted Hulie, and he'll outsmart you."

"I'm going to stay with him until he's finished eating, gnat brain," she said. "So what are you going to do? Shoot me? You're good at shooting people."

High brandished his pistol, hesitating, as if undecided about what to do.

"What's the matter?" she asked. "Haven't you ever shot a woman? If you haven't, go ahead. That would be the ultimate thrill, wouldn't it? It should be no problem to a man that's killed as many times as you have already, your mother included."

Blin turned to see High step back, as if hit. "I didn't kill my mother. She just died."

"According to what Papa told me, you drove her to her grave, dumbbell," Eva said sharply. "Now it looks like you've done something that'll kill your father, too."

High leveled the Beretta at Eva and for a moment, Blin believed he was going to fire, but he again hesitated. She kept her eyes set on his, defiant and unafraid. Her face was flushed, and her eyes were puffy.

"Don't do it, High," Hulie said. "We need her to look after Papa as long as he's alive. And you've got plans for her, remember?"

"Well, idiot?" Eva demanded. "What's it going to be?"

High lowered the gun. "That was a bad thing you said about me killin' my mama." His voice was shaking. "You shouldn't have said that. And for doin' it, I'm gonna hurt you real bad as soon as we get our money." He slammed and locked the door, telling Hulie, "She hadn't oughta said that."

"Let it go, High," Hulie said. "You can get even with her later. Any trouble at the pickup spot? What did the guy say when you told him one of us was gonna stand guard out of sight?"

"What could he say? He wants the cop. I took off the license plate just like you said I should to keep 'em from finding out who we are. But you almost blew it, lettin' the runt jump you like that. What was you gonna do with his money if he had any? Keep it all for yourself?"

"I would've split it with you, of course. Cool it, man, so you can check on things at our shack. We left there in such a hurry we didn't spread the net or check on our new batch of meth. While you're over there, feed the hybrids. Here, have a joint."

"Okay, but you gotta promise me you won't go against me like Papa and Uncle Emmett did."

"Okay. Keep your radio and phone on in case I need to talk to you before you get back."

There came a hard kick on the door, and High's voice cut through the gathering darkness. "Eva, don't forget about that little party I said we're gonna have as soon as I get everything settled with the cop. Get your rest and build up your strength, because you're gonna need it." He laughed and walked away.

Blin turned to Eva in the near-darkness. "Am I glad to see you. How do you feel?"

"Lousy. My leg and tummy hurt, and I ache all over, but I'd be much sicker if you hadn't helped me. From the looks of you, I'd say I'm no worse off than you. I brought you something to eat." She set a jar of water on the ground and gave him a wet washcloth. "For your hands."

She leaned down to gently brush the dirt off his face "I'm sorry I used your real name."

He wiped off his hands, face, and neck. "They've been in contact with the crooks I gathered evidence on. You took a big chance, coming out to feed a cop."

She set the metal pan containing the food on the ground and pulled a short candle from her dress pocket, lighting it with shaking hands. A tiny reflection in front of her bosom told him she was still wearing the golden cross.

He opened the jars and drank several swallows of the cool liquid without taking his eyes off Eva's solemn face. In spite of the limited light, he could see that it was drawn and pale. He reached for the food. "Did the venom make you nauseous?"

"A little. Don't worry about me. Concentrate on getting away from this place."

As he ate mashed potatoes and sliced ham, she watched in silence and her shadow jumped about on the end wall in cadence with the candle's unsteady flame. It was very quiet.

Finished, he drank more water. "Thanks. When I heard you singing over in the woods, I thought an angel had landed in a tree to check on me. Nothing's happened since to change my mind."

"It's a shame things aren't always what they seem."

A sound near the front wall caused Eva to glance away and lay her finger across her lips. "We'll have to whisper now."

The setting did not diminish her beauty. Her perfume was refreshing. She leaned closer. "I have to tell you not to count on Papa getting in touch with his friend in town because the phone isn't working. That also means I can't call out. I'm too weak to walk out. If I wasn't, I couldn't leave Papa. Hulie wouldn't let me if I could. Jimmy can't go for help because of what High told him he'd do to me if he did. We're all prisoners now."

"Emmett didn't come back yet? Maybe you can talk him into taking you and Jimmy away from his place before High gets back."

"Since he didn't come back with High, I'm convinced High murdered him. With Emmett gone and Papa too ill to take charge, High'll do as he pleases."

There was a hint of resignation in her voice he hadn't noticed before. It made him want to say something that would restore her to her former self. "You'll be back in Beaumont soon. Life'll be good again."

"Too bad life was so bad here I had to leave."

"When was that?"

"I was twelve when I went to live with my aunt in Beaumont, but I always worried about what was going on out here. I visited Mother on occasion, and when I did, she'd tell me about everything that happened here."

"Come on out, Eva!" Hulie yelled, banging on the door.

"Blin's not through eating," she said.

"Well, make him hurry up!"

She leaned closer. "Don't count on Hulie helping you. He's too afraid of his brother. He gets more afraid of him every day, just like Papa and the rest of us." She looked around with a shudder. "This is where Papa locked up High to get him off heroin cold turkey. Mother said Papa and Uncle Emmett searched the woods for days looking for him. They tied him up like a wild animal and pulled him back home. Papa whipped him with his bullwhip before he locked him up. He did the same thing three more times before High quit the stuff. That's when he went back to smoking pot, taking uppers, downers, and using crack cocaine. I'm afraid Jimmy will turn out just like him and Hulie if I don't get him away from here soon."

"Jimmy told me you were taking him to Beaumont." He thought changing the subject would lift her spirits. "I could tell he was happy about that."

"Please forgive me for burdening you with my family problems again, but you're the first decent person outside the family I've had the opportunity to talk to for a long time." She sighed. "From the time Mother married Papa, my life has been a nightmare. High wouldn't keep his hands off me. I'd tell Mother, but High denied everything, and that was the end of it. Besides pawing me, he'd make me watch him play with himself, the pervert. Shortly after that, his appetite changed, and he tried to rape me. That's what caused Mother to send me to Beaumont."

Her voice broke and she bowed her head, apparently too overcome by bad memories to say more. It made Blin wish he could help her, or at least say something that offered hope, if he could do so without allowing sentiment to overcome good judgment. He studied Eva's expression for an indication of a motive behind telling him things so personal. He said, "I didn't think women told men about such things, particularly strange men."

She raised her head quickly, apparently stung by his remark. "I'm sorry," she said. "It just slipped out. Maybe it's your caring manner, or that you treated me for snakebites. Maybe it's because I've never known anyone I thought might listen and understand."

"I'm not saying I don't know where you're coming from, or that I don't want to help you. But as you can see, I'm in no position to help you or anybody right now." He immediately wished he hadn't been so sarcastic. Her expression told him she was hurt.

"I'm sorry for making you feel imposed upon," she said. "You have burdens enough already. With what you know, and the things Jimmy and I could add, you could put High in an institution for the rest of his life. He'd be out of our lives forever."

Her statement raised his suspicion of hidden motives to new heights, disappointing him. "Sounds like you believe what your crazy half-brother has believed all along—that I'm still working for the feds."

She picked up the broiler and stood up. "I'm sorry it sounded like I had an ulterior in being so open about things. I'm tired." She regained her composure. "I'm also sorry I allowed myself to believe that there are still a few good people in the world interested in what happens to others and for thinking that by now you had as good reason as I did for ridding the world of High Fancher."

He picked up the candle and followed her to the door. "Please don't leave angry. There's never a good excuse for bad manners, Sorry. Just please try to understand why I'm so edgy. I do care very much about what happens to you and Jimmy, your mother, and stepfather."

Tears welled up in her eyes.

He gave her the candle. "Thanks for being so good to me in so many ways. If I do find a way to break out, I'll help you if you'll let me, but before you go, please tell me one more thing about you and High."

"If it has something to do with what he told you he did with me, it's probably a lie."

"It's the way you talk to him. If you're so afraid of him, how can you order him around like you do?"

When she moved closer, her shadow on the wall became larger. "He's afraid I'll tell Papa what he's been doing to Jimmy. Papa would kill him."

"High likes little boys?"

"Boys, girls, goats." Her eyes were defiant. "He'd have sex with a snake if somebody would hold its head. Does that answer your question?"

There came a sudden rapping on the door. "That's it," Hulie shouted. "Come on out, Eva."

The door opened barely enough to allow Eva to squeeze through. "What's that cop been doin'? Suckin' your little belly again?" He shut the door and locked it.

Blin placed his eye against the crack and saw Hulie wrap his arm around Eva's waist and pull her tightly against him. "What was all that whisperin' about?"

She looked at the house, not answering him. He tightened his arm. "You owe me a kiss for lettin' you stay in there. Gimme."

Unable to push him away, she hit him on the side of the head with the broiler. He dropped his arms and staggered back, cursing and moaning, as she ran to the house.

Recovering his balance, Hulie lit a lantern and hung it on a post next to his chair. Blin resumed digging.

"What are you doing in there, cop?"

"Smoothing out a place where I can lie down." He had to make less noise.

"You had to do something real bad to those city crooks for them to pay so much for you."

"You should ask yourself what they'll do to you and High when they pick me up." He continued to dig. "Or what the law will do to both of you if they *don't* kill you. You'll be old and grey when you get out of prison."

Hulie didn't respond for a moment, causing Blin to think he might be giving his remarks serious thought. He said, "If I am still working for the law like you and High believe, somebody knows where I am, and they'll send other lawmen to look for me."

"According to what your ex-sweetie told High, you're not on the best of terms with the law, either. It's your butt in the crack, not ours."

"Did you see that red airplane circling over the woods the day before Emmett's hybrids got on my trail? They were looking for me."

"Planes fly down that pipeline easement over there, and the timber company buzzes over their property now and then."

"But what about your Uncle Emmett? Are you going to stick by High when you find out he murdered him?"

Hulie threw a can against the door. "That's some of Eva's lies. She likes to stir up trouble. Uncle Emmett has been to lots of places with High, and he's always come back later. He has to ride with one of us, 'cause he can't get a drivers license."

"Your uncle is dead, Hulie. And if you do nothing about it that makes you an accessory."

"Our family's affairs are none of your damn business. High'll make Eva pay for tellin' you all those lies. So will I."

After digging until exhaustion stopped him, Blin stopped to rest. He had just stretched out on the dirt floor when he heard a beautiful sound coming from the house. A choir was singing with an orchestral accompaniment.

Puzzled, he rolled his head and made out some of the words of the hymn "Higher Ground." He'd heard it many times at the little Methodist Church he and Mama attended. Although comforting, its beauty in such a tragic setting stuck him as out of place, macabre, even. Apparently played on Papa's stereo system, it suggested the possibility of a change in the father's condition.

He resumed digging as another hymn began. "Rock of Ages." "Swing Low, Sweet Chariot," and "Old Black Joe" followed it. Were the songs a dying request from Papa? Perhaps Eva was playing his favorites to improve his outlook on his deteriorating family.

Though he was near the point of collapse, Blin's hole was no more than a foot deep. He needed a sharper digging tool. It would take all night to tunnel under the wall without one.

He removed his belt and began digging with its wide buckle, and when he had loosened enough dirt to fill one side of the hole, he pulled it out to repeat the procedure on the opposite side. It was a slow process, made more difficult by having to do it by the narrow strips of lantern light coming through the cracks in the wall between him and Hulie. As the pile of dirt grew, he was in constant fear of Hulie peeking inside.

He continued digging, ignoring torn fingernails and cuts from gravel and bits of glass. He lost all track of time, and he dug harder and faster, expecting High to return at any moment.

When the hole was finally deep enough, he began tunneling beneath the wall, but stopped when he heard footsteps and the faint rattling of a chain. He heard Hulie say something to the dog, and the creak of the chair as he sat back down. Blin resumed digging.

Some time later, he stopped digging and stretched out on the dirt floor to rest. His hands and arms ached so badly they were becoming numb. His injured groin and side ached fiercely, and his thigh wound and bumps smarted from the dirt and sweat. A headache added to his discomforts.

He resumed digging, and sometime during the early morning hours, he heard what sounded like a four-wheeler approaching and saw its lights stop at the carport. High was back. Blin heard a knock on the back door of the house. The door opened and closed, and moments later opened again. When footsteps approached his prison, he stopped digging to spread his dirty shirt over the pile of dirt and lay down in front of it.

High said something to Hulie, and his voice told Blin he was excited. Blin couldn't make out anything he said. When Hulie spoke, his voice was strained. One of them walked away, but Blin couldn't tell which. The lantern was blown out, leaving his prison and its surroundings in total darkness. A flashlight suddenly snapped on, its beam centered on the door. Blin tensed at the thought of the remaining brother moving up to the wall and spotting the piled dirt, but the chair creaked again, telling Blin the remaining brother had settled down to wait. When the light turned off, Blin crawled back into the hole and resumed digging.

He dug until the hole was deep enough for him to lie down on his back and dig upward beyond the wall. With each handful of dirt, he feared he might have to stop from sheer exhaustion. The thought of certain death should he fail made him continue.

He was badly in need of a bath before he started, but now he was utterly filthy. His entire upper body was covered with dirt, turned to mud by his sweat. He felt more animal than human.

After what seemed like hours, he mustered the strength to break through the surface outside the wall, and when he did, he found it was full daylight. He had run out of time, but if the brother guarding him was still asleep, he might still be able to slip out undetected and get to the woods.

With trembling hands, he enlarged the hole above his head, trying to keep the dirt out of his eyes and mouth. Moments later, he raised his head into the fresh outside air, stopping suddenly when he struck a hard object. Puzzled, he looked up and found himself staring over a pistol at High's grinning, bearded face. He froze, unable to believe his eyes.

High laughed and jammed the pistol hard against Blin's head. "We don't have us a runt cop, after all. We've got ourselves a stinkin', belly-crawlin' gopher!"

Numbed by pain, fatigue, and shock, Blin was unable to move. "Damn you, High Fancher. You knew what I was doing, but you let me do all that damn work anyway."

High's expression became fierce and threatening. Leaning forward, he snarled, "Cop, I knew ever since I smelled that greasy dirt you dug up while I was gone. I ought to know what it smells like. I tried the same thing when Papa locked me in that stink hole."

"Damn!" Blin moaned, shaking his head. If he'd had the strength, he would have tried jerking the gun from High's hands, not caring if he was killed.

High jabbed him again. "I even kept ol' Logan there with me so he wouldn't start sniffin' around back and make you stop. I had to see the look on your face when you crawled up out of that hole and bumped your head into my gun." He laughed, kicking dirt into Blin's face.

His legs still in a bind under the wall, Blin couldn't grab the gun. At that moment, he hated High more than he had ever hated another human. Brushing dirt from his eyes, Blin looked along the top of the gun at High's ugly face and said, "You sorry, demented bastard! You'll pay for this!"

High kicked Blin's head. "Cop, the only reason I haven't already shot you is because you're worth more to me alive than dead. Now, crawl back in there and fill up that damned hole."

Chapter XVIII

Squirming backwards into the smokehouse, Blin pushed the loose dirt into the hole as the gloating High watched from the open door. When the task was finally finished and the door locked, Blin fell forward on his stomach, completely spent. Taking deep breaths, he gained the strength to roll over on his back, but was still too exhausted to be concerned about how filthy he was, or how soon Doss Zaavedra's killers would arrive to pick him up. He fell into a troubled sleep.

His next awareness was that of a woman's voice calling his name. Half asleep and disoriented, his first thought was that he had died and was being called by Mama. Reality overcame fantasy when Eva's face materialized over him.

Blinking to clear his vision, he focused on her concerned brown eyes as she peered down at him in the light of the morning sun streaming through the open door.

"My God," she exclaimed, looking at his bleeding hands and dirt-covered stomach and chest. "What happened to you?"

He blinked some more in the glare and upon looking around found he was still in the smokehouse, too weak to sit up. He asked, "You mean that idiot didn't tell you already about the fun he had at sunup?" He looked through the door, and when he didn't see High, he rose to his hands and knees and crawled toward the exit.

"You can't get away," she said. "Hulie's just outside the door."

He leaned against the wall. "What time is it?"

"Eleven-thirty. Here, drink some water."

He took the jar and began drinking as he studied her face. It was still a bit pale, and her eyes were red and puffy. She looked tired.

He asked, "Does your stepfather know I'm still being held prisoner out here?"

"He's still very weak and barely conscious, but he did ask about you. He wanted me to call his friend in town, and when I told them the phone was out of order, he got very upset. He asked for Emmett, but I was afraid to tell him he didn't come back with High. I don't dare tell him what's going on out here except to say you're still here. I'm afraid he's dying. He believes he is, too, apparently, because last night he had me play his favorite hymns and songs. I also read some passages from his old Bible."

The golden cross hanging from her necklace caught his eye. "I heard the pretty songs and wondered how he was getting along. Sorry."

His eyes met hers when he took the plate of eggs and sausage, wishing he knew if her sadness was caused by what he said the night before or her concern for her stepfather.

She said, "Sorry I forgot to bring a wet washcloth. I wouldn't have been allowed to bring the food if High hadn't left."

"He probably left early to meet the guy that's bringing them their blood money."

"I couldn't help overhearing some of their talk about that. I'm sorry. Wish there was something I could do. He said Hulie was in charge 'til he got back this afternoon. He took Jimmy with him, the pervert. Wrapped duck tape around his arms and ankles and covered his mouth. When I tried to stop him, he pulled his knife and threatened to cut Jimmy's throat. Said if I tried anything while he was gone, I'd never see Jimmy alive again."

"This ordeal will be over soon, one way or the other, if that's any consolation to you. How are you feeling? Are those fang wounds still hurting?" He began eating with the wooden spoon provided.

"Some, and they're swollen. Stayed up much of the night with Papa, but I'm feeling better. The thing bothering me most is not how I feel, but how helpless I am."

Glancing at the door, Blin swallowed another mouthful of food. "I've got to get out of here before High gets back. Can you bring me a pistol or some kind of knife?"

"I can't even bring you a fork because they're searching me before they let me in. Hulie practically undressed me this time. I tried to bring you a paring knife with that breakfast, but he found it up here." She pointed at her bosom. "And after last night—" She gave him a cautious look.

"You mean after what happened out here?"

"No. Hulie came into the house and started pawing me. I grabbed a butcher knife."

He couldn't tell by her expression if the knife had stopped Hulie. She must have read the question in his eyes because she suddenly seemed near tears. He put his hand on hers, but pulled it back, remembering the suspicions that plagued him the previous night. It puzzled him that none of the women he had known had provoked such troubling conflicts. He had to blame that on his never having met a woman he wanted so much to meet all his expectations.

Buoyed by the food and her presence, he looked at her bosom, hips, and legs. When he looked up, her eyes were fixed on him.

"So tell me," she said calmly. "How do I compare with your city lady friends?"

Her remark contained a hint of the strength he had seen on previous occasions. It was another of her attributes he had come to admire. "One thing's for certain," he said. "Those city women couldn't read my mind like you can. I apologize for gawking. You are such a contrast to what I've seen out here."

She held his gaze, not responding.

He added, "And no woman I've ever known has helped me like you have. I guess that's the real reason I find myself becoming attached to you. The fact that you are also very attractive, well—" He wanted to tell her more, but such talk was absurd and pointless under the circumstances.

"You have a way with words." Her face was brighter now. "Maybe you should be the writer."

Hulie appeared in the doorway. "Come on out, Eva. Our prize cop has had plenty of time to eat."

"He has not. Close the door if you want to, but get back away from it if you don't."

Hulie slammed and locked the door, and the room became dark again as Blin resumed eating.

Eva said, "When I was looking in that metal box of yours for more medicine, I found that envelope of old letters. What should I do with them?"

"Did you read them?"

"Not past 'My dear grandson' in the first one. Hope you don't mind."

"No problem. I'd appreciate it if you'd hide them somewhere. If get out of this alive, I'll want them. If I'm killed, I want you to read all of them and take them to my grandmother's relatives on the reservation. Will you do that?"

"Time's up!" Hulie yelled, kicking the door.

Picking up the plate, she said, "I will if I don't get killed, too. I don't know what'll happen to me and the others if Papa feels like confronting High about Emmett and the telephone line and finds out what's been going on out here."

When the door swung open, she held his gaze as if she suspected it was their last meeting. "I'll try to come again. Bye."

She stepped outside and disappeared. Hulie gave Blin a contemptuous look and slammed the door shut. "I hope you enjoyed your last meal, cop."

Blin stood up with a groan and limped over to peer through a crack in search of Friend. When he didn't see her, he suspected she had finally left for good.

He lay down with a sigh, feeling terribly alone and helpless. It was much the same way during his first years in elementary school after his mother died and Mama moved in to care for him. He was a sickly, growth-deprived, part-Indian outsider in a hostile land. An ideal target for bullies. Much later, upon building a successful business and much-needed self-confidence, he remembered how good it felt to have escaped poverty and family turmoil. He had finally arrived at a place in life where he felt in complete charge of his fate. He realized later that he had allowed his newly acquired affluence to serve as a wall between him and his memory of what life was like before the transition. He had forgotten the comfort that comes from knowing that the simple things provide the essentials for meaningful living. In his hurry to make money, he had failed to realize that a man could achieve no goal higher than a contented state of mind. That should have been his quest; it was one of the things Mama had tried to explain long ago that he hadn't understood.

He shook his head in disbelief, bitter at having to suffer so many hardships in order to understand something so basic, something taught for free when he was a child.

If he survived his ordeal, he vowed, never again would he forget that contentment is not found in wealth alone, and that freedom should never be taken for granted. How good it would be to be able to move about as he pleased, choose his associates, stay clean, and rejoice in knowing that he was his own man, that he would never again be the victim of violence and greed. He also vowed to never again lose the power to defend himself against brutal, morally inferior men.

He wondered how much longer he could tolerate his present circumstances without becoming as warped as High Fancher. The fear and frustrations of his early years were nothing compared to the loss he now felt: abandoned and forgotten by his government and all his fellow citizens for whom he had taken a stand.

He could think of no one who had reason to care what happened to him. Maybe it had been that way longer than he had realized. It was very possible that during the good times, there were only those who *pretended* to care because he had something they wanted. A depressing thought.

Was Eva the light of hope he needed? She did appear to be genuinely concerned about his welfare. Hadn't she helped him at great personal risk to her own safety? He wished he could forget recently learned facts about women so he could avoid hasty suspicions about Eva, but a man has to keep his guard up. Eva might not have helped him because she saw him as a valuable human being, but because he was someone who could provide her with something *she* wanted or needed, like so many other women he had known.

He thought of the old man on his deathbed in the house. He got the impression at their first meeting that Jim Fancher was once a proud and productive man, but now was little more than a prisoner of his insane son and the promise he'd made to that son's mother, long dead.

There was Jimmy, bewildered, afraid, and abused, his own identification as a male hanging in the balance. There was Lily Fancher, dying amidst family members torn by crime, violence, and insanity. Had she fulfilled her expectations of life? Had the promises made to her been kept?

His thoughts turned back to what Mama told him about the unusual things that sometimes happen to a man when he is at the lowest point of his life. She said a Great Power would come over him and save him if he had been living in harmony with the natural world. That power would sustain him, she said, give him the strength required to survive.

He wished he had that kind of moral strength now. He wished he possessed half the inner strength always present in his mama, Laura Bartee. If only he'd had sufficient insight back then to fully understand the things she told him regarding such profound matters.

The possibility of someday having to turn to the one she called the Great Father and the Great Power had never come to mind prior to his coming to the big woods. He now dismissed the idea, chiding himself for even thinking such a thing. During his struggles in the real world, he had come to suspect that matters of the spirit were merely the creation of man's imagination, born of disappointment and fear. He had never taken the time to explore the possibility of his being wrong about the matter. Until he got lost in the forest, he had never felt the need for self-examination.

Something on the underside of the roof's decking caught his eye. All areas of the roof, except one spot, were obscured by shadows. He could not have seen it had it not been pinpointed by a reflection of the sun's rays streaming through a crack in the wall.

Lying in the silence, his eyes locked on the spot, he thought of something else his grandmother told him. "When the special power comes, you will see a sign. It will come when you believe all is lost. And when it comes, I will be there."

Remembering that sent a rush over him. *Could it be?* Was he watching something more meaningful than a mere spot of light on a board? Just as he thought he might be experiencing a spiritual revelation, cynicism rushed in, regaining control of his thinking. The cruel realities of his circumstance could not be denied, not even for a moment. But the lit spot remained clear, as if challenging his pessimism. He was glad, for in the spot he saw something that gave him real hope. Without taking his eyes from the mysterious light, he climbed to his feet to more closely examine the decking.

The spot on the board was dark with rot, telling him there was a leak where the two twelve-inch boards came together on the rafter. The longest board appeared rotten near the rafter only, but the short board extending from that point to the rafter at the front wall appeared to have been softened its entire length by decay.

His adrenaline flowing, he mustered the strength to pull up on a ceiling joist and swing a leg over it. Pulling himself higher, he pushed his left hand against the shortest board and found it soft enough to cut with his thumbnail. The tips of the roofing nails protruding through the decking there were loose enough to push upward. He lowered himself to the dirt floor and studied the spot more as the light on it moved slowly across the board and faded. Within seconds, it disappeared completely.

He was amazed by the mysterious appearance of the light. In spite of the hope it offered, he was still a prisoner. He would be turned over to those who would kill him unless he could break out.

Moving closer to the back wall, he peered out at the beautiful day and wondered if he would live to see another. He was about to turn away when he saw a slight movement along the tree line. He smiled. It was Friend. She was sitting down, looking in his direction like a silent sentry, waiting for his response to the mysterious light on the decking. Mama's words, *And I will be there,* came rushing back. Could it be?

Naah! No way. Such things don't happen in the real world. "Mama is buried in West Texas, far from this place. I've got to remain rational if I'm to get out of this alive."

Going to the front wall, he peeked out at Hulie to see if he had spotted Friend. The brother sat, chin on his chest, as if asleep; the radio near his chair sputtered. He apparently had not seen the hybrid.

He believed he could pull up and kick off the rotten board, but he couldn't do it as long as High or Hulie were close enough to hear the noise. He had to wait and hope both brothers would be called into the house or become distracted. Some time later, he was awakened from a troubled sleep by the sound of an empty can bouncing off the door and Hulie's voice. "Want a beer, cop?"

The brother slammed another can against the door. "Well, you're not gonna get one. I'm not wastin' cold beer or good dope on a man that's gonna be dead before the day's out." He turned the radio's dial to a clear station playing country music.

Peering through the crack, Blin said, "You and High will be, too, most likely."

"Not the way we've got it figured, cop." Hulie turned down the volume. "We'll be enjoying our sudden wealth long after you're gone."

"You're as sick as your brother."

"You'll think we're angels when them city crooks get their hands on you."

"I told you already, big city crooks don't strike deals with petty thieves."

"You'd better hope so, cop. Because if they don't, High'll take you back in the woods, cut you up in little pieces, and feed you to the wild hogs."

Blin urinated in the corner he had used only once before. Because he had eaten, he also felt the urge to relieve his bowels for the first time in two days, but decided he had to wait until he could escape. He sat down by the front wall.

By the time short shadows of near-noon appeared, he was again very thirsty and hungry, and wondered if Eva would be allowed to bring him more food and water. She might not, for fear she would be forced to submit to another body search.

The heat became more intense, and Blin was perspiring profusely. That and the stifling humidity made him feel dizzy again. Hulie went to the house and came back shortly with a plate of food. County and western music continued to play on his radio.

"Hey, cop!" Hulie yelled. "How about a steak and some iced tea? We'll have plenty left over from lunch. Eva started out here with a plate, but I threw it off the porch to my dog when she told me I couldn't search her."

Blin leaned over to see Hulie opening another can of beer. His slurred speech told Blin he was already drunk or stoned.

The brother looked Blin's way and said, "Don't know what Eva sees in you, cop. What promises did you make her? No woman is that good to a man unless she thinks she can get somethin' out of him. You might've turned her head with your slick city talk and big promises, but High told me he's gonna put her in her place. That'll show her who she's got to reckon with around here from now on."

"And what will you and your brother do to her after High humiliates her? Kill her? Maybe he'll make you drop her in that pit in the woods and throw lime on her like he did the other one."

"What other one? You don't know nothin', cop. Even if there had been another one, we wouldn't waste a pretty thing like Eva."

"That's another one of your crazy brother's witty observations, I suppose."

"I've noticed your eyeballs zeroin' in on her finer points when she came out here, so don't talk like you're different or somethin'."

Hulie took several more swallows of beer with a mouthful of food. Perhaps the alcohol and sun would put him in a deep sleep so Blin could kick through the roof before High returned.

Hulie didn't go to sleep, but as Blin became drowsy from the heat, he sat down and relaxed against the wall, hoping the time would pass faster if he could just sleep. Some time later, he was awakened by the sound of High's truck driving into the yard out front. The lengthened shadows outside told him it was near sundown.

High appeared, smiling and rubbing his hands together like a happy child.

"I've done it, little brother," High said with a giggle. "Them Houston big shots showed up in a chopper. After flyin' around a while, they landed in the pasture out front, and I showed 'em where I parked your car. They liked the setup."

"So when do we get the dough?"

"Ten in the mornin'. I told 'em I'll be waiting in the car with the cop and you'll be in the bushes with your shotgun, just as we planned. We'll rush back here through the back roads and hide our money 'til we're sure they've left the county."

Hulie stamped his foot. "Yahoo! That calls for a celebration. What do you want, beer or a joint?"

"I've got a joint." He turned the radio's dial to pick up some country rock music. "Let's hear some real music."

"Jimmy didn't hear you make any of them calls, did he?"

"Naah! He didn't do nothin' but pee in his pants, the sissy. I kept him tied up and gagged in the back seat all the time I was gone. Every time I got out, I told him I was lookin' for Uncle Emmett. I don't think he woulda run off because he's afraid of what I'll do to Eva, but was afraid to leave them two together while I was gone. I locked him in a closet when I got back, and I've got the key."

Hulie's expression remained somber. "You shouldn't have done that, High. It's too dark, and he'll be wantin' to go to the bathroom."

"I put Papa's chamber pot in there with the wimp. Stop worryin' about him. We've got more important things to think about."

"Okay, but I don't want Jimmy hurt. You didn't run into Uncle Emmett anywhere? If he's still in town, he deserves part of the payoff."

High's expression reflected a sudden mood swing. "Now, don't start talkin' about poor Uncle Emmett again. I already told you he's out of the deal and why. You're just like Papa. He's all shook up about Emmett, too."

Hulie's expression told Blin he wasn't pleased with his brother's thinking, but the alcohol had dulled rational thought. "We can get into the business big time now," he said. "We'll find a place where we can plant more weed and make more meth. And I know where we can get lots of crack and smack to sell."

High's face reflected another sudden change of mood when he looked at the smokehouse. Leaning forward, he said something to Hulie Blin couldn't understand and walked over to slam his foot against the door.

"Wake up, runt!" he snarled. "You're gonna have a reunion with your old pals in the mornin'. Their man said they're gonna be real happy to see you." He laughed, pulling out his penis.

Going around the corner, High pushed his organ through a knothole in the side wall and began urinating four feet from Blin. The crazy brother laughed. "Thought I'd sweeten up them smells you already got in your little house, runt cop," he said. "Didn't want you to think I forgot you in all the excitement about the big pay-off."

Too angry to consider the consequences, Blin slammed the heel of his boot against High's organ, and the brother screamed and fell back, yelling, "Kill him, Hulie! Kill him! He broke my pecker!"

Hulie calmly walked over to High rolling on the ground, his hands over his privates. "Are you crazy? I'm not gonna shoot him now and lose all that money."

"Screw the money!" High screamed. His face was contorted in pain as he rolled about. "Shoot him, I said!"

Hulie shook his head. "I won't, and I won't let you, either. Besides messin' up the payoff, it would be goin' against what we promised Papa and Uncle Emmett. You wouldn't want to kill him if you'd quit rollin' around like a baby and pour some cold beer on your root."

"If your pecker hurt as much as mine does, you wouldn't care if you lost a million dollars. Shoot him!"

"If you had a man-sized pecker, you couldn't have put it through that little ol' hole. I've never been rich, so I'm not gonna let a little thing like that come between me and gettin' that way."

"But he broke it, I tell you," High moaned. "It's turnin' blue. Look!"

"It's not broke," Hulie said, leaning down to take a closer look. "It can't be, stupid, 'cause a pecker has no bones in it. And yours has always been nearly black."

High pulled his pistol from his pocket. "Then I'll do it myself as soon as I can stand up."

"If all you want to do is get even, I can tell you a better way to do it, and it won't mess up our money deal."

"It'll have to be something real good, 'cause what he did is a killin' offense."

"You remember Papa's bull whip, don't you?"

"How could I ever forget it?"

"I'll help you tie up the cop so you can whip him with it. That way, you can get even with him for everything he's done to you, in addition to stompin' your wiener. And he'll still be alive for the big swap."

"That's a good idea, Hulie," High's face lit up. "I like to beat up cops and anybody else that orders me around. Let's do it."

High got to his feet with a groan, returned his pistol to his pocket, and gently pushed his penis inside his fly. Still standing in a stooped position, he pulled a small metal box from his pocket and took out a crudely wrapped cigarette. He lit it with shaking hands. Inhaling deeply, he gave one to Hulie and headed for the smokehouse door.

Banging on the door, High called, "I'm gonna whip the hell out of you, cop, just like my daddy used to do me. You'll wish you was dead before I quit. You'll be sorry you came into them woods to check us out, and you'll be even sorrier for kickin' my joy stick."

Blin steeled himself for the moment the door opened, determined to jump the brothers and get one of their guns before the other shot him. If he could do that, he would be a free man; if he failed, he wouldn't lose anything he wasn't going to lose the next morning.

By the time Hulie returned with the whip and ropes, High was feeling the full effects of the weed. He beat on the door, laughing and hurling insults at Blin.

Hulie said, "All we need now for a real celebration is for Eva to show up. All we'd have to do to get her out here would be to tell her she can feed the cop."

"I'm not in no condition for that kind of celebratin'," High replied with a grimace.

"You'll be ready by the time you get through whipping the cop."

Blin was waiting with a bottle in each hand, and when the brothers swung the door back and saw them, they stopped short. High leveled his pistol at Blin. "Come on out, runt. You've been a bad boy, and bad boys always get punished real good. At least, that's what Papa always told me."

Blin drew back his right arm.

High pushed off his gun's safety. "Then I'll shoot you where you stand."

"Dammit, High," Hulie said, pushing the pistol aside. "I told you I'm not lettin' you shoot me out of a fortune. Cool it."

"Then you go in there and pull him out."

Propping his shotgun against the outside wall, Hulie picked up a short two-by-four and moved through the door. Drawing back the board, he said, "Cop, you can walk out on your own, or you can let me drag you out with two broken arms."

Blin threw a bottle at Hulie's head, but the brother ducked, and it shattered against the wall behind him. Blin sprang forward with the other bottle raised to strike, but Hulie's club slammed into his ribs, then his arm and head. He fell, groggy and helpless, and the brothers tied his wrists together in front of him.

"We'll take him out to the big oak behind the barn," High said. "They can't hear us from the house out there. Take the lantern. It'll be dark soon."

Blin tried shaking the cobwebs from his brain as Hulie formed a slipknot in another rope and dropped it over his head. By the time he was jerked to his feet and pulled outside, he had revived enough to see that the sun had sunk to treetop level. He hoped he was still alive when it came up in the morning. It was a question he had asked himself every night since coming to the big woods.

Chapter XIX

*H*igh inhaled deeply, holding the marijuana smoke in his lungs until he had to breathe again, then exhaled loudly. He told Hulie, "Lead on, brother. This is gonna be fun. It's gonna be almost as much fun as killin' the runt."

Hulie jerked hard on the rope, choking Blin and pulling him off balance. High followed them, prodding Blin in the back with his pistol, laughing and cursing. It was dark by the time Hulie pulled Blin around the barn.

Lighting the lantern, High hung it on a low limb as Hulie transferred the rope from Blin's neck to the short one binding his wrists. He threw the other end of the long one over a big limb of a gnarled oak, and both brothers pulled until Blin's toes barely touched the ground. They tied the free end of the rope to the tree's trunk.

Hulie leaned his shotgun against the tree as High moved to within inches of Blin's face. There was wildness in his eyes, like Blin had never seen before in a human.

"It's gonna hurt like hell, runt cop," High snarled. "I know, 'cause it's been laid on me lots of times. The first licks will be for knockin' me down over there in the woods. About the next dozen will be for nearly kickin' my pecker off, and the rest will be your reward for bein' a lousy cop."

Blin spat in his face, and High jumped back, screaming obscenities. He attempted to kick Blin's groin, but Blin raised a leg to ward off the blow. Jerking the whip from Hulie's hands, the crazy brother walked behind Blin and began swinging the braided leather lash against his bare back.

Blin clenched his jaw against the pain to keep from crying out, but soon was moaning through each blow and praying for unconsciousness. Breathing hard, High stopped and leaned against the tree to rest. Regaining his breath, High walked over to face Blin, snarling, "How does it feel, smart aleck cop?"

Blin remained slumped, his weight supported by his arms, too numb to respond.

Moving behind Blin, High looked at the welts. "Damn, they're pretty," he said. "Ain't they pretty, Hulie?"

Hulie said nothing as High walked in front of Blin. "A whip has a way of cuttin' us all down to nothin' but a bag of shit, don't it, cop? And it takes pigs like you off their high horse, by God."

Blin's head was spinning. His back felt like it was being probed by hot nails.

High asked his brother, "Want to give him a few licks?"

Blin raised his head in time to see Hulie give him a cautious glance and shake his head. High sat down next to a tree, still breathing hard. He had just settled down when Blin heard something move in the brush nearby. He spotted a reflection of the lantern's rays off the eyes of what he guessed to be a small animal. It was too dark to tell, but he believed it was. *And I will be there.*

Blin turned his head toward a new sound between them and the smokehouse. Someone was running toward them. High jumped to his feet and ran to the outer edge of the light. "Who the hell could that be?"

Eva burst into view, stopping abruptly when she saw Blin hanging from the limb. "You animals!" she screamed. "Let him down!"

She ran toward Blin, but High grabbed her, lifting her off the ground. She kicked his ankles and scratched his face, screaming, "Let me go, creep!"

High laughed. "Puttin' you in your place might be as much fun as whipping the cop."

Eva sank her teeth into High's arm, and he cried out, dropping her. She made a dash for Hulie's shotgun.

"Stop her, Hulie!" High yelled.

Hulie dived into her, and they fell into the leaves. The brother shoved her over on her back and pinned her down. Drawing his face close to hers, he said, "You won't get away this time, hot stuff, because there aren't any butcher knives out here. Now, be still, so I won't have to hurt you. Give ol' Hulie a big kiss."

"I'd rather kiss a pig!" she said, turning her face. "Get off me! Both of you are stoned out of your heads. Let me up so I can cut Blin down."

High walked over and looked down at Hulie and Eva. Tapping his brother's shoulder, he said, "If you can't handle her, get off, and let me take over."

Hulie made no move to get up. "You had a go at her already and let her get away. I'll take her down a notch or two."

174

Blin strained against the rope holding him up. Convinced it wouldn't stretch enough to allow him to pull his hands free, he attempted to lift himself up, but he was too weak. He could do nothing but hang there and watch.

Hulie told Eva, "I ain't lettin' you get up until you give me a big kiss."

"Never!" she said. "Stop acting like your crazy brother and let me go."

Grabbing her chin, Hulie jerked her face around and pressed his lips against hers, but immediately drew back with a cry of pain and rolled off, spitting blood. "You stuck-up wench!" he moaned. "Take her, High!"

High attempted to grab her, but she was too fast, jumping up and disappearing in the darkness. High left in hot pursuit, yelling at Hulie, "Now look what you've done! She'll wake up Papa and Lily for sure."

Hulie stared at the blood on his fingers and moaned, "Damn!" He turned to Blin. "At least I've still got you, cop. That's more important than something I can get later."

Hulie picked up his shotgun and cut Blin down. When Blin fell, the brother kicked him in the leg and ordered him back to the smokehouse. Blin's legs were weak and he was dizzy, but he managed to do as ordered.

By the time Blin staggered into the smokehouse and fell to the dirt floor, he was barely conscious, but he was alert enough to realize Hulie had pushed him inside without untying his hands.

He lay in the dark in a semi-conscious fog, numbly aware of the pain along his back and the extreme dryness in his mouth and throat. He made a feeble attempt to get the rope off his wrists, but gave up. After what seemed an eternity, he passed out. His last conscious thoughts were of Eva being chased by her crazy stepbrother, the darkness, and Doss Zaavedra's enforcers, who would arrive soon to pick him up.

Chapter XX

*B*lin regained consciousness sometime during the night with sharp pains shooting up his arms and back. The pain was so intense that when he attempted to sit up, he fell to his side, disgusted and angry. Unable to move, he listened for sounds that might tell him what was happening outside. When he heard no one moving about, he assumed he had not awakened whoever was guarding him.

Where were Saavedra's gunmen? Had they followed High back to his father's farm the previous day? If so, they might be joined by more gunmen at daybreak to take him away from the brothers. If they did, they would murder all witnesses. If not, he believed it was because they'd decided to wait until he was delivered to them. They would be anxious to perform their grisly chore without any slip-ups, so they could send the good news to their bosses.

Did Eva get back to the house before High caught up with her? Perhaps she, too, was lying alone on the ground after being brutally assaulted. It was a depressing thought. He became aware of the steady rush of gas from a lantern outside and wondered which brother was sitting by it. A more pressing concern was the lack of circulation in his hands and his need for fresh air.

Remembering the bottle that had shattered, he rolled over to it and rose to his knees. Slowly sliding his fingers through the dirt, he found a shard about four inches long and began pulling it back and forth across the rope binding his wrists. He stopped when someone stirred out by the light.

There came a sleepy groan, then a long yawn. It was Hulie, and he apparently was still asleep.

Transferring the shard to his left hand, he resumed sliding the glass against the rope. Some time before dawn, exhausted and wet with perspiration, he cut through, and it fell off. Standing, he flexed his fingers and swung his arms over and around until the tingling faded, but his exertions made the pain from his lash marks more intense.

Looking at the cracks in the east wall, he saw the dim light of a new day. The sight prompted him to remember what was in store for him, causing him to forget his pains for a moment. He had to break out.

He heard Hulie move and get up to urinate. Moments later, he heard footsteps approach the door. Blin lay down on his side, in case his captor snapped on his flashlight and peeked inside.

"Wake up, runt!" Hulie said, kicking the door. "You don't want to miss the last day of your lousy life."

Blin remained still as more footsteps approached the smokehouse. This time, it was High who spoke. "Take one of these pills, little brother. It'll perk you up."

"I need it. My neck's nearly broke from sleepin' in that damn chair most of the night."

"Has our prize pig been a good boy?"

"He couldn't be anything else in his condition. He stayed passed out all night. But right now, I'm more interested in whether Eva has our breakfast ready or not. I'm starvin'."

A woman's voice cried, "Come to the house quick, Hulie! Hurry!"

It was Eva. Blin was relieved she wasn't lying on the ground somewhere and was well enough to be up and about.

"Is that a breakfast call, or what?" Hulie said, laughing. "She doesn't sound the worse for wear. What did you do to her when you finally caught up with her last night?"

"What do you think?"

"I'm thinkin' I don't know, otherwise I wouldn't have asked. Did she beat you to the house and tell Papa what we did to the cop?"

"She couldn't have, because Papa didn't wake up all night, according to Lily. He's in a coma or somethin'. Go get your breakfast. We've got lots to do before we get rich."

Blin peered out and saw Hulie walking to the house. High sat down in the chair with a long sigh and laid his Beretta on his lap.

Hulie immediately reappeared on the footpath with a worried look on his face and upon approaching High said something Blin couldn't make out. The message apparently shocked High, because he jumped up and ran to the house.

Blin watched the back door where High disappeared, and moments later, saw the brother came back outside, drawn and pale. Rejoining Hulie, he said glumly, "She wants you again."

"What for? There's nothin' I can do now. There's nothin' anybody can do."

"You'll have to take 'em to town in my truck. But what about the cop? We've got to figure out how to get him to the drop zone. Nothin's gonna keep me from bein' rich."

"The one drivin' Lily and Papa into town can't take him in. I'll wait here with our prize while you do that."

"Hell, no. I left you with him before, and he almost got away. I'm stayin' with my fortune 'til I get that money in my hands."

"Which you won't get until we deliver him at my car. You can't do that without wheels."

"Then you'll have to drop Lily and Papa off at Bastrop's, meet the pay-off guys out there, and bring 'em out here." High smiled and clapped his hands. "That'll work. And you said I couldn't figure out nothin'."

"That will be too risky."

"You've no choice, little brother." High's eyes flashed, and he patted the pistol. "Now get back in there and do what you have to, but make sure Eva stays here, and that Jimmy is still locked in that closet. Eva won't try nothin' as long as I've got him."

"She won't leave without Jimmy, anyway. But what about Lily? Do you think we can trust her in town?"

"She's too sick to cause us any problems. Besides, she knows nothin'. She doesn't even know we've still got the cop."

Hulie headed for the house at a fast walk and the excited High sat down, lighting another cigarette. He inhaled several times. His courage restored, he stepped over and kicked the door. "You didn't die, did you, cop?"

Blin sat down next to the door as High moved his eye up to a crack. When Blin didn't answer, the crazy brother asked, "Are you hungry, runt cop? Eva outran me back to the house last night, but I told her if she'd make me the right promises, I wouldn't hurt Jimmy, and she could bring you some breakfast. What she doesn't know is I'm taking my delivery first." He laughed. Blin didn't respond.

High kicked the door. "Damn you, cop! Why ain't you talkin'? Did that whip clean all the sass off your lousy tongue?"

Mouthing obscenities, High moved away from the door, and Blin got up to peer out as the truck started up at the house. Moments later, it passed through the yard fence. He couldn't tell how many were in it. He peeked out to see what High was doing.

The crazy brother was sitting in the chair, calmly puffing on a joint with his pistol in his lap. His eyes had their usual fierce glow, but there was a hint of bewilderment in them now. Otherwise, his appearance was the same: dirty jumpsuit unbuttoned to his waist, long black hair tied behind his head in a ponytail, a soiled Copenhagen cap sitting askew on his head. He apparently never shaved.

Hearing footsteps, Blin looked up the path to see Eva approaching. Her face was pale and grim in the early morning light, and there were dark circles under her eyes.

Stopping in front of High, she said, "You saw me coming, moron. Why didn't you unlock the door?"

"Because you've got to make good on that promise you made first."

"You're talking like an idiot as usual. Open it."

High grabbed her arm, allowing his pistol to fall from his lap. He said, "Your mama ain't around now to take up for you like she did last night." He pulled her closer.

She tried to pull away. "I'm warning you, High. If you lay a hand on me, I'll kill you!"

"With what? You can't even hurt me, let alone kill me." His smile vanished. "But I can hurt you, and I will. It'll be more fun than I've been allowed to have around here in a long time on account of Papa and Uncle Emmett always tellin' me what I can and can't do."

Her expression suddenly became less defiant, suggesting to Blin that she was too tired or ill to continue fighting. She said, "All right. But first, I have to give this food to Blin."

Smiling in victory, High patted her right buttock. "Okay, but only if you promise you won't try to pull any more tricks on me or bite me when we get to it."

She nodded, and he released her to unlock the door. When High stepped back to allow her in, her expression bore a desperate look of defeat and she was crying.

The room darkened when the door slammed shut, requiring them to stand still for a moment to allow their eyes to adjust. She gave him a metal pan containing the food. "I'm sorry I couldn't bring something for pain."

"Thank you for bringing breakfast. I would've said good morning, but that look on your face told me it wouldn't help."

She dropped her eyes without speaking and moved around him to look at his back. When he sat down to begin eating the eggs and sausage, she leaned down to study his wounds more closely. "I'll try to bring something for these welts later."

"I hope I'm still here when you do. Those killers are coming, you know." He turned. "I've never seen you look so beat. Is that caused by what happened to you last night or what happened in the house just now?"

"Both. Papa died." Her sad eyes met his.

"I'm sorry." He set the food on the ground.

"Me, too. I guess the fatal blow came when he finally had to admit late yesterday that he could no longer control High, and his only brother either had run out on him or been murdered by High. He told me he no longer had a reason to live, poor thing. He asked about you, and I told him the truth. Perhaps I should have spared him that. He asked what they planned to do with you, but I couldn't place that burden on him. He wanted me to call the sheriff, but he knew the line was cut. The last thing he said before he died this morning was that he wanted me to find a way to get the word out about what was going on out here and then save myself, Jimmy, and Lily. You, too, if I could."

"It's bad when a man has to admit all his best efforts have come to nothing."

Something about her eyes told him she might have been struck suddenly by that same thought about him.

She said, "Papa was very old, living on old memories. He may be better off, the poor dear."

High shouted, "What's all the mumblin' about in there? I said you could feed him, Eva, not play nurse. Come on out. It's my turn now."

Blin saw the pleading in her eyes, and knowing he couldn't help her made him forget how hungry he was. "Isn't there someone in the house who can hear you scream?"

"Nobody but Jimmy, and he's still locked in a closet. Even if he wasn't, he's too afraid of High hurting me to come out here. The only time I've talked to him except through the door was when High let me tell him about Papa. He was terribly upset and very frightened. I tried opening the door later, when High wasn't watching, but couldn't. Jimmy needs his mother."

High swung the door open, leveled his pistol at Blin, and told Eva, "I'm tired of waitin'. We've got to get through partyin' before Hulie and our rich friends get here."

She leaned over and kissed Blin's cheek, saying, "Good-bye. Thanks for being so respectful and nice."

She passed through the door, which was immediately slammed shut and locked. Blin crawled over to put his eye to a crack, realizing this might be the only chance he would have to kick through the roof. He was sorry the opportunity had come at Eva's expense, but he couldn't help her if he couldn't break out.

High snapped on the radio and turned to a rap station. "This occasion calls for special music," he said. "Come here." He pulled her over to the chair and sat down, his pistol pointing at her head. He pulled her down to her knees in front of him and took another long drag off his joint. He pushed the joint against her lips. "Take a drag off this. It'll make your chimes ring louder."

She turned her head.

High took another drag off the joint and tossed it away, laying his pistol on his right thigh. Crossing his ankles behind Eva, he released her arm and began caressing her breasts. She tried to jerk free, and he tightened his legs around her. Her eyes were closed, and she was sobbing.

Blin stood and searched for the rotten spot in the decking in the subdued light, but couldn't find it. He could barely hear High pawing Eva above the music.

"Look at me," High ordered. "Don't pretend you haven't done this for a man before."

Blin heard a slap. Moving back to the crack of light by the door, Blin saw High grab Eva's hair and jerk her forward. The pistol fell off his lap.

Spotting the board, Blin climbed to the top of the joist beneath it, as Eva cried, "No! I won't do that! I'll die first!"

Blin heard another slap, followed by, "Stop fightin', dammit! And don't you bite me again unless you want me to cut you real bad. You promised."

Blin rubbed his eyes to clear the imprint of light that tainted his vision, made by looking through the crack into the sunlight. He moved closer to his target and slid his fingers over the decking in search of the rotten board.

Blin heard High's voice rise to a higher pitch. "Go ahead. Fight and whimper. That'll make it even better for me, Miss Uppity." His voice trembled with anticipation. "Ouch! I told you not to bite me! Just for that, I'm gonna teach you a real lesson. And it's gonna hurt real bad. You won't bite me no more after I get through with you!"

Sounds of a struggle and High's curses passed the side wall of the smokehouse, and moments later, from out back, High shouted, "Lay down, dammit! This bottle won't hurt as much if you'll be still. After I'm done with this, I'm gonna bite and pull all your pretty parts 'til I see lots of blood. Then I'm gonna smear it all over your pretty face. That'll teach you not to be uppity with me." Eva was crying.

Blin walked his feet up the underside of the decking and slammed his right boot against it. It tore loose from the rafters, but not far enough, so he kicked it again and again, until there was an opening large enough to squeeze through.

Eva's screams were ringing in his ears as he pushed his head and shoulders through the opening. Ignoring the splinters tugging at his body, he climbed out on the roof, and without taking the time to see if High had heard him escape, he jumped to the ground and ran toward the pistol.

When he heard High cry out, he glanced around and saw the crazy brother also running toward the gun. Blin reached it first and scooped it up just as High tackled him from behind. He was barely able to stay on his feet and shove High away.

Pointing the Beretta at High, he said, "Back off, pervert!"

High pulled a long knife from his pocket and snapped it open, and as Blin fumbled with the gun's safety, the crazy man lunged at him, slicing the air near his face. Rap music still played over the radio.

The gun's safety off, Blin pointed the pistol at High's chest. "Drop the knife, High! Don't make me kill you!"

High stopped, and a sick smile appeared on his face as he fixed his dark eyes on Blin. "Them bullets won't hurt me, runt! Besides, you ain't got the guts to shoot nobody."

"That's the weed talking, High. Drop the knife and back off."

"There ain't no do-gooders around this time to keep me from killin' you, runt cop," he said. "You ain't worth as much to me dead, but I'll be just as happy." Knife raised, he sprang forward.

Eva screamed as Blin pulled the trigger. The bullet struck High in the chest, stopping him. He staggered backwards a step as shock and disbelief swept over his face, and then teetered about like a drunken man before taking a step forward. He stopped. He moved his lips, but only gurgling sounds and blood came out. He took one more step toward Blin and stopped again as his face paled.

Blin stood, poised to shoot again, but instead of advancing further, High turned toward the house. Dropping the knife, he held out both arms and pleaded, "Help me, Papa!" then fell forward, face down.

Blin let his gun hand drop to his side, and after he was convinced High wasn't going to move, he pushed the pistol's safety on and snapped off the radio on his way to Eva. He found her sitting down and staring about numbly, as if unable to fully comprehend her situation. She appeared not to realize she was nude from her waist up, or that her skirt was pulled up high on her thighs. Her eyes met his, but she was in such shock she could not speak.

He knelt and wrapped one arm around her as she began to cry uncontrollably. "It's okay now," he said. "High won't bother you or anybody else any more."

At the sound of his voice, she suddenly became aware of her plight and began pulling frantically at her skirt. Blin saw the red, swollen fang marks on her white skin.

She said, "I'm so ashamed!"

Blin gave her the torn blouse, and she turned and pulled it on. Seeing a large round brown bottle near her feet, he asked, "Are you all right?"

She grimaced when she closed the blouse in front and began buttoning it. "I think so, but I wouldn't have been if you hadn't broken out when you did."

"I'm sorry I couldn't get out quicker."

"I was afraid you weren't going to shoot in time." She shuddered and looked past the corner of the smokehouse at High's body.

"Hulie and those gangsters will be here soon," he said. "That means I've got to get out of here fast. You and Jimmy should leave, too, because they won't leave any witnesses. You and Jimmy can stay until Hulie gets here if you prefer, or one of you can go with me. My horse can only carry two and I'm in no condition to walk out of here to let both of you ride. Moving out with me will be very risky, too, because they'll come after me for sure."

"Please let me go with you. I know what Hulie will do to me if I'm here when he gets back, and you need help finding where you're going. Jimmy knows these woods. He can hide in them until we send help."

"What about your mother? Won't she need you?"

"Mother will stay with ladies from our church in Dooly."

"You could walk away with Jimmy."

"I'm still too weak, and I don't want to risk Hulie's dogs finding me before he puts them on your trail."

Blin recalled what it was like when he got lost in the forest. If he left alone, he would be overtaken for sure, and his smarting back wounds told him they needed to be cleaned and treated. "I'll get my horse."

"Before you do, you have to get the key to Jimmy's closet out of High's pocket. I can't do it." She shuddered.

She followed him to High's lifeless body. He knelt down and searched for the key. "Are you sure he's dead?"

"I'm sure." He found the key and six cartridges for the Beretta. He gave her the key and studied the pathetic face of the man he had been forced to kill. There was no man he had ever hated more, but in spite of all the degrading experiences suffered at his hands, he found no pleasure in what he had done. Instead, he felt a twinge of sadness for the insane, evil man, and for those whose lives he had ruined.

"Death is never pretty, is it?" Eva said. "But if anybody deserved to die, he did. I'm just glad Papa didn't have to see it."

He looked at Catcher in the pen. "Be ready by the time I get to the house."

"I'll get some things we'll need after I get Jimmy out and explain what he has to do." She started up the footpath.

Blin found the saddle, bridle, and blanket inside a small, dusty crib. Picking them up, he approached Catcher in the weed-infested lot. "Whoa, boy. Remember me?"

Catcher's ears flipped forward, but he didn't move, allowing Blin to slip the bit into his mouth and slide the bridle over his ears. A glance at his back showed Blin scabs formed over his wounds.

He placed the blanket and saddle on Catcher's back, pulled the cinch tight, and led him out of the pen, climbing into the saddle. Catcher shook his head a couple of times and calmed, and Blin turned his head toward the house. "Good boy." He patted the horse's neck.

Blin searched the outer edges of the clearing for Friend, but didn't see her. The shot had scared her off.

Eva was waiting for him near the back steps with a large paper sack under her arm. She had put on another blouse and skirt, but apparently hadn't bothered with another brassiere. He admonished himself for having noticed such a thing under the circumstances. "Get my letters?"

She nodded. "Everything's in the sack."

Jimmy appeared in the opened door with paper sack and rifle in hand, sad and shaken. Eva said, "Go deep in the woods, opposite to the way we leave, and stay there 'til you hear the strangers leave, okay? But stop at the edge of the woods to make sure they didn't leave someone with Hulie. There'll be lots more cars here when we get to town and call the justice of the peace about High."

"Okay, Eva. I'll be all right, but I wish Mother was here." He looked down the trail at High's still body. "Hulie won't hurt me."

"I put enough food in your sack to last 'til supper. If for some reason Hulie leaves before I get back, wait in the house until Mother comes home or I send somebody to get you. I'll return as soon as I show Blin the way out and do something for the cuts on his back."

"What'll happen to Mother now?"

"We'll take her to Beaumont with us. We'll take care of her."

"I miss Papa," Jimmy said, voice breaking.

Eva wrapped her arm around him. "I do too, Jimmy, but now that he's gone, we have to be stronger than ever. That's the way he'd want it, don't you think?" She pointed. "Now, better get going."

Jimmy wiped a tear from his eye and headed for the woods beyond the side fence. "Bye, Eva."

Blin took his left foot from the stirrup and reached down to pull Eva up behind him.

She said, "Oh, my! He's so wide!"

"Are you going to be able to ride with that sore leg?"

"I think so. Ouch!"

He nudged Catcher with his heels. "Put your arms around my waist so you won't slide off."

Catcher took them around the side of the house at a brisk walk, and when the front porch came into view, Blin fixed his eyes on an old wooden rocker. "Papa's?"

"Yes. He liked to sit in it and read or listen to his favorite records."

A gentle breeze moved across the yard, causing the chair to rock slightly, as if some invisible force from its dead owner was making one last plea for recognition.

"Poor papa," Eva said. "He was a good, brilliant man. He deserved more out of life than he got."

He looked at the lane beyond the front gate. "We can't take a chance of meeting Hulie and those crooks. Which is the fastest way to Dooly under cover?"

"The highway." She pointed.

"Then the highway it is. It also offers us the best chance of running into a sheriff or state trooper that would make our ride a lot shorter. I've got to report what happened out here and make some calls to the feds."

She pointed at the woods bordering the open field in front of the house. "It's faster to the state highway that way."

He turned Catcher in the opposite direction. "Then we'll head this way and cut back after we pass through that gap they brought me through coming in here. Maybe that'll throw off Hulie's hounds long enough for us to get away."

"The only way to keep that from happening is to shoot them now."

She was right. He reined Catcher to a stop near the hounds under the edge of the front porch. They looked at him with sad eyes, a picture of harmless indifference. But Blin knew their capabilities.

He moved his hand to the Beretta in his pocket, but pulled it back when he recalled fond memories of the dogs of his boyhood days. Hearing a movement behind them, Blin turned to find Friend sitting next to a shrub, calmly watching them. He smiled. "Hi, girl. Am I glad to see you! Want to go with us?"

Friend wagged her tail as he turned the horse toward her. Climbing down, he held out his hand. "We're still friends, aren't we?"

Friend limped to him, wagging her tail, and lowering her head in an ingratiating manner. He was pleased to see her putting more weight on her injured foot. There was new dried blood on her belly, but no other signs of recent injuries.

Patting her head, he said, "I'll fix that new wound as soon as I can stop long enough." He glanced at Eva and wondered what she thought of a man who talked to animals in such a manner. Mama's words came back again. *And I'll be there.* He said, "It's uncanny how she keeps showing up."

"Papa always said God moves in mysterious ways."

He gave Eva a concerned look, and the cross on her necklace caught his eye. He remembered her telling him that Papa was a religious man and wondered how much his beliefs had influenced her. It was something he felt unprepared to discuss. "Some very puzzling things have happened to me since I came to these woods." He climbed back into the saddle, nodding at Friend. "Too bad I don't have something to feed her."

She pulled a piece of bread from the sack. "Will this help?"

"Sure. Thanks." He tossed the bread back to Friend, and she caught it with her mouth in midair. Looking at Hulie's hounds, he told Eva, "I don't have enough cartridges to waste on dogs."

They passed through the gap and circled back toward the state highway. He told Eva, "I'll flag down a car on the highway so you can be taken to a safe place, and after you do what you need to do with your mother, I'll talk to the authorities."

It was vital they make the fastest time possible, because Saavedra's men would use their helicopter to search for him when they arrived at the smokehouse and found him gone. And Hulie would put his dogs on their trail in pursuit of his lost fortune.

While working undercover, Blin had learned how diligent and efficient organized crime bosses were in seeking out and destroying their enemies. They would allow Hulie to live long enough for his hounds to find him for them, and if anyone arrived at the Fancher place before they were finished with their grisly errand, they would murder them as well.

Blin decided not to alarm Eva further by mentioning the odds against their reaching safety before being overtaken. That gloomy prospect had already taken away much of the relief he felt after escaping crazy High Fancher.

The difficulties encountered to date, worsened by knowing what the gangsters would do, made Blin again fear he might not live long enough to fulfill his sacred promise to Mama. He glanced behind him and kicked Catcher into a trot.

Chapter XXI

*T*hey rode at least an hour over and around hills, through big trees and undergrowth, before Blin had to stop for a rest in the bushes. Eva slid off the horse with a sigh of relief, immediately setting about straightening her clothes and smoothing her hair. She had held her head close to him to avoid low-lying branches, but hadn't been able to protect her legs, left bare when she mounted the horse. He saw several nasty scratches about her knees and outer thighs when she slid to the ground.

He asked, "How are your legs?"

Her surprised look made him realize his mistake. "I know they're pretty, but I'm more concerned right now about the cuts and scratches I saw on them."

"Oh. They're okay, but your back looks bad. Some of those cuts appear infected already. I'll treat them with Neosporin as soon as we can get to water and clean them."

He turned up his nose. "What I really need is a good, soapy bath." He gave her the reins. "Nature calls. Be right back."

He walked out of sight into the bushes and relieved his bladder and bowels, cleaning himself with wide green leaves and scrubbing his hands with a mixture of sand and dead leaves. He returned to the waiting Eva.

"Sorry about that," he told her. "I guess you could call it my second step to recovery."

She smiled, pointing. "If you want to take a bath where I can treat your wounds, there's an old mill pond less than a mile up ahead."

He looked at Friend who had caught up with them and lain down nearby, panting heavily. Climbing into the saddle, he said, "That would take too much time."

"It's not out of the way, and your back has to be treated before the infection spreads. And it'll give your horse some time to rest."

"He needs that, and some water. Anybody live around that pond?"

"Not for years and years. But I haven't been over there since I was a little girl. It's probably grown up with weeds and full of snakes by now."

188

"I'd get in a tank of alligators to take a bath, but if I didn't have to rest and water Catcher, I wouldn't take the time. Point the way." He pulled her up behind him and urged Catcher into a fast walk.

"Everything's so grown up since I was through here last," she said. "The woods seem to go on forever, and it's so quiet it's scary."

"I thought the same thing that first day I rode into the big woods. It was awesome to me, and gave me the feeling that living in them would be the worst thing I'd ever have to do. That was before I fell in that pit and was locked up in that smokehouse. Any chance of Hulie doing something sensible for a change when he finds High dead, like calling the sheriff instead of taking out after me?"

"It's hard to say what Hulie will do without Papa and High around to give him orders, but I know he's not brave enough to do anything that would make those gangsters unhappy, which means he'll help them find you. But if you're worried about what'll happen to you when the sheriff does find out about High, you shouldn't be. I'm your witness."

Her voice held none of the sadness he'd noticed before. She seemed to have regained the gentle demeanor he had come to admire. He said, "You're getting more important to me every day, whether you like it or not." It just slipped out, and he immediately regretted saying it. It was no time for sentimental blabber.

"Other than my mother and little brother, I've never been made to feel I was needed by anybody. I like it."

"A girl as pretty as you must have been told lots of flattering things."

"But always for the wrong reasons."

"How do you know my reasons are any different?"

"By the way you talk to me, treat me. And don't make fun of my woman's intuition."

"I think I forgot what fun is. Am I still headed in the right direction?"

"Head a little more to your right. I'll keep a lookout for signs of the pond."

Blin listened for barking dogs in the distance or the flutter of a helicopter's rotor, but so far heard neither.

Progress was slow in the thick underbrush, but most of the time, Blin was able to keep Catcher in a fast walk. He didn't dare push him into a gallop out of fear of what the heavy brush and low-lying limbs would do to Eva.

There was little talk during the next half-hour except for Eva's directions, but Blin became increasingly aware of her arms around his lower abdomen and the occasional touch of her bosom against his burning back. She occasionally released him to point, but quickly replaced her arms around him.

They crossed a dip in the ground's surface in a grove of small trees and tall grass. A stream flowed into it.

Eva pointed to the thicket downstream. "It's down there, unless it's all filled in."

They circled the area until Blin saw water through a small opening in the heavy growth of weeds and saplings. They soon found themselves in a weed-infested clearing near the remains of a rotting frame building smothered by a mass of vines, bushes, and small pines.

"The old gristmill," she said.

Blin reined Catcher to a stop at the center of an opening where the weeds were not so thick and offered his hand to Eva. "Off we go."

He led Catcher into soft, wet sand near the incoming stream's sandy bank and let him drink. Moments later, he pulled up his head and returned to the waiting Eva. Tying Catcher to a sapling surrounded by tall grass, Blin loosened the saddle's cinch and removed the bit from the horse's mouth so he could graze.

He found a fallen tree branch about four feet long that would serve as a club in case he encountered snakes. "This dirty boy is gonna get back a little closer to being civilized. You can watch, turn around, or run. It makes no difference to me."

She reached into the paper sack and pulled out a shirt, a pair of faded khaki trousers, and some socks. "I hope you don't mind wearing something that belonged to Papa."

"You're incredible," he said. "I don't mind."

"There's a bar of soap and some clean shorts in one of the pockets."

He wondered whom the shorts belonged to, but it didn't matter as long as they were clean. When his hand touched hers, he sensed tenseness between them like none he had noticed before, and when their eyes met, she quickly looked away. That told him she felt it, too.

With stick and clothes in hand, he walked through the tall grass and vines to the edge of the pond, anxious to be clean again. He glanced back and saw both Eva and Friend watching him.

The weeds were thicker and taller near the pond's edge, and the grass so dense he had difficulty passing through it. Breaking through, he stopped and pulled the bar of soap from a pocket of the khakis and draped the clothes over a bush.

He slipped off his boots and blue jeans and began pulling down his shorts, stopping when he realized the weeds might not block Eva's view. Stepping behind a hanging branch of a willow tree, he pulled off the dirty garments, crinkled his nose, and tossed them into the weeds.

Moving slowly into the moss and lily pads along the water's edge, he worked his way toward a small clearing at the approximate center of the little pond some twenty feet away. It appeared to be free of weeds and stumps.

The water was cool, refreshing, and very clear in the spots not covered by lily pads. He held the stick at the ready, but saw no snakes. A frog jumped from a nearby lily pad with a loud squawk that made him jump back a step, and he saw a turtle's head slip beneath the surface in the clearing, but no snakes.

The bottom was very soft, so with each step his feet sank ankle-deep into the mud, but he continued walking. A few more steps into the muck and he began scooping water with his free hand, splashing it on his crotch and belly.

Dropping the stick, he got down on his knees to splash the cool water over his body, but stood up when the welts on his back began to burn. He wet the soap and vigorously rubbed it between his hands until there was enough lather to clean them, then repeated the procedure to rub thick foam on his arms, armpits, face, and neck. His eyes closed, he repeated the process on his head, immersing it to rinse the soap away. The soapy water running down his back caused his back wounds to burn more severely.

He made more lather and washed his privates, rinsed them, and applied soap to his thighs down to the water level. Rinsing again, he teetered about on one foot at a time to wash his legs and feet.

Keeping his back toward the bank in case the clearing could be seen from where Eva stood, he moved to deeper water to more thoroughly rinse himself. When he stopped with the water lapping at his waist, he looked back and found Eva watching him. "Sorry I can't draw the curtain."

"Ready for me to clean and treat those cuts?" She had a towel draped around her neck.

He immersed himself to wash off the remaining soap, glad to be clean now except for his stinging back, which he couldn't reach. "You don't mind getting wet?"

She kicked off her shoes and waded into the pond, stopping often with a surprised, "Oh, my!" to regain her balance and push down her ballooning skirt. By the time she came to within fifteen feet of him, the water had risen past her waist, causing her to stop and give him a concerned look. He walked toward her and was almost within her reach when he discovered the water level was approaching his privates.

She held up her hand. "That's far enough. I'll come to you."

Her blouse was immediately saturated, becoming transparent where it clung to her bosom. She was so absorbed with keeping her balance she seemed not to notice.

He gave her the soap and turned around. She dipped the bar into the water, vigorously rubbed it between her hands, and began to gently wash his wounds. In spite of her soft touch, he could not help flinching; each time he did, she stopped and said, "Sorry," or "Excuse me." When she was finished, she scooped up water to rinse him off, and the burning became less severe.

"Hold still for a few minutes more," she said, pulling the towel from her shoulders to gently press it against his back. She then applied the antibiotic salve from a small tube. "This will fight infection," she said.

When he turned, she was washing her face, arms, and neck. She filled her mouth with soapy water from her hands, swished it about, and turned to discharge it. Her performance puzzled him until he remembered her encounter with High by the smokehouse. She apparently felt contaminated by his touch.

He said, "Thanks for taking care of my back. With that and a good bath, I feel like a human being again."

She leaned down to rinse off the soap. "You're welcome." She didn't meet his gaze. Although outwardly calm, he noted a hint of nervousness in her voice. "Since I've done what I came to do, I'll go to the bank and wring out my clothes."

He watched as she struggled against the water and mud. She had taken only a few steps when she lost her balance and fell with a big splash and a sharp, "Oh, damn!"

He moved over to her and pulled her up, sputtering and gasping for air. She wiped water from her face and pulled her hair to the back of her head to squeeze it out, clearly embarrassed.

"I really am a sight to look at," she said. She pulled at her blouse, which was clinging tightly to her bosom.

"I don't see anything you should be ashamed of." He pulled her tightly against him and leaned down to kiss her, but just as quickly drew back. "Sorry."

She appeared surprised. "Thank you for not taking liberties. But when you stopped, something about your expression told me it was because you remembered something unpleasant all of a sudden."

Her uncanny ability to read his mind was unsettling. How could she possibly know he'd drawn back because he suspected High had forced her to kiss him or perform acts of perversion?

"Was it something High and Hulie said, or what you thought High made me do before you escaped?" Her gaze didn't waver.

He hesitated. "It's not because I don't still find you attractive. Nothing could spoil that."

"Thanks, but that doesn't settle anything. I'm not dropping the matter and having someone I've come to admire believing anything bad about me that's not true."

He couldn't lie to someone who had been so helpful. If he answered her, he had to tell her the truth.

She said, "You are repelled by what you think High made me do outside the smokehouse, aren't you?"

"If that *was* the reason, it's over and done with now. You had no control over what happened."

"I appreciate you saying that, but it doesn't settle anything. I don't know what you heard or saw, or what you think he might have made me do then or later, but I want to make one thing perfectly clear. I did not do anything to or for High. He *tried* to make me do something perverted, but I refused. I would've died first. When you heard him cry out, it was because I bit his hand. You saw the condition I was in behind the smokehouse, so you couldn't help knowing what else he was trying to do to me back there, but you saved me from that, thank God. And now, after washing off in the pond, all places touched by my crazy half-brother are clean, even my mouth, which I washed out to get rid of the taste of that weed he stuck in my mouth. Okay?"

His held her gaze, impressed by her sincerity. His concerns about the matter faded. "Okay."

When he stepped toward her, she glanced down and turned quickly. "Oh, my!"

Glancing down, he found the water level so low he was exposed. He sank to his knees. "Sorry."

She walked toward the shallow water at the shoreline and disappeared in the tall weeds. Was she angry or merely embarrassed? He'd find out soon enough.

He waded ashore, and as he approached the clean clothes, Eva reappeared briefly, walking behind a clump of bushes by his horse. She didn't glance his way. Friend lay near Catcher, apparently asleep.

"There's a towel in the sack," she said. Her voice carried no hint of resentment.

He wiped his body dry, worried about the time they'd lost. "You need this towel, too. I only used one end of it."

"I'm okay. I brought it for you."

She brought it for me. How could he doubt the word of a woman who was always putting his welfare ahead of her own? But he had to be careful not to succumb to foolish, romantic notions in their rustic surroundings. It was no time for such nonsense. Hulie and the dogs might already be on their trail. In spite of his concerns about being overtaken, however, he could not deny how exciting those refreshing moments with Eva in the pond had been. His troubles and concerns were pushed aside for a few minutes.

He looked her way. "Eva?"

"Yes?"

"Now that certain misunderstandings have been cleared up, I can't help thinking about what I might do if I got that close to you again in my birthday suit."

No response from behind the bushes.

"I'm doing my best to handle this, but it's not easy. You're a very pretty woman."

When she still did not reply, he suspected he had been too bold, or that she had taken offense at the implications of his remarks. Finally, she replied, "You'd say the same thing to any woman under the circumstances."

"Maybe. But I wouldn't have allowed just any girl to walk back to the bushes by herself."

She fell silent again. He finished drying himself off and pulled on the shorts and pants.

She said, "I appreciate you letting me walk out of the pond alone. After what happened at the shed, I was afraid you might see me as some kind of cheap party girl."

"Party girls don't take risks for strangers." His pulse pounded as he reached for the shirt. His wounds weren't hurting as much as before, so he hoped the garment didn't rub off all the salve and caused them to begin burning again.

He had just finished dressing when Eva reappeared in the clearing, fully dressed. Her wet hair lay flat against her head.

He took the towel to her. "The dry end is clean. I'll get the horse. We've got to move on." Their eyes met briefly before he turned away, and he saw no hint of resentment in hers.

When he returned with Catcher, she gave him a look that suggested she wondered what his next move would be. Then she said something completely unexpected. Thanks."

"For what? Being dumb?"

"For treating me like a lady. I may not be by your standards, but if I'm not, it's not because I didn't want to be. I'm what I am because way back there, when certain things were very important to me, I wasn't given a choice."

"It's that important to a woman, this choice business?"

"It is, and will always be to me. But since I've met you, I've been telling myself that just because somebody pulled me down a long time ago there's no reason to think I can't climb high again. If somebody drops me a ladder, that is."

"You've been a good ladder for me." He gave her a sober look.

She began wiping her hair with the towel as he continued to study the pretty woman he had become so dependent upon, the one he had come to respect more than any woman friend he had ever known. Should he believe Eva was different from those women who were affectionate and accommodating only as long as he provided them with the things they wanted? Perhaps, because he was weary of dead-end searches for the emotional contentment that could come only with knowing there is someone totally committed to him, to whom he could respond in kind. It was amazing how tragedy and the threat of death could so quickly change a man's priorities.

He asked, "What if I hadn't given you a choice? What would you have done?"

"Only what I had to do after a struggle. Then I would've known I was wrong about you and that ladder. After we got out of these woods, I wouldn't have wanted to see you again, ever. Life would have gone on, but there would be nothing special about mine any more."

"After making so many bad choices lately, it's good to know I made one that pays such big dividends." He listened for sounds of the hounds, but didn't hear them. They had to get moving.

She pulled a small bottle from her blouse pocket. "I have to put more lotion on those bumps and that rash on our face and arms."

He beckoned her to silence and listened. The fluttering sound was faint, but unmistakable. A helicopter was approaching.

"No time for that now," he said. "Let's get mounted."

They had dallied too long.

Chapter XXII

*H*e pushed Catcher into a slow lope through trees and heavy undergrowth, no longer concerned about low-hanging branches and briars. Turning his head to the side, he asked, "How much farther to that state highway?"

"About two miles." She tightened her arms around his waist.

"Getting shot is a big price to pay for a bath."

"But even if they spot us, they can't land in the woods, can they?"

"Not unless they find a large clearing. But they can shoot without landing. And they'll send in somebody on the ground as soon as they spot us. But it's me they want, so when they get close, I want you to jump down and run away. They won't follow you."

"You said they'd kill all witnesses. That means they'd just hunt me down. I'm staying with you. Our chances are better if we stay together."

Her response didn't surprise him, but it made him feel guilty for allowing her to accompany him.

Concentrating on the area ahead, he found himself stooping and weaving to avoid slashing limbs, and each time he did, Eva leaned with him. It was impossible to dodge everything, but she didn't complain. He heard her gasp a few times and felt her move an arm from his waist from time to time to ward off a passing limb, but she didn't allow herself to be bounced from her precarious position.

Approximately a half-hour later, he slowed Catcher to a fast walk, and after traveling at that pace for another ten minutes or so, reined him to a stop. Climbing down, he said, "We have to walk a while to rest Catcher."

She slid off into his arms and straightened her rumpled dress and hair as they set out in a fast walk. He cocked his head to listen for the helicopter, but didn't hear it.

"Are they still coming?" she asked.

He cocked his head to listen, not answering her. Moments later, he heard the chopper's motor and the distinctive flutter of its rotor. "Yes,

197

and they're closer. They're flying in ever widening circles out from the Fancher place until they spot us."

She opened her mouth to speak when he stopped and signaled her to silence. "I hear something else now."

It was very faint, but just as ominous. He resumed walking. "Hulie's hounds are hot on our trail. We've got to move faster, because the men in that chopper will follow those dogs."

He remounted and pulled her up. "We have to get to that highway before the dogs overtake us."

"I'm scared, Blin!"

"We're not caught yet. Somebody'll pick us up once we reach the highway. It can't be more than a mile away by now."

He pushed Catcher into a gallop. "Even if they spot us from the chopper before the dogs find us, it'll take a while for them to find a place to land. Hold on tight. We'll make it."

He meant it to be reassuring, not a statement of fact, because when she climbed up behind him, he saw the terrified expression on her face. It was the same look he saw when High allowed her to come into the smokehouse that last time. He didn't want her to know it would take the helicopter only a few minutes to spot them once the dogs arrived.

Noting Catcher's heavy breathing and a faltering step, Blin reined him to a stop. "We've no choice now. We've got to walk."

They had walked only a short distance before a panting Friend overtook them. She wagged her tail when Blin spoke to her. "Good girl. Glad to see we're still family. Sorry my horse doesn't have a rumble seat."

About twenty minutes later, they remounted, but shortly thereafter Blin had to pull Catcher to a slow walk in heavy underbrush. The hounds' barking was much louder now. He had heard enough hunting dogs on a hot trail to recognize the growing intensity of their yapping. It told him they were pressing harder in anticipation of a quick kill.

He glanced behind them for signs of the dogs, and had just turned forward again when the hounds broke through the brush on either side and made a dash for Catcher's legs. His horse reared sharply, causing Blin to grab the saddle horn to prevent them from being thrown off. His front feet back on ground, Catcher began to kick and whirl wildly, trying to escape the snapping dogs. Blin slapped Catcher with the reins and yelled at him, but couldn't make him move forward.

Blin jumped to the ground and caught Eva when she slid off the horse's rump. She dropped the paper sack, but scooped it up before jumping clear. She screamed at the dogs, but they appeared not to hear her.

Above the melee, Blin heard the drone of the chopper's motor closing as he struggled to keep the reins from being jerked from his hands. He looked for cover, spotting a large oak nearby. He pulled Eva and Catcher toward it, but the two hounds didn't fall back. Pulling the pistol from his pocket, he squeezed off a round at the closest dog, and it let out a yelp and disappeared into the brush. Taking hold of Eva's arm again, he said, "Follow me!"

He tied Catcher to a smaller tree nearby and had joined Eva under the big oak when the two dogs charged again. He said, "We'll have to go around the tree to keep it between us and the chopper when it gets here."

"Blin, I'm so scared!" Her fingers dug into his arms. "Those dogs! Can't you just shoot them? If you did, maybe the men in the chopper wouldn't find us!"

"They can see a dead dog as well as a live one, and I don't have enough bullets. Besides, I think they've already zeroed in on us."

Apparently frightened of the chopper, the hounds became less aggressive, but when one grew brave enough to charge again, Blin scared it away with the dead limb. The chopper was almost overhead now, but Blin couldn't see it through the heavy foliage.

The chopper approached their location cautiously, finally hovering no more than a hundred feet above them. Blin pressed Eva tighter against the tree, the pistol pointed upward, waiting for the gunmen to appear in an opening. The Beretta wasn't effective against the flying machine, but it would kill a man sitting in an open door.

The noise and the downdraft were too much for the dogs. They stopped barking and ran into the brush. Blin was glad, because he could now concentrate on the more serious threat.

He remained still against Eva, hoping they wouldn't be seen if they didn't move. He flicked off the pistol's safety and waited, but saw no openings in their cover.

The noise caused Catcher to rear, break his reins, and gallop down the slope. Blin whistled and called to him, but he continued running. The chatter of an automatic weapon was heard above the noise from above, and Catcher fell.

"They killed my horse!" he moaned.

"And they'll kill us next," Eva shouted. "What are we going to do?"

"You stay here until they start following me then run in the opposite direction. Don't stop until you get to the highway. Flag down a car and go to town for help."

"No! I'm staying with you!"

"I told you. It's me they want. Do as I say!"

A hail of bullets ripped through their cover, clipping off leaves and small limbs and kicking up dirt around them. Blin pushed Eva closer to the tree.

The helicopter moved closer, and more bullets ripped through the limbs and leaves of a large tree next to the oak they were under, telling Blin the gunmen weren't sure of their exact location. He raised the pistol.

The chopper began circling, and on its way back to the oak, it paused above a small opening in the canopy, giving Blin a clear view of a large man in a white shirt sitting in the door, his feet resting on a landing strut. It was Walrus Walsaka, one of Zaavedra's enforcers, and he was holding what appeared to be an AK-47 automatic rifle.

Blin took aim, but before he could fire, the chopper moved out of sight, causing him to shake his head in disgust at being so slow. Leaning down to Eva's ear, he said, "Stay here!" He kissed her cheek and ran from cover, her screams ringing in his ears.

Because he was directly beneath the chopper and had run towards its tail section, he was able to run some forty feet before the pilot swung the aircraft around to follow him. Walrus resumed firing as Blin dived behind a dead tree.

Bullets kicked up dirt and split chunks off the log as Blin hugged the earth, and when the firing stopped, he peeked over his barricade in search of a target. The flying machine moved slowly out and around, apparently looking for a spot that would give Walrus a better view of his position. When it passed an opening in the leaves, Blin fired at the gunman. Walrus fell from the door, landing nearby with a large *thump* as a second gunman moved up to replace him. The door passed from Blin's view, but not before he recognized Graveyard Boze, the black Saavedra enforcer.

The chopper approached from the backside of the log, and Blin rolled over it and raised the gun to wait for another chance to shoot. He would aim at the pilot through the windshield. The cockpit appeared, and he aimed and pulled the trigger. The gun was empty.

He jumped up and run to a tree to Catcher's left as Graveyard began firing. Leaning against the tree, he pushed the six shells from his pocket into the pistol's magazine and threw a round into the firing chamber. He peeked around the tree to see if he had a clear view of the chopper.

All he saw was limbs and leaves. He looked at the oak for signs of Eva, but didn't see her. He was glad, because that told him she had run out of range, after all. The men in the helicopter wouldn't look for her until they disposed of him, and she would be too far away to be found by then.

The pilot pulled away and began circling, and Blin followed the sound, gun poised, determined to shoot as soon as a human target appeared. He heard the dogs barking still, and out of the corner of his eye, he saw them milling about, still too afraid to charge. He wondered where Hulie was.

The chopper moved so far away Blin believed the pilot was looking for a place to land so he and Graveyard Boze could come after him on foot, but it turned and moved toward him from the opposite direction, with Graveyard firing through the foliage.

Blin moved around the tree that suddenly seemed much smaller, and when the chopper slowed to begin a tight circle, he ran to a large pine some forty feet away. Peering around the trunk of his new cover, he aimed at an open spot, where he believed the helicopter's cabin would appear when it followed him.

The chopper began moving slowly across the opening, and when its cabin was in clear view, Blin placed the sights of the Beretta on Graveyard and fired twice. He quickly turned the sights on the pilot and fired the remaining rounds.

The chopper banked wildly and disappeared from view, causing him to believe he had missed. If he had, he no longer had the means to defend himself and would be killed when they spotted him. After that, they would find Eva and kill her, too.

He waited anxiously for sounds that would tell him they were landing or turning to come back, and seconds later, he heard treetops and limbs being broken by a great force. A loud crash and an explosion followed.

The chopper was down.

He breathed a sigh of relief. "Thank God!"

He walked from his cover, and when he heard running footsteps, whirled, expecting to see Hulie and more gunmen closing in.

It was Eva. Her face was pale, and her brown eyes wide with fright. "Are you all right?"

"I think so. How about you? I thought you ran away."

201

Upon reaching him, she held onto his arm for support, gasping for air. "Besides being scared to death, I'm okay."

He wrapped his arms around her. "Great. For a moment there I wasn't sure if either one of us would make it."

He turned to see what the hounds were doing, but they were gone. He believed the shooting and the noise from the crash had frightened them away until he saw Friend standing on her three good legs near where he had last seen the hounds. She was panting heavily, as if she might have been in a fight, but she wagged her tail when he spoke to her. When he whistled, she limped over to him and licked his fingers, whining softly.

"Good girl," he said, patting her head as he again recalled Mama's statement. *When the darkest time of your life comes, I will be there.*

He glanced at Eva, wondering what she would think of him if she knew he suspected the spirit of his grandmother was present.

He looked for new wounds on Friend, but didn't find any. "Thanks for sticking with me, ol' girl, and for chasing those hounds away. I'll get you something to eat as soon as I can."

He looked toward the crash. He had to find out if there were survivors. "Be right back."

"Stay here. You're bleeding!"

He looked at his arms and legs. He didn't see any blood, but he felt a sharp pain in his right cheek and an aching along his right side. Both places were bloody.

She pointed to his side. "That's the most serious, but I'll pull that splinter out of your cheek first."

"Before you do, I've got to make sure there's nobody in that chopper still able to finish what they started. Be right back."

He found the pilot and Graveyard Boze lying unconscious inside the flame-enveloped cabin. Convinced he could not save them, he walked away from the intense heat in search of Walsaka, finding him where he fell. Blin believed him to be dead, too, and he had turned to walk back to Eva when the big man groaned and moved.

Blin approached the gunman and saw his head move slightly, then noticed his eyes were open. His body was twisted. Both legs appeared to be broken, and one arm, but he appeared to be breathing normally, and there was no external bleeding.

When Blin leaned down, Walrus groaned and rolled his head from side to side. "Help me. I'm dyin'!"

"Probably. If you'd had your way, it would be me lying there."

"Where's Graveyard?"

"In that burning chopper down there. His luck ran out, just like mine will if I don't get out of here before another load of your friends gets here." He turned to leave.

"Please! Don't leave me here to die. I was just followin' orders. If you'll help me, I'll tell the feds everything. Please?"

Blin turned. "You'd testify against Doss and the others?"

The gangster nodded. "And all their connections. Just don't let me die. Please?"

"They'll kill you if you testify against them."

"I'm gonna die for sure if you don't get me to a hospital." He grimaced. "I'd at least have a chance. And I'd have time to talk to a priest."

Blin gave the spreading fire an anxious look. "I can't move you, and it'll take me a while to get out of here and find somebody that can. But you may live if I can get you to a doctor."

Walrus raised his good arm and pleaded, "Just promise me you'll do it. I ain't ready to die."

"Okay, it's a deal." Blin leaned down to pat Walrus' pants pockets and slide his hand along his belt. "Where's your pistol?"

"Lost it, I guess."

"I'll stop that fire so you won't get roasted before I can get help out here."

Breaking off the top of a pine sapling, he walked through the smoke to the outer perimeter of the fire and began snuffing out the flames, not stopping until he'd completed the circle. The helicopter was still burning, but with nothing to feed on, the flames would die after the machine was consumed. Blin had never smelled burning human flesh before. It made him nauseous.

Coughing from the smoke and breathing heavily, he walked over to Catcher's body and gazed grimly at the many places where the gentle horse had been struck by bullets. Shaking his head in disgust, he said aloud, "I'm sorry I let that happen to you, my four-legged friend."

He looked for Walrus' gun, but didn't find it. Emotionally drained and physically exhausted, he turned to rejoin Eva, and as he passed Walrus, he said, "I'll be back with medics as soon as I get into town, unless more of your friends show up to stop us."

He found Eva ripping off the bottom of her blouse. When he sat down next to a pine tree, his legs almost collapsed. It was the first time he'd realized how weak he was.

She opened his shirt to reveal a wound where a bullet had grazed him just below his ribs. It ached fiercely. "Looks like nothing vital was punctured," she said. "I'll stop the bleeding and clean it."

She sponged away the blood and pressed a small, folded piece of cloth against the entrance and exit wounds. "You really took a chance, running away from me like that," she said. "How about those killers? Are they all dead?"

"All but one, and he's in bad shape. Told me he'd turn states evidence if I'd help him."

"And what did you tell him?"

"That we had a deal. But we have to get to that highway before more shooters get here." He glanced around. "Or Hulie."

"You don't have to worry about Hulie. I'm sure he went back to the house as soon as he heard the helicopter go down. Without the gangsters, High, or Uncle Emmett to push him, he's too big of a coward to act on his own."

"Staying with me could've got you killed."

She removed the blood-soaked pieces of cloth and wiped the wounds. "If they'd killed you, maybe I wouldn't have cared if they did."

While pleasing to hear, her statement surprised him. "If you said that just to make me feel good, it worked. But you're a hard one to figure."

"And so are you." She looked at his cheek wound. "Did you try to save me because you had a crazy notion about owing me something, or for some other reason?"

"I didn't want to be the cause of you getting hurt after all you've done for me. What other reason would I have?"

"Nobody would blame you for getting as far away from this place as you can and forgetting everybody connected to it."

He wanted to believe her mood change was prompted by remembering Papa and worrying about Jimmy, but knew it could also mean she was like many of the other women he had known, after all. If that were the case, it meant she no longer had a reason to be warm and attentive. She didn't need him any more.

He said, "High is out of the picture, but I'm still not in a position to help you and Jimmy. The loss of that chopper and three gunmen won't stop those gangsters. They'll keep sending killers after me until they shut me up for good, unless the feds figure out a way to stop them."

He glanced around, expecting to hear more gunmen moving in on the ground or the flutter of a helicopter's rotor. "And according to what

I heard on the radio, the U.S. attorney in Houston might file charges against me for skipping out on them. If I save Walrus, I can get on good terms again. He'd get a conviction this time for sure."

"Looks like things are gong your way for a change." She met his gaze, as if by doing so she would find the answer to a question she had not yet asked.

"Hope so. But there's also that matter of clearing up what happened with High, and those dead killers in that chopper, and Walrus. I'll be very busy for a long time trying to stay out of jail myself." He looked at her. "What will you do now?"

Taking hold of the splinter, she pulled it out, causing him to grunt and jerk back.

"Sorry," she said, pressing a piece of cloth against the wound. "I'm sorry I lost the lotion. I'll put something on your back and the new wounds as soon as we get to town. The first thing I have to do is check on Mother and Jimmy. After Papa's funeral, I'll arrange to take them to Beaumont. I'll get my old job back." She gave him a cautious glance. "But I won't leave for Beaumont until I tell the sheriff and the district attorney up here about how High and those men in the helicopter tried to kill you."

"Great. I need that. I appreciate everything you've done for me." Appreciation didn't adequately describe his feelings toward her, but stronger words might strike her as presumptuous, or maudlin. A professional woman customer told him when he was tending bar that he was prone to allowing sentimentality to overplay reality. He must avoid that. She also told him she sensed a hidden fear that prevented him from forming the kind of romantic relationship he was looking for. She said it could be his fear of not finding one as pure and lasting as what he had with his grandmother. She said that while they were different kinds of loves, they were both founded on basic needs. She said he was looking for guarantees.

Whatever the reason for his failure in love, he could not express his true feelings without first receiving further assurances of how she felt about him. She wasn't likely to do that in their present circumstances.

When she leaned over to look at his side wound, he found himself looking at the golden necklace again. When she noticed, she sat erect and said, "I couldn't help noticing how my little cross catches your eye. Care to tell me why?"

"I'm not sure." He shrugged.

"Could it have something to do with all the cynicism that's been building up in you for so long?"

205

"It shows that much?"

She nodded. "Maybe it's trying to break out."

"I'm not qualified to talk about such deep subjects. You're not one of those woman preachers, are you?"

"No, but when I lived at home, Papa read the scriptures and talked about a person's spiritual needs. I never would've understood if he hadn't."

"My grandmother did the same with me. You go to church?"

"Used to. It gave me hope."

"A powerful thing, hope. Maybe that's what kept me going back there in that stinkin' smokehouse."

"I know men don't feel comfortable talking about how they feel about such things. But Papa was a strong man, and he did."

"I don't know if I've never talked about it because I'm weak, but if hasn't kept me from *thinking* about what Mama told me. She talked a lot about man's inside person. Matters of the spirit, she called it."

He watched as she turned her attention back to his side wound. Her fingers trembled, as if she might still be afraid, or struggling with deep inner feelings she was afraid to mention. He said, "I'm sorry about all the bad things you've been put through because of me."

Her hands trembled more, but she still didn't look at him. Finished with sponging away the drying blood, she paused to stare at her shaking hands. Without looking at him, she said, "Remember that ladder I mentioned?"

"Yes."

"The bad thing about ladders is that they're sometimes jerked away when you need them the most." She stopped, near tears.

He said, "I'm still a couple of rungs short of climbing to the top of that ladder you dropped to me, so I know the feeling. I wouldn't be alive now if you hadn't done all those things for me. I won't jerk away my ladder unless you want me to, or unless you jerk yours away first. You'll have plenty of time to decide, because I don't plan to disappear like a puff of smoke. I want to keep seeing you after this is over, if I can. If the sheriff allows it, I'll be at the reservation a while, then I'll play it by ear from there, after getting things straight with my relatives and a certain federal prosecutor."

Wiping away tears with the back of her hand, she looked at him. "Will you please hold me, Blin? Just hold me."

He pulled her tightly against him as she began to cry. He stroked her hair and kissed her cheek, and when her sobbing stopped, he raised her face and kissed her lips, relieved that the coolness in her manner was gone.

Her head against his chest, she was quiet for a moment. Moments later, she said, "I'm sorry I acted like a typical female a moment ago. I don't know what came over me, unless it had something to do with being so scared lately. Seems I've always been afraid of something. Afraid of High, afraid for my little brother and my mother. Afraid I'd never be loved by a good husband so I can have children."

He pulled her face up. "There's still plenty of time left for that last item."

She drew back. "I'm twenty-eight years old. Do you know what it's like to be a woman that old without getting it together?"

"I'm a few years ahead of you. I was anxious to do some things in a hurry, too, and on the way find myself a good wife. Look what rushing got me. Right now, I'm in a hurry to get out of these woods, but don't believe I can do that, either, without my horse because my legs are too wobbly."

"You're very pale, too. You've got to rest." She picked up a piece of cloth and swabbed away the fresh blood oozing out of his cheek. "When you ran from that tree over there, I just knew I'd never see you alive again. And now—" Her hands began to tremble again. Recovering her composure, she asked, "What makes you think those bad people in Houston won't just forget you now?"

"Because I know how criminal minds work. The men in that chopper and their bosses are just the tip of the iceberg. There are more criminals in this country than there are termites in all the old houses in Texas, but if I can save Walrus and get lucky at a new trial, there won't be quite as many to worry about. No, they won't forget. Walrus and I'll have to hide in a safe place somewhere until they need us for the trials."

"Where will your safe place be?"

"The first place that comes to mind now is the reservation, but I don't know if I'll be welcome there, or how long I can stay without bringing down trouble on Mama's people. Don't know where I'll go when I leave the reservation." He looked around with a sigh. "I used to think the big woods my grandmother told me about would be the safest place in the world. Now I doubt there is such a place anywhere."

"No family?"

"No. I might find some cousins at the reservation. I don't even have any friends. Regardless of all that, I guess you could say there's a good side to this dirty business. It's made me take a new look at things."

"I can tell that's good by the way you said it. I have a two-bedroom apartment in Beaumont. It's not much, but you're welcome to stay there if you think you can share a bed with Jimmy."

"Thanks, but your apartment is the second place those hoods will look for me. Too risky for you and Jimmy. And your mother."

She gave him a questioning look. "If your concern for our safety is the real reason you won't join us, I could find a bigger place in a different town."

Sensing the unspoken question, he said, "If I didn't care about what happened to you, I would've accepted your first offer. As for your second one, well, let's wait and see. If I'm still alive a couple of months from now, I'll look you up, and we'll get better acquainted and talk about something more permanent. Is that okay?"

"It is, if that's a promise."

"Scout's honor." He held up his right hand.

"Then I'll be expecting you."

He looked up and around and listened, but didn't still didn't hear another chopper or killers approaching. He heard Walrus groan. "We've got to go. Walrus won't last long in the shape he's in. Got to get him to a hospital."

He stood up, but his legs buckled, causing him to lean against the tree to keep from falling. "I'm a little dizzy."

She jumped up to take his arm. "No wonder, after what you've been through the last few days, and losing so much blood. I'm surprised you made it this far. You're in no condition to go anywhere."

He looked at the smoke boiling up from the crash. "That fire is going to bring in lots of people, and I won't be able to tell the bad ones from the criminals." He looked up and around again. "And there's that matter of a second chopper. I'm sure the guys that hit us were in radio contact with their boss."

"Sit down. I'll get that sack and give you something to eat. After eating and resting a while, maybe you'll feel like moving on. Try to quit looking for a monster to jump out from behind every tree. You can stop being so afraid now."

"Not until I get out of here and save my star witness." He listened a moment. "I don't hear him groaning any more. I guess that means he passed out. Wish I could do something for him."

208

She knelt in front of him to take a closer look at his face when he sat down.

He said, "Like you, I've been afraid of some things too long. It started with my first day of school. But after everything I've been through since I came to these woods, I don't think I'll ever be afraid of anything again."

Her eyes met his. "So out of the bad, there sometimes does come some good. Why do you think that happened?"

He shrugged. Guess it's one of the things Mama tried to explain to me that I didn't understand. She was always talking about what she called a man's inside person. She said the only thing more beautiful than the pretty butterflies she chased as a girl was the healthy spirit of a good person at peace with himself."

Eva suddenly raised her eyes to look over his head at something. "Don't move!"

He whirled, expecting to see Hulie or one of Zaavedra's gunmen poised to shoot him.

Chapter XXIII

"Oh, no," Eva moaned. "You moved and scared it away."

"Scared what away?" He saw no one.

"A butterfly." She pointed at the top of his head. "A large one with red, white, and black markings." She pointed. "It's over there on that bush now. Isn't it beautiful?"

He sighed with relief and watched the butterfly move its wings up and down, as if to stir up a breeze or regain its balance on its delicate perch. Eva walked over and reached out for it. "Did you ever catch a butterfly?"

"No, don't!"

She stopped, giving him a puzzled look.

His eyes were still on the butterfly. "My grandmother told me a long time ago to never catch a butterfly. She said it caused the colors on its delicate wings to come off and it would die. She said its beauty is its most valuable possession, and taking it away is like taking away a man's spirit, which is his most beautiful possession."

When he saw no hint of skepticism in Eva's expression, he added. "She told me that men won't admit to having beautiful qualities, because they see beauty as something that belongs to women. Admitting otherwise is a sign of weakness, like a butterfly's wings. She believed it's why most men have trouble finding peace with their inner person." He threw her another cautious glance. "Pretty heavy stuff for a country boy, huh?"

"Maybe. But you must've considered it important; otherwise, you wouldn't have remembered it. Makes sense to me." She rejoined him. "I can appreciate your grandmother's appreciation of beautiful things."

He felt more relaxed now. "Her people called her Girl Who Follows Butterfly. She told me that when she was a little girl, she found them in many sizes and colors and wondered how an insect so small and delicate could be blessed with so many colors and designs. She told me she caught them and played with them at first, but they died. She put some in jars, but they still died. She said that made her very sad."

"You really loved your grandmother, didn't you?"

"Still do. She gave me everything. Love, a sense of belonging. She was my anchor, my blood tie to my past. She taught me rules to live by and the value of patience. But being young and stupid, I didn't appreciate it at the time."

"Oh! I forgot her letters in the sack. Since I'm getting you some sandwiches, I'll bring them, too."

She walked to the tree where they first took cover and returned with the sack. "I'm sorry it's torn. But your letters and our sandwiches are still okay."

The envelope containing his grandmother's letters slipped through a split in the sack as she sat down. She picked it up and pushed it back into the torn sack.

"Would you like to read some of the letters?"

She nodded. "If it's okay with you."

"It won't take long. You can do that while we're eating. I'd like you to get better acquainted with Mama. They're all dated, so you can read them in the order they were written." He shook his head. "On second thought, read only the last one. Most of the others would be dull for a stranger because they're full of the usual stuff a mom writes to her boy. She always looked upon me as her son. The last letter pretty much sums up things."

She removed the letters from the envelope, unfolding each one to check the dates. Selecting the most recent one, she looked at him to make sure he still approved and turned her eyes back to it.

"Read it out loud," he said. "Hearing something Mama said will sound extra good right now. It might help me figure out what's best to do."

She began, "Dearest Bright Light in Night." She stopped, giving him a puzzled look.

He explained what happened the night he was born. "Mama told us what the Indian version was, but nobody could spell it. Mama said my dad didn't even like the English version, but finally agreed to it after my ailing mother insisted. He had to have a name for my birth certificate. But when I started to school, they only used the first letter of each word." He shook his head. "The kids in school thought it was a dumb name."

"I like it." She turned back to the letter. "My grandson. Although I did not bear you with a mother's pain, I have always looked upon you as my son. You are blood of my blood, bone of my bone, and soul of my soul. You made my life good. Without you, the road I have traveled would have gone nowhere.

211

"I will now write about things I never mentioned, things that have always been heavy on my mind. They must be said while there is still life. It might help you with things that have troubled you though the years that you have kept to yourself. I know, because I saw the signs in your eyes. I will mention things that might help you understand why I always tried so hard to teach you the right ways, the ways of my people and all others that are wise. No man can know himself unless he understands such things. By writing now, it might keep you from making mistakes of judgment as I did when I turned away from the proven ways and the rules handed down by our Great Father."

Eva glanced at him and found him looking out into the trees, as if alone. She continued. "Live a quiet life of simple pleasures and moderate appetites, my grandson, and follow the proven ways. The road of life has many forks. Some are dim and narrow. Some are wide and bright. Some we choose, and forces we cannot control push us into others.

"If we hear the words of those who walked the long road before us, we stay on the main road. When we do not, we take the wrong fork. My road was narrow but straight before I shut my eyes to the wise ways and took the fork that was wider and brighter, but I found that it ran under many chinquapin trees. Their burrs were sharp."

Blin sensed Eva's eyes on him, and when he turned, her expression told him she was moved by Mama's words. He looked into the woods, and she continued.

"When I was fifteen, I met your grandfather in town one day, searching for excitement in the white world. I did not listen to the old ones when they warned me about such things. My parents forbid me from seeing the young man I met that day, the man who became your grandfather, but I went back to town anyway. Soon, my innocence was gone, as was the respect of my people. When I married your grandfather, the chief and his council banished me and stripped me of all things I was entitled to as a member of our tribe."

He turned to see Eva shake her head. When he turned away again without speaking, she turned back to the letter.

"My people never accepted my husband as family, and they looked at me with angry eyes. So your grandfather brought me to this place. My heart was heavy because I was separated from my people and because there were bad feelings for my kind out here. It was not long before the man I married became as one with them. Evil lies in the hearts of many.

"Your mother's skin was not as fair as some liked, so she also suffered the wounds of arrows shot by angry eyes. My heart sang when you were born with much lighter skin. Your mind proved bright, too. You would have had many friends in school if I had been like all the other children's grandmothers. But I was proud when I walked with you to school that first day, and I looked forward to all the other days when I would walk down the road with you in sun and rain, but I was made sad later when I heard the names the other children called you. Yes, I knew. They called you Squaw Boy, Red Trash, and Teepee Peewee. It was just another way you were made to suffer because of me."

Eva looked up from the letter to again test his reaction, and when he made no comment, she continued.

"Nothing ever brought me so much pain. I cried for you because I knew that my mistakes were the reason you were pushed without shoes down the fork of the road that ran under the chinquapin trees. I suffered pain many times greater than you felt when I learned of the blows that fell on you during the fights you had because you are part of me. But we had many talks, and you listened, and I thought you learned to stay on the main road of life. That made me proud. But when you were grown, your eyes told me you were not at peace with your inside person. I knew there were many things of the mind that a person cannot see until he has traveled his chosen road for many miles. Perhaps I will be dead by the time you come to that place in your road, but if you remember the things I have taught you, you will turn back to the main road one day and stay on it, and you will find peace.

"Now I must tell you the other reason for teaching you the proven ways, and when you hear this, I hope you will not be angry with me for my selfish ways. You are my only hope of being redeemed in the eyes of my people. When they see and hear you, they will know I have not betrayed them after all, because you are trained in their ways, and you are good. That's one of the reasons it is so important you keep your promise to me, my grandson. When you go to the reservation and ask the chief and his council to lift the banishment on me for the misdeeds of my youth, plead with them to put my name back on their list of honor so I can rest in peace in the afterlife. Trusting that you will do this, I hereby bequeath to you all my tribal rights and privileges.

"And after you have done this, come to where I lie in the earth that has reclaimed me and say words to the Great Father over me so I will be at peace at last. With much love, Laura Bartee, Girl Who Follows Butterfly."

213

Blin turned to see Eva's reaction to the letter, wondering if it had changed her opinion of him. Would she now see him with the eyes of those Indian-hating bullies in grammar school?

She gently refolded the letter and returned it to the larger envelope. "It's a beautiful letter," she said. There were tears in her eyes. "Your grandmother was a very wise person, and she loved you very much."

He relaxed. "Thanks. She always was so pleasant around me; I didn't realize she was hurting inside. I never saw her angry. Until I got that last letter, I always took that to mean she was content with her life in West Texas. I didn't tell her about the bad names the other kids called me, or about all the fights, because I didn't want to make her sad. I didn't know she found out anyway."

Blin studied Eva's face as she wiped away a tear and realized she had wiped away his reservations about her and destroyed the last of his long-held opinions about women in general.

She leaned over to check his wounds. "We've got to get you to a doctor."

"And I have to find somebody that'll take my witness to the hospital before he dies."

He turned to find Friend sitting nearby, quietly watching him. "Before Friend showed up after I broke out of that stinking smokehouse, I was beginning to believe she'd decided I didn't need her any more."

"Do you need *me* any more?"

"Why did you ask that? Of course I do. And it seems, the better I get to know you, the *more* I need you. Does that make sense?"

"Yes." She held his gaze. "Now don't let this scare you off, but I want you to know. Regardless of how things turn out between you and me, I feel the same way about you."

"That's a relief. I was afraid you might not want to have anything to do with a loser called Teepee Peewee, the Squaw Boy, after reading that letter."

"The more I learn about you, Blin Burge, the more I'm convinced you've got a lot to learn about women. *Some* women, anyway."

"I'll admit I've been a slow learner in that department, but I believe I've finally got it right. But I should tell you that I haven't much left to offer a woman now. Thanks to gangsters, a not-so-friendly mortgage holder, and bankers, I could lose my businesses and my home. My car. I have very little money stashed away I can call my own, and if Walrus dies, I might have to stay in hiding for a long time."

He listened for sounds from the injured gunman, but heard nothing. He regretted being unable to leave already.

She said, "Try not to think about all that bad stuff right now. You're alive. What could be more important? Concentrate on that and more important things, like what your grandmother told you in that letter, and the fact that you've got me and Walrus to help you now. And Friend."

"You have some of my grandmother's qualities."

"Thanks. Hungry?"

"You bet. As soon as we eat something, we've got to move on."

He had finished a sandwich when he heard the distant flutter of an approaching helicopter. "We've got to leave *now,* ready or not."

Grabbing her hand, he shoved another sandwich into his pocket and pulled her up, limping toward the highway. They had gone less than a hundred yards when he became so weak he had to slow their pace to a walk, and the approaching flutter told him they could go no further without being spotted.

Breathing hard, he told Eva, "They'll spot us for sure if we don't stop moving. We'll find a place to hide and hope they believe we left already."

"Just don't leave me and let them shoot at you again."

Leading Eva down the gentle slope, looking for a place to hide, he spotted an uprooted dead tree and turned toward its exposed roots. He found a large hole filled with leaves and pointed. "Jump in."

By the time the chopper arrived, they were half buried on their sides in the leaves, Blin nestled tightly against Eva's back. He said, "I'll pull more leaves in over us."

She sneezed. "I don't know if I can lie in this stuff."

He raked more leaves over their legs and bodies. "Breathe through your mouth. If you have to sneeze after they land, cover your face."

He settled his left arm around her as a large helicopter swung in over them and slowed to hover. Rising up just enough to see over the rim of the hole, Blin saw it hovering above the fire. He saw three men in its cabin. When it began to circle the area, he ducked down in the leaves.

He said, "They're looking for a place to land. Think you can keep from sneezing until they get through checking out the fire and looking around?"

She smothered another sneeze. "Does that answer your question?"

"We won't have to lie here very long. When they don't spot me or find their friends alive, they'll go back up and start looking farther out."

"And they'll have your star witness with them."

"If he doesn't move or make a sound, maybe they won't see him."

She moved closer. "I'm so frightened!" After she smothered another sneeze, Blin saw her look up through the treetops at the circling chopper.

"Blin?"

"If you're about to sneeze again, get down quick." He raised his head to see what she was looking at.

"Why would gangsters fly around in a camouflaged helicopter with a U.S. Air Force star painted on its side?"

"What?" He followed her gaze, but the chopper moved behind a tree. "What are you talking about?"

She pointed. "Look!"

The chopper swung into view, looking much like those he had seen in war movies and news programs. Near its open side door, he saw a large blue and red star in a white circle with short horizontal bars extending from its sides.

He sat up. "That's a military helicopter."

"Can I sit up, too?" she asked. "I'm dying in this stuff."

"We can't leave the hole until I'm sure it's not more shooters in a stolen machine."

Moments later, the camouflaged aircraft found an opening up the grade and descended. When it came to rest amid a swirl of dead leaves and swaying bushes, Blin ducked down of sight, slowly rising again to peer over the rim of the hole as three men climbed out.

They looked respectable enough, clean-shaven, and neatly dressed in casual attire. All appeared to be in their late twenties or middle thirties. Two looked familiar, but because of the heavy ground cover, he couldn't determine if he'd seen them before, or if they favored someone that he knew. They carried no guns, but he saw holstered pistols on their belts.

"Who is it?" Eva whispered.

"Can't tell yet. Lie still."

The men moved out of the heavy undergrowth on their way to the fire, giving him a full view. He was shocked when he recognized George Madsen. One of the other two was the DEA agent he'd worked with in Houston, but he didn't recognize the third. He was wearing a big hat, khakis, and a badge.

He muttered, "What's going on? Did that gang buy Madsen, too?"

"What are you mumbling about?" Eva whispered. "May I please get up now?"

"I think so," he said. "If these guys are on the level, the cavalry has arrived."

"Good!" She sat up and sneezed, causing the three men to whirl.

Blin jumped out, waving his arms. "Over here, Madsen! It's me, Blin Burge."

A surprised Madsen said, "So it *was* you hiding in those woods over there." He pointed.

Blin joined them, offering his hand to Madsen. "Never thought I'd be glad to see you again after what happened in that Houston courtroom."

"I figured you blamed me personally for that," Madsen replied. He pointed to the DEA agent. "You remember Joe Walk. He's also a chopper pilot. The other gentleman is Elvin Langham, a local deputy sheriff. Boys, this is the undercover agent I've been looking for."

Blin nodded, shaking their hands. "I'm glad to see you, too." He remembered what the Fanchers said about the local sheriff being a Holsomback man. He told the deputy, "I hope your boss doesn't go to hard on me for tangling with one of your star citizens."

The deputy's expression was solemn. "We hovered long enough at the Fancher place to spot a man on the ground. Looked like he was dead. You're saying you had something to do with that?"

Blin nodded. "That's High Fancher. He was trying to kill me." He pointed to Eva. "She's my eye witness." He introduced her.

The deputy smiled. "High Fancher is dead?" He smiled faded, and he tipped his hat to Eva. "Sorry." To Blin, he said, "Lots of folks in our county will want to give you a medal."

Blin said to Madsen, "What happened to bring you here? How'd you find me?"

Madsen looked at Blin's bloody cheek, face, and side. "You're white as a sheet. From the looks of you, somebody's been giving you a hard time. What happened?"

"It's a long story." He told him about the fight with the men in the helicopter and gave him their names. "I'll tell you the whole story later. I'm too beat now."

"How did I find you? I received a weird telephone call from a guy with a high-pitched voice asking if I knew anybody with the initials B.B. I told him the only man I knew was Blin Burge and asked the purpose of his call. He said I could have you if I was willing to pay him lots of money."

"That was the dead man, High Fancher. He was a crazy, small-time dope dealer. He locked me up and whipped me with a bullwhip. He, his brother Hulie, and their Uncle Emmett were holding me for a ransom from that Houston gang I gathered evidence on. What happened after that?"

"Told him I was a United States attorney and couldn't pay anything for you, but that I very much wanted to talk to you about a critical matter. I asked if he knew where I could find you, and he laughed like a child and hung up."

"That means he called your number first. After that, he called my ex-girlfriend, who referred him to the gang that chased me out of town."

Madsen looked at the fire down the hill. "Did all the shooters die in that fire?"

"All but Walrus Walsaka. He's still alive, but he won't be for long unless you can get him to a hospital in a hurry. He promised he'd turn state's evidence if I didn't let him die."

Madsen's face brightened. "Really? That's very good news, and a good piece of work on your part. But how—"

Blin pulled the empty Beretta out of his pocket. "They flew in close, and I got lucky."

Turning to his two companions, Madsen said, "If Walsaka is conscious, tell him he's not under arrest, but give him his Miranda in case he changes his mind about testifying, or if Blin decides to file on him in sate court. We'll get a deposition from him in the hospital."

Blin pointed. "You can't miss him. He's as big as an ox." He turned to Madsen. "These woods cover most of the county. How did you find me?"

Madsen gave Eva a cautious look. "How does Miss DeBerry fit into this puzzle other than being present when you shot High Fancher?"

"She was living at the Fancher farm, taking care of her ill mother and stepfather. If it hadn't been for her, I would've died. She was being abused by High when I broke out of a locked smokehouse. She saw him charge me with a knife." He patted his pocket containing the Beretta. "He'd dropped this, and I beat him to it."

Eva said, "I also saw those men at the fire fly in and try to kill Blin."

"Very good," Madsen said. "You and Blin can give me the details during our flight to the nearest hospital. We'll put it in writing later." Looking at Blin, he added, "I have to give part of the credit to my caller

ID and the rest to a cooperative telephone company and the timber company's pilot. After determining where that call came from, I called the DEA in Beaumont to see if they were working any cases in the area. They told me they had nothing solid, but they suspected an operation in or around Dooly. They, in turn, referred me to the local sheriff and the pilots that keep an eye on the pipeline and timber company's interests. The sheriff told me all about the Fancher family and about High and his Uncle Emmett in particular. That's when I requisitioned a helicopter and set out for the Fancher place."

"How did the pilots help you?"

"The one flying for the timber company told me he saw animal tracks in the pipeline easement put there by something larger than a deer or a hog. Thinking they might be some campers on horseback, he circled around for another look. He spotted two piles of fresh manure."

"I was afraid he'd spotted that. It's too bad he didn't swing by later and see the pit High and Hulie pushed me into."

"I had the FBI check out every place that sold or rented horses within two hundred miles of Houston, and they reported a man fitting your description buying a trailer, horse, and pack mule a couple of weeks ago in a little town northwest of Houston. They remembered you because they had such hard time transferring money from your account."

Blin sat down and told him about the patch of marijuana in the woods and the fire in the pit as the other two officers struggled back up the grade with a moaning Walsaka.

Madsen said, "Deputy Walk, will you please radio in the location of those smoldering leaves down there? There must be a volunteer fire department somewhere in the area." He turned to Blin. "As soon as we get our prime witness under guard in a hospital and get your wounds taken care of, I want you to direct officers to that weed field." He glanced at the men attempting to load Walsaka aboard the helicopter. "I'll help them with that gorilla."

As Madsen sprinted over to join Walk and Langham, Eva knelt beside Blin, giving him a look of concern. "Are you okay? You don't look so good."

"I'm okay now, I think. But if you don't mind, I'll sit out this dance." He shook his head with a sigh. "It's hard to believe the nightmare is finally over."

"I'm glad for you, too, and happy you didn't get hurt any worse than you did. But they'll get you to a doctor, and you'll be fine after you rest some more."

"What I can't figure out is how I can feel so good and so bad at the same time. I hurt all over, I'm woozy, and my face, back, and side feel like they're on fire, but I've never felt better. It's another of those strange things that's come to mind lately that I don't understand."

"You'll work out everything in due time."

He nodded. "I believe I can if you continue sticking by me like you have since I found you by that spring in the woods."

"I plan to do that as long as you need me and want me." She nodded at something behind him. "Just like she has."

He turned and found Friend sitting close by, watching him. "Hi, girl. I'll take you with me if they'll let me."

Friend wagged her tail and looked at the sack in Eva's lap.

Eva said, "I know Friend is special to you, but she's still a half-wild animal. I doubt she'd allow you put her in that noisy flying machine. Even if she would, there'd be the problem of taking her from place to place. Wild creatures don't like to be shut in."

A sense of foreboding swept over him at the thought of never seeing the old hybrid again. "You're probably right, as usual, but I wouldn't feel right leaving her in her condition. She's crippled and old. It would be like leaving a member of my family."

"When things settle down, I'll come back to the big woods with you and help you find her if she's still alive. She's near the end of her days."

He looked at Friend. "You'll be around 'til I get back, won't you?"

Friend wagged her tail.

"I'll take that for a yes." He glanced cautiously at Eva. "I started off talking to a horse and a pack mule and ended up talking to a hybrid wolf. Another of those strange things that's happened to me in the big timber."

"So how about another sandwich to celebrate? You need nourishment."

Remembering the sandwich in his pocket, he pulled it out. It was mashed and covered with bits of leaves. He held it out, saying to Friend, "You first, ol' girl. It's not much of an offering for all you've done for me, but it's all I've got except my love and gratitude. You'll always have that."

Friend limped over and took the sandwich, retreating several steps before dropping it in front of her. She paused, looked at him, and picked it up to gulp it down.

Eva gave him another sandwich and took one out for herself.

They were finished eating when Madsen approached them. "Ready?"

Looking at Eva, he said, "I'm ready if my chief supporter is."

"I'm with you."

"And that makes me a very happy man."